I0672371

Uroboros Saga

BOOK FOUR

By Arthur Walker

For Elle

Get updates on my books by following me on Twitter.
@arthurhwalker

Divine Union Deriding, And Denying Immediate Communion with God,
The Spoilers say, "Where are his Works That he did in the Wilderness?
Lo, what are these? Whence came they?" These are not the Works of
Egypt nor Babylon, Whose Gods are the Powers Of this World, Goddess
Nature, Who first spoil & then destroy Imaginative Art, for their Glory is
War and Dominion.

~Blake

CHAPTER 1

Mars Colony, Processing Facility 09

Receiving Department - July 3rd, 2200 – More than a year after Shutdown

The mining company transport was as dirty as it was cramped. The dozens of workers lying side by side across the narrow chamber didn't stir as the craft came to rest against the docking clamps. Each was fitted with an apparatus that put them into stasis for the long journey. Dragos alone had opted to stay awake for the six months it took for the transport to arrive. The confinement and isolation had done Dragos some good, where it would have driven another man to the brink. He'd had a lot to think about after leaving Port Montaigne.

Even as the hydraulics engaged to open the transport doors, he wondered if Truman had survived, and if Tullia would ever be able to forgive him. More than that, he hoped they were simply alive. Other than the dim illumination from his mining helmet, it was the first light he'd seen in months. Squinting did little good as several individuals appeared at the egress to check the interior.

"Looks like all the miners made it in one piece. Stasis harnesses are still engaged. Seem to be breathing okay," one said.

"Well, except that long-haired fellah toward the back. He looks like he might have woken half-way. Keep a bar at hand in case he's gone feral," another said, taking up an implement in one hand.

Dragos lowered his head, keeping his duffle out of sight behind him as he pulled the mining helmet on and fastened the strap under his chin. The impressment agents strode forward, stepping on unconscious men as they did, only pausing to hover over Dragos where he sat. One held out his hand to receive a pry bar, the other obliging the gesture with a heavy hunk of metal.

"You got the madness? You're supposed to keep your stasis harness on and active the entire voyage. It can break the strong as easy as it breaks the weak," the man with the pry bar said with a sneer.

"You know nothing of strength," Dragos whispered, brushing off his shirt sleeve.

"What'd he say?" One agent asked the other in twisted amusement.

Dragos had spent six months rehearsing how this would go, practicing the movements, his demeanor, the feigning of infirmity after months of alleged inactivity. The truth was that he did nothing but exercise and think about every contingency. He knew that he would be at a disadvantage because the long voyage would leave him very light sensitive. As the agent brought the pry bar over his head to strike, muscle memory took over.

Standing with practiced agility, Dragos brought his shiv up into the cluster of soft tissue under the man's arm. He stepped aside letting the stabbed man stagger between him and the second individual standing in the cargo hold. Reversing his stance, Dragos caught the pry bar as it tumbled toward the floor. The man reached reflexively for the shiv under his arm as his comrade standing behind him put his hand on a holstered sidearm.

Swinging as hard as he could, Dragos brought the pry bar across the man's head, then stepped past him. The other man had just cleared his holster and was bringing the pistol up as Dragos caught him across the temple on the back stroke. As the two impressment agents fell to the floor, Dragos went limp and fell as well, putting the one he'd stabbed in a choke hold.

"Don't pull the shiv, you'll just bleed out," Dragos whispered, pinching the agent's neck between his bicep and forearm.

They wrestled for a moment in a pool of blood as the impressment agent tried to pull the shiv from his armpit. He went unconscious first, his brain quickly deprived of oxygen, as Dragos squeezed as hard as he could. He took two quick breaths before he released the agent and pulled his inert stasis harness over his face. Being winded, it was hard to stay still, but Dragos had practiced that as well.

Two more impressment agents rushed into the cargo hold from the receiving area beyond. They were carrying rifles with illuminators swaying back and forth as they struggled past the many miners still lying about in stasis. Dragos deftly palmed the sidearm dropped by the agent he'd concussed, pulling it down to his right side and, he hoped, out of sight. He held his breath and closed his eyes as the armed impressment agents loomed over him.

One of them bent down to check their fallen comrade, nearly losing his footing in the blood. Dragos opened his eyes, shooting him from the ground and rolling to one side to get a clear shot. The second agent brought his rifle up, but not before Dragos shot him in the head. They both fell, the recoil from the rounds pulling them off their feet. Dragos rose, quickly grabbing up both rifles. He holstered the pistol in his waistband, and slung one rifle over his should and held the other at the ready.

Recovering his shiv, he made sure none of the impressment agents were going to be a problem in the future. He tried to end them as humanely as he could, pushing his anger down deep to keep himself professional and efficient. His old habits lay about under his new ones like old soldiers still eager to find a battlefield.

The compartment went quiet, with only the barely audible breathing of the other miners breaking the silence. Dragos' ears rang from firing the handgun in such close quarters and he hoped the isolated passenger compartment was sound proof enough the crew was still unaware. Pushing the impressment agent to one side he searched them all for some sort of identification badge or code entry. Written in black marker on the palm of one of the men was a six digit code.

Walking to the access hatch for the crew compartment, Dragos entered in the code and waited as the indicator lights slowly turned from red to green across the top of the hatch. When it cycled, a very surprised pilot was standing on the other side. Dragos stepped quickly inside, pressing the rifle to the man's belly and a handgun toward the surprised members of the crew waiting in the adjoining corridor.

"We had a deal," the pilot whispered, looking down at the rifle.

"New deal. You take miners to the right receiving terminal. You take them where they belong. Otherwise, you all die," Dragos growled, his accent abnormally thick as he pushed the muzzle of the rifle harder into the pilot's stomach.

The pilot nodded quickly, bringing his hands up. Dragos followed him past several stasis chambers and into the cockpit so he could listen to every word he told Martian flight control. As the transport craft pulled away inside the port, Dragos looked out to see several other transports languishing at the dock. Each had a thick layer of ore dust draped across the top as though they had been there for some time.

He didn't doubt the Shutdown on Earth had made people desperate, but the notion that mining crews were hiring mercenaries just to make sure they made it to their destination seemed far fetched. Easy money, he thought. It should have been a free ride to his destination and some quick money. Looking down at the blood covering his work suit, he was glad he'd prepared to do the job just in case.

As the transport docked at the proper destination, Dragos clapped the pilot on the shoulder, startling him. He held vigil until the ship was powered down, docking clamps were engaged, and the access point was open. Once he was satisfied everything was as it should be, he escorted the crew to the cargo compartment. Mining company officials were already onsite with paramedics waking up the miners.

"We'll take the crew into custody now. Mr., um… Dragos, I assume you had a pleasant journey?" one of mining officials asked, looking down at the pool of blood amidst the unconscious miners.

"Yes, was okay. Thank you, Mr. Graham," Dragos said, laying the rifle and handgun across the men he'd killed to get them.

"You going to head right back? We can make arrangements to take you in three days. I apologize that it can't be sooner, but our shipment schedule has had to be altered of late," Mr. Graham explained.

"Is okay, I am going to stay awhile I think," Dragos said, picking up his satchel and heading for the door.

"Wait, Mr. Dragos," Mr. Graham said, holding up an envelope. "Your payment?"

"Right, sorry. Was thinking about where I must go next," Dragos replied, taking the envelope.

"We've tried to be discreet, but Mars is an incestuous place. They likely know you're coming. That transport leaves in three days, don't forget," Mr. Graham said, tapping the tip of his nose.

"There will be others?"

"Yes, but it is the *soonest*."

"Why do you worry for me? Just mercenary working for mining company credit vouchers," Dragos asked.

"You seem decent, and you didn't rape anyone or doing anything else unseemly while on board those six months. Usually, we have problems when we augment security on personnel transports. The mostly noble actions you took while working the detail set you apart from the usual individuals willing to take such work," Mr. Graham explained.

"Glad you like. I will try to do what I came to do, and be back before transport in three days," Dragos stated, unleashing a genuine smile.

"Maybe we can help by providing a courier or escort?"

"No. This I must do alone. A matter of honor."

Mr. Graham nodded, waving the mining company personnel through to continue waking the workers.

Dragos walked through the heavy refining area next to the receiving dock, his boots kicking up stone dust as he made his way for the exit. Miners pushed past him as they arrived for work early in the Martian day. Each of them walked by with barely a glance upward. He was attired and as dirty as they were. A few noticed the blood he had on him, but said nothing, averting their eyes quickly.

The Martian streets were like silt traps as condensation rained down persistently from the massive biological enclosure overhead. Many of the living spaces were built into the supports holding up the curved biological shielding high above. The adjoining buildings were built to mimic that architecture, giving the place an organic feel, buildings curling up toward the dome, like metallic orange bean stalks.

The Martian sky was clear, allowing the great dome over the port district to glisten against the stars. Habitation spires sparkled with ore dust blown through industrial filters, which provided the whole area with a breathable atmosphere. Sandy orange colored transports slowly moved fluidly and in ordered rows high above, carrying workers into other districts, and ore in from others.

There were makeshift shelters, and open air markets selling goods on the pedestrian walkways outside more formal commercial storefronts. Each was dark, looking to have closed recently, a red indicator light above the entrances signaling that they were awaiting Central Global Government repossession that would likely never come or be resolved. Walking toward the wall of raincoat-clad pedestrians, Dragos took up pace to match, doing his best to blend in.

There was no visible civic surveillance, but that didn't mean it wasn't there. Dragos kept his head down, drifting to the awnings and overhangs where he could. As the crowd fell away, so did the markets and makeshift shelters. The orange of the port district surrendered to grey as he drew close to a Martian Authority control zone. Ahead, a heavily armed checkpoint marked the egress from the mining orange where Dragos stood, to the teal of the first of many penal zones.

The biological shielding over that area was dark, with only a few spotlights and roaming patrols giving the area illumination. The guard at the checkpoint barely gave Dragos a second look after he put half the money he'd earned guarding the mining transport on his clipboard. It shouldn't have been so easy to enter the penal facility, and Dragos wondered if the bribe was even necessary. He wondered now if he was expected, and how far beyond the sally ports of the prison that expectation reached.

The penal manufacturing structures kept opposite hours from the rest of the colony so that if there were breaches, decent folk would be safely asleep behind locked doors. There was little in the way of trash as inmate cleaning crews constantly patrolled the passages and streets between structures. The whole area squatted beneath a huge penal facility that was only the face of the institution that lay beyond. Heavily armed prison guards walked every parapet and ledge of the teal and grey edifice.

Like a row of square teeth along the bottom of the structure, there were many sally ports and overhead doors leading within. Dragos quietly counted to get his bearings and headed for the seventh sally port from the left. The guards on patrol paused for a moment, dropping down advanced optics from their helmets to gaze at him. He paused, holding up his satchel and an empty right hand as they did so.

After being waved over, he approached the sally port, the overhead door beginning to open before he even got close to the threshold. The interior was painted white, with a control booth to one side. On the other side was a locked down lift vehicle for receiving cargo from trucks. Dragos grabbed the edge of the dock and lifted himself up, pausing just outside the door.

A pair of baton wielding prison guards came out of a security door beside the booth, the door cycling shut behind them like a vault door. One of them gestured for Dragos to come further in. The other leaned casually up against the wide steel frame around the vault door, which led further into the institution. Dragos walked in, keeping his hands and the satchel in plain sight.

"You Dragos?" the prison guard asked.

"Yes."

"You here to see Archie?"

"Yes."

"You have what he asked you to bring?"

Dragos paused for a moment and regarded the prison guard somewhat impatiently. "Yes."

The sally port closed slowly behind Dragos, a sheet of solid steel dropping in behind it as an extra precaution. Orange warning lights began to strobe as the prison guard leaning against the wall bolted upright, the vault door to his side began to cycle and come to life. Several heavy hydraulic presses retracted, allowing the vault door to open with a mechanical click. The whole of it was fifteen feet in diameter, and five feet thick but it seemed to open on the wide hinges as if it were weightless.

Dragos watched as a small contingent of men wearing numbered teal jumpsuits stepped through, the man in the center being familiar to him. Of the four men, Archie was the largest, well over six feet tall and three hundred pounds. He had short black hair and a well-trimmed black mustache that sat in the center of his square and imposing visage. His steel-blue eyes seemed to cut the air as they darted back and forth.

"I see you have brought what I asked for, at last," Archie said, stroking his thick mustache.

"Yes, it should all be there," Dragos replied, looking with no small degree of anxiety past Archie into the penal facility beyond.

"Mr. Soames?" Archie said gesturing to one of the prison guards.

The prison guard approached Dragos and frisked him before checking the contents of the satchel he carried. He held the vacuum sealed bearer bonds aloft as though he'd found buried treasure, making sure the internal sensors could clearly see the exchange. Archie nodded, seemingly satisfied with the exchange. He walked over to Dragos, arms held wide to embrace him. Dragos returned the embrace, clapping Archie on his shoulder.

"This is over then?" Dragos asked.

"No," Archie replied, dropping a savage body blow on Dragos that sent him to the ground.

The other inmates moved in to give Dragos a good stomping, but Archie held out his arms blocking their advance. "No, I need him relatively healthy."

Archie knelt down beside Dragos, again smoothing his black mustache thoughtfully. "Have you ever wondered why we are here?"

Dragos shook his head, turning over to clutch his badly bruised ribs.

"I think sometimes it is to act as consequences for each other, when nature falls short. In your case, nature fell very short. The package looked awfully light. Did this Vance Uroboros get the better of you? It was my understanding that you were to do many jobs and find a way to take control of his finances. Now, I am hearing the economy on Earth collapsed in dramatic fashion. This is not good Dragos," Archie said, tapping his index finger on Dragos' temple.

"Uroboros had no memory, and nothing to steal. He was not one of the merchant class we hate, just a man. The intelligence was bad from beginning," Dragos rasped, trying to sit up.

"I am insulted you think I would believe these lies after you tried to cover up what Truman did. Oh yes, I know all about him killing one of our fellow freedom fighters. These things are simply not done, which is why I'm *not* going to kill you," Archie said, grabbing a handful of Dragos' jacket.

"That mustache… so ridiculous," Dragos hissed, flashing a sinister smile.

Archie looked hurt by the comment at first, but his face broke into a wide smile a second later.

"Try not to be jealous. When you're older, you might be able to grow one," Archie replied sardonically.

The prison guards watched apathetically as Archie pulled Dragos across the threshold beyond the vault door into the penal zone beyond. Lights began to flash as his cohorts hurried inside behind the closing door. Hidden mechanisms turned within, sealing Dragos inside the facility. The interior housed an empty processing facility where inmates would normally be processed, check in their belongings, get fingerprinted, and so forth. The various stations and checkpoints were deserted, not a soul left standing about.

"You left money with guards," Dragos hissed, breaking free of Archie.

"They are going to deposit it for me. I've been running currency on the outside for quite some time now. After the Financial Liberation Front collapsed, I took all we had sequestered and moved it into legitimate investments," Archie explained, patting Dragos affectionately on the arm.

"You… will leave Tullia and Truman alone," Dragos growled, after catching his breath.

"That isn't how it works, and you know it. I have forgiven their debts because that is what we do, we forgive. However, there is still the matter of what Truman did to Zechus. Strangling him over a woman? It isn't…"

"Truman loved that woman. Zechus spit on that love saying he would sell her to skin merchant. They argued and fought. Zechus lost," Dragos explained.

Archie paused for a moment, looking back at the others arrayed around him. They all shrugged slightly and nodded. Massaging his eyebrows, Archie lowered his head as he considered what to do.

"Tullia and Truman are clear. No debts, and no retaliation," Archie said, beckoning for Dragos to follow him.

"This is good for both of us, yes?" Dragos growled.

"Possibly. I'd prefer to have the leverage, but everyone has to have a code. Do you have a code, Dragos?" Archie asked.

"I protect my family, and do my job, whatever that is," Dragos replied.

"Indeed? We'll just see how loyal to that you truly are."

They walked into the processing facility where possessions were processed. The other inmates forced Dragos down to deprive him of all his earthly possessions, stripping off his clothing, and throwing it into a storage box. Dragos didn't fight them, but sighed loudly at the indecent way he was being treated.

"He has a lot of mining company vouchers on him, recent and legitimate," one of the inmates reported.

"Put it in the bin with the rest of his belongings," Archie ordered.

"But boss—"

"Remember what I said before about having a code? We are not thieves," Archie insisted, looming menacingly over the inmate.

He quickly put the vouchers and the rest of Dragos' belongings in the bin, sealing it for storage. The other inmates glared at their cohort disdainfully as he put evidence tape across the top of the container. Dragos rose from the floor, humiliated to find Archie standing by with a bundle of prison clothing.

"Put these on, please," Archie asked in an ingratiating tone.

Dragos glared at Archie angrily as he donned the prison garb and slip-on shoes. The others nodded their approval as Dragos buttoned up the coveralls and pushed his hair back out of the collar. Archie clapped his hands together like a proud parent, then ushered Dragos past the cage to the far side of the processing area.

"Your sister ever marry? She find herself a nice man to be with?" Archie asked.

"If you or any of our associates go near her, I'll break legs and pry fingernails with pieces of knee bone to tie with sinew, and seal with blood. I'll kill you and yours until rest are left to drown in endless red. Heaven will weep at every scream, until I am sure she is safe," Dragos growled.

"Manners!" A burly inmate snarled and swung a fist at Dragos.

Dragos turned into the blow, letting it graze his jaw before taking a reverse grip on the man's neck with his right hand. He twisted quickly, shattering the man's trachea. Gasping for air he pawed helplessly at Dragos' coveralls before sinking to his knees. Grabbing the shiv out of the man's waistband, Dragos stabbed him over and over again until he was a bloody wreck on the floor. The others froze while Archie watched without emotion or a hint of distress.

"I play along, to find out what it is you want for this to be over. After that, I go, we never see each other again," Dragos warned, dropping the shiv on the ground.

"Ha! This is why I like you so much. So dramatic! Yes, yes, one last job, and then the FLF will be dissolved and your obligation to it will end," Archie said, smiling warmly at Dragos.

They lingered near a locked door at the far side until a loud buzzing sound indicated the door was clear to open. Stepping through, they entered the central cell block where rows of small cells were arrayed four stories high along the twenty foot wide hallways. Large LED lamps hung from the ceiling, shedding bright light throughout the area as a couple hundred inmates looked down from the railings at Archie and his entourage.

"Welcome to my kingdom!" Archie declared, holding his thick arms out at his sides.

"It smells like piss. Big surprise," Dragos replied.

"Always so negative! Don't worry, I'm going to turn that frown upside down," Archie said, cheerfully clapping Dragos on the back.

Each of the cells held a bunk bed, an exercise bike bolted to the floor, and a large touch-capable display along the wall. The place was incredibly clean and inmates could be seen cleaning and making repairs to the facility. Dragos looked curiously at the arrangement and took note of the obvious deference paid to Archie by every single inmate as they parted like a human sea to let him pass.

"What's with the bikes?" Dragos asked, pushing his long hair out of his face.

"We've got about three and a half million cells equipped with those now. The average rider can produce about 950 watts of power per hour of cycling. More proficient riders can do even more, earning additional credit with the institution. They can use that credit for a variety of things like supporting family members on the outside, earning access to education, rehabilitation programs, special food when it is available, and so forth," Archie explained.

"Why would murderers and rapists serving life sentences care about such things?" Dragos whispered, keeping a close eye on the inmates following them up the corridor.

"If one gains enough credit to complete all the rehabilitation programs and earns at least an undergraduate degree, they can be released. This, provided they hurt no one while they are inside," Archie explained, nodding occasionally to an inmate with a smile.

"And what if they hurt someone while already in prison?" Dragos asked.

"You mean like when you crushed that convict's throat?" Archie replied, amusement dancing across each word.

"Yeah, like that. Or if I decide to do the same to you," Dragos said, pointing toward the ceiling.

"Mostly, they die. Mostly. There are many ways of dealing with individuals that are dissatisfied with the program I negotiated," Archie explained.

"Why don't you leave, do these things we used to talk about?"

"Oh, I have far greater power on the inside than I ever did on the outside. In here, I'm a king, a Savior, and a man of esteem... a God," Archie explained.

"Nice to see you're staying humble," Dragos said, watching the upper levels carefully.

Archie smiled. "Of course, I have an exit strategy. Have a little faith, Dragos."

They continued on to a well-appointed cell block where the cells looked to have been without normal occupancy for some time. Each one contained numerous desks that harbored stacks of paperwork and office chairs spread about haphazardly. Inmates worked busily to file paper work with one another that seemed to eventually follow a route that ended with a wheeled cart on the main floor. Everyone paused for a moment as Archie approached, his entourage breaking off to head back to their assigned positions.

"What are you really doing, Archie?" Dragos asked, squinting up at the dizzying amount of bureaucracy at work.

"Sharp like a razor. This is why I went to considerable trouble in bringing you to Mars. Also, you know me like few other living people do, and understand how I work," Archie bragged, like a proud father speaking of his son.

"Cut crap, please. What am I doing here?" Dragos growled, looking around suspiciously.

Archie smiled, wagging a finger at Dragos as if the question only affirmed what he'd been saying a moment before.

"Principal to the colony are the various mining companies. Each is ruled by a board of directors that represent the shareholders and a CEO. They are like normal companies in that you can also purchase shares. Inmates on track for release are allowed to purchase company shares with a portion of the credits they earn pedaling the bikes," Archie explained.

"It can't account for much. The companies are composed of billions of shares," Dragos replied, shaking his head.

"Let me worry about the math," Archie continued, straightening one of his eyebrows with his index finger.

"This is about money then, not freedom?" Dragos mused, looking around at the paperwork arrayed across the cellblock.

"It's about the sum of my legacy. It always was," Archie admitted, doing his best to seem humble.

"You look like a usurper to me, the same as we used to fight," Dragos said, shaking his head as he pushed a stack of papers to the floor.

Archie frowned. "I find your lack of vision deeply disheartening. All the same, I still need your help to make it work or I'll rescind my earlier statement regarding your wayward siblings. Refuse, and I'll have our old agents still on the outside slit their throats and jettison their corpses into space," Archie explained, smiling as if he were talking about a sunny day.

Dragos frowned, his eyes betraying an intense desire to do Archie harm. "What do you want me to do?"

"I need you to kill two women. They are both hard targets. One is a Custodian, a Marshal in charge of enforcing the law on the Martian Colony. She is the only police officer on the planet, and will likely try to interfere with my plans. The second calls herself Enyo," Archie stated, turning to a desk to gather up a sheaf of papers.

"This Enyo, who is she?" Dragos asked, anger still corrupting his every word.

"She is the daughter of the Ares Omega Class Artificial Intelligence. My agents on the outside say she is a terrestrial intelligent agent, an artificial intelligence with an artificial body that allows her to look like a human being. She is rarely seen, but drawing her out in the open isn't hard. Simply go anywhere near the industrial compound where the Ares System is housed and she will be along shortly to kill you dead," Archie explained, casually.

"Daughter?" Dragos asked.

"Yeah, I'm told that's the relationship between them, even though they are just advanced machines. Not sure what the backstory is on that," Archie said, shrugging.

"I have seen some of what they can do. These terrestrial IAs are not to be trifled with," Dragos replied.

"Oh, I'm aware you've had contact with one. That's why I chose you specifically for the job. No one else I'm aware of in our organization has the experience you have. Everything else we know is in these documents," Archie said, handing Dragos the sheaf of papers.

"This thing you are doing with the mining companies and the shares, if Vance Uroboros finds out, he will come here. It was his mission, like us, to stop the usurpers and the merchant class getting fat off the poor," Dragos explained.

Archie smiled. "This Vance Uroboros wasn't just a suit after all?"

"Far from. He is idealist, and fighter when need be. I know you, Archie. Whatever it is you do, Uroboros would not like," Dragos explained.

"Then, if this Vance Uroboros comes to Mars, we'll kill him."

CHAPTER 2

Uroboros Financial Corporate Headquarters

Port Montaigne - March 24th, 2200 – Almost four months following the Shutdown

Kale's Private Records, Part 1 –

I write this knowing it may never be seen or read, but in the interest of giving myself perspective for introspection later. I lack the luxury of assuming I'll always be around to relate these things to Vance Uroboros in the aftermath, so I take these notes down for that purpose as well. I hope that he can forgive me for all I've done.

In the wake of the global economic apocalypse, there has been little to suggest the world will recover in the near future. I met with one of our analysts this morning in Vance's office about the current outlook. While I understand that Madmar met his end on the Moon Colony some weeks ago, his madness continues to undermine our efforts.

"I've checked the satellite topography against previous records and gathered all our financials from the last week," Jason Mortimer explained.

Understand that I don't like Mr. Mortimer, which is why I have him bring me the bad news. I retain him because he is loyal, and as I write this, there is nowhere for him to go. Most of the world doesn't have power, let alone a comfy job working in a cubical.

"Mr. Mortimer, analytics seems to rarely have good news for me," I said, doing my best to look and sound like Vance Uroboros would.

"Very little of the global economy has survived, and some of the places we thought were going to join the new global initiative went dark last week. We've no one on the ground that has been able to report back yet," Mortimer stated. He placed his data slate on the edge of my desk and summoned several interactive holographic graphs and charts with a wave of his hand.

"Tell me about mainland Asia and the Pacific Islands," I inquired.

I nearly lost my calm looking over the figures.

"All dark, as are Russia and Ukraine. We haven't seen a single light from space, nor received a radio transmission from that half of the world. Europe and Africa have a handful of cities with the lights on and the capacity to transport goods. South America and Mexico seem largely unaffected, except as a result of the trade deficit," Mortimer stated, gesturing to one of the floating holographic graphs.

"We have significant holdings in South America. Why is the flow of goods so constrained?" I inquired, already knowing the answer.

"The graphs are scaled to show demand relative to our ability to move goods. We have transports running around the clock to move food but we can barely keep Port Montaigne and the surrounding area fed, even with rationing."

The most dangerous symptom of the Shutdown was not a lack of communications or the ability to move freely. Restoring communications, the ability to travel freely, and access to medical care was important, but it would have to wait. Even before the world went mostly dark, hunger was a problem worldwide. More people would starve in the next ninety days than all other causes of death combined if we didn't change the trends I was observing.

Vance Uroboros had put me in charge of making sure that people wouldn't starve in the aftermath of his plan to wrest control of the global economy from a very greedy few. One nanotechnological replica to figure out how to feed billions of people. Vance knew this would be a problem, but he couldn't have known how precarious things would be if his plan didn't go exactly as intended. I had to remind myself I wasn't human in that moment, just to stay objective. Even then, I often failed to be civil when I was stressed.

"Mortimer, did you even bother to shower this morning? We have running water in most of the city, do we not?" I growled, dismissing the holographic data floating in front of me.

"Yes, of course," Mortimer replied hesitantly.

"Then it's only your reports that stink? It is, alone, your incompetent handling of data and econometric analysis that floods my office with the stench of failure?" I asked, adjusting my tie.

"We've staff returning from South America tomorrow, they should be able to assist me in getting more accurate findings," Mortimer stammered, gathering up his data slate.

"See that they do."

Mortimer scurried out of Vance's office, an unseen hydraulic closure pulling the richly adorned wooden doors shut behind him. I settled back down into Vance's chair and turned to gaze at the small Drone huddled beside me. Brook looked up at me, her face displaying her displeasure at having raised my voice.

"Why are you so mean to him?" Brook asked.

"He's incompetent. I can literally smell failure wafting about around him wherever he goes," I explained, wrinkling my nose.

"I don't smell anything. He smells like a man, and not even a stinky one. For all your yelling, I think he bathes twice before coming to work," Brook said softly, scolding me slightly with her tone.

"Truly, I don't know why my mind translates frustration into aromatic sensation," I replied, deadpan as possible.

"Your mind really does that?"

"No, but wouldn't that be neat?"

Brook smiled quietly at the thought. She was my only comfort in what was a very dire situation. If it wasn't for her vouching for Mortimer's loyalty, I would have dispensed with him long ago. Vance Uroboros clearly valued loyalty, even before I robbed him of his memory, and so I continue on in that same tradition. Mortimer might stink, but he would die before betraying the firm.

"Shall I continue looking for Vance the Younger?" Brook asked.

"If you haven't been able to find him in the last three weeks, I'm inclined to believe he isn't in Port Montaigne. What I am certain of, is that he will return and try to take control of Uroboros Financial," I said, taking my suit coat off and hanging it on the high-backed chair.

"Why would he come back?" Brook asked innocently.

"It's what I would do," I replied, removing my cufflinks and rolling up my shirt sleeves.

"Taylor thinks he's probably taken a full dose of the catalyst. He will be pretty bad to deal with."

"Tomorrow, when our transport returns from South America, I think you and I should get back aboard for the return flight. We're going to need to try to find some of Vance Uroboros' assets abroad and pull together the individuals loyal to his original vision. All the data and analytics in the world are meaningless without the personnel to do something about them," I said, trying to change the subject.

Brook stood beside me fidgeting as I looked out the window at the late morning sun, blurred radiance spread out over the Atlantic Ocean. I shared her anxiety knowing something of how dangerous and unpredictable Vance the Younger, was before he took a dose of the nanotechnological catalyst designed to upgrade the firmware governing our bodies. I'd been offered the opportunity, but declined knowing how dangerous I already was. Being already able to relieve someone of their memories was a terrifying power I hoped to never use again.

The rest of that day passed quietly as I made my usual rounds, attending meetings, and replying to interdepartmental mail. The mundane things gave me balance when I thought about how the world had crushed Vance Uroboros' dream, like Atlas utterly failing when his shoulders were needed most. I wished I could have been there to watch Dr. Madmar draw his last breath and watch his eyes fade to lifelessness.

For many in Port Montaigne, little had changed since the Shutdown, the city being uniquely insulated for the event. There were riots over lack of food and unrest at the port for paying work but these new civic uprisings just replaced old ones. I had begun to feel a cold indifference to it all except that I had been entrusted with sacred work, the sort one did not deny. Nanotechnological replica, Drone, or human being, we rarely get a chance to make a difference, or serve a higher ideal.

I was determined to not squander what chance I had left.

Brook and I grabbed a few hours of sleep on the leather couches in Vance's office while waiting for the transport. She needed far less sleep than I and spent much of that time keeping vigil over me. I'm not certain why she was so protective. It was probably something intrinsic to her design. She was created to rescue people from smoking wreckages, and some part of her knew that I was trapped in one, even if just allegorically.

Secretly, I was glad for it. After being injured and healed by Taylor's own nanotechnological influence, I had begun to sleep very deeply. I would awake sometimes to see Brook standing there, her hand on my chest making certain I was still breathing. Always she would look into my eyes, as if she was just doing what she was supposed to. Ezra One told me that his tribal leader believed Brook was supposed to be above ground for a reason, that she had a purpose or destiny to fulfill. I didn't believe in such nonsense openly, but I would often be glad to consider the notion privately.

In the weeks since we left Matthias' laboratory, Brook had changed. I knew it was likely impossible, but she seemed slightly taller and more feminine. I was terrible at making small talk or starting conversations about personal matters, and I declined to ask her about the changes. It was in her voice and demeanor as well, as all the things that made her childlike were fading with gained experience of the surface world.

"Why are you so sad? We're going on a fun trip," Brook asked me, as I gathered up my briefcase.

"Do I seem sad?" looking up at the wall length mirror between two bookcases in the office.

"You smell a certain way when you are, almost like tears would form if you knew how," Brook observed, handing me my coat.

"Contentment is a sort of living death. Sadness isn't the thing people think it is. It isn't meant to be treated with pills or by filling your living space with things. My sadness is my vital force, the thing that gives me motion," I explained as gently as possible.

"I like what I do. It makes me happy," Brook replied.

"You've never hurt anyone, and never would. You're allowed," I said, wishing desperately I could be as unburdened as my companion.

"I hurt Madmar, or tried to," she said indignantly.

"He doesn't count."

As the transport descended slowly, I was filled with a terrible foreboding. The exterior was dimpled across the bottom with small arms fire, and blackened by soot. They were supposed to have left

Rio de Janeiro as their last stop on the journey. That they may have encountered unrest there was as alarming as it was disheartening. Blake Messer was the first off the transport, his suit rumpled, and he smelled of smoke.

"Mr. Messer, why is my transport all shot up and my employees otherwise spindled?" I asked, adopting Vance's persona.

"Mr. Uroboros, I didn't realize you'd be here to meet us," he said, coughing into his fist.

"Why is that?" I asked.

"Oh, well, no reason I guess. I'm just not used to being met on the landing pad by anyone and…"

"Your report please, Mr. Messer," I interrupted.

"There are riots in Rio over a lack of work and the government allowing refugees into the country from the north. Our influence there is stable and our assets secure, but that may not persist without intervention," Messer replied, gesturing to the other executives to come out on the landing pad.

"Isn't South American your responsibility? Why is there unrest in a place that you are supposed to be watching over?" I asked, betraying no emotion whatsoever.

"If it were not for our efforts, the riots would be far worse. We've kept unemployment to the low teens," he reported, transferring his report from his mobile to mine via near field communications protocol.

"I want it to be single digit by next week. Get inside and aid Mr. Mortimer in analytics. No one sleeps until we have a clearer view of our stake in Brazil and a means to bolster the local authorities. Go, now," I said clapping my hands to hurry them along.

I watched the executives scurry across the landing pad and out of sight, allowing Brook to emerge from the utility stairs under the landing pad. We walked up the loading ramp into the transport to find the pilot, Gregor Mundt, performing a check of the systems. He looked up from the wall mounted terminal in the cargo hold, obviously tired from the journey.

"I need to get back to South America tonight."

"Ah, Mr. Uroboros! I see you've brought the charming Miss Brook with you this time as well. Let me make us some coffee, then we will be on our way," Mr. Mundt replied cheerily.

"You alright to make the journey?" Brook asked.

It was a valid question. Mr. Mundt was a pale man, in his late fifties, with thick black hair he usually kept combed straight back. That night, he looked even more pallid, his normally clear eyes were bloodshot and tired. He did not look well.

"I will sleep when I am dead, no?" Mr. Mundt replied, gesturing for us to follow him.

The kitchen aboard the transport was no larger than a hallway with an array of appliances built into one wall. Mr. Mundt began brewing a new pot of coffee while he hummed some song I didn't recognize. Brook looked on intently as she always does, devouring the movements and mannerisms of everyone around her.

"Very nasty in Rio right now, Mr. Uroboros. You sure we shouldn't bring more people for the journey?" Mr. Mundt inquired.

"It'll be fine. If things go well, our security will be augmented for the return trip," I replied, checking the time on my watch.

Mr. Mundt nodded as he filled his thermos with coffee. He'd learned in recent weeks that it was better not to question me, but he seemed to lack any other way to make conversation. Traveling with him was a patience building exercise, but only a few could fly a transport as he did.

"Mr. Messer smelled like fear. He reeked of it," Brook whispered, blowing on her coffee.

"That's strange," I said, trying to fathom why someone that traveled the world for the firm would be afraid of anything.

"I think he was afraid of you."

"He shouldn't be, he is fully vested and his last assessment was positive. Something to look into when we get back," I said, finding a seat in the passenger compartment.

Mundt's heavy transport lifted slowly into the air, engines vibrating loudly enough that Brook had to cover her ears. I watched over Mundt's shoulder as he brought us around to face south down the coastline before pressing the throttle down slowly to bring us up to speed. The world raced by below us as the heavily modified craft that carried us climbed higher and higher. I loved to fly.

"Mr. Uroboros, if we skirt Venezuela's airspace we can cut a few minutes off our flight time," Mr. Mundt said, looking back at me over his shoulder.

"No. I won't gamble with our lives over thirty minutes, Mr. Mundt," I replied, looking at Brook strapped into a crew seat beside me.

"As you say, we'll be there in about seven hours," Mr. Mundt reported.

I could tell Brook didn't like flying and did my best to comfort her, even though I've no clue how one actually does that. It seemed to matter to her that I cared, which was good enough.

"What about flying bothers you?" I asked.

"I saw a bad wreck once, remember?" Brook explained.

"I remember."

"Why are we going to Brazil?" Brook asked.

"To find a man," I replied.

"What sort of man?"

"At the bad wreck you witnessed, there was a man there."

"With the cybernetic eyes?" Brook replied, turning to meet my gaze.

"Yes, him."

"We're looking for a man like him?"

"No, we're looking for him specifically."

"He was bad," Brook said worriedly. "Ezra One said so."

"I'm counting on it. Also, not all augmented individuals are bad, Brook. Some are very useful."

"How do you know where to look for him?" Brook asked.

"I know many things that the real Vance Uroboros knows, not just what I was imprinted with, but things he told me as well."

"Someday, you'll have to explain all this to me."

"The man's codename is Perfidy. He worked for the organization you told me about."

"The one with the monks, that Dr. Helmet told Taylor and me about?"

"Yes, that one."

Brook paused, her face turning toward the floor for a moment.

"They seem bad to me, too," Brook whispered.

"If there's anything about this you don't like, we'll leave and try something else. Okay?"

She seemed satisfied with that. Her anxiety wasn't unfounded and she was extremely good at calculating risk and liability in most situations. I think that many discounted Brook as being naïve, but they couldn't be more wrong when it came to bad people. She could almost smell them and had helped me expose many of them at Uroboros Financial in the weeks previous. If Brook was uneasy about Perfidy, I was wise to be as well.

"Wouldn't he be old now?" Brook asked.

"Yes, I suppose he would. Still, he has a vast knowledge of our employer's former organization and the assets managed therein. We will need his help to fix the world, Brook."

"Okay."

Rio de Janeiro was an interesting sight from the air. There was a large statue of a man in a robe overlooking the city, and many fires burning in the streets. Unrest and rioting had marred what appeared to be a restful place, and there were many displaced individuals squatting in alleys and spaces between buildings. Mr. Mundt brought the transport down toward the airport, slowing his descent as he drew close to the private portion of the airfield.

After we set down, Mr. Mundt opened the hold so we could exit. After unbuckling myself, I helped Brook get free of the crew seat and made sure her kerchief was oriented in such a way to hide her nature. Mr. Mundt just nodded, pulling his cap over his eyes for a snooze.

"Heh."

"What?" Brook asked, pulling on a pair of leather gloves.

"A nanotechnological replica and a genetically engineered rescue worker just flew halfway across the world. We're here to hire security for food shipments humanity desperately needs, but that other humans will probably try to hijack."

"Yes?" Brook replied, smiling.

"It's all very absurd. We could go anywhere, couldn't we?" I said, looking out at the city.

"I want to help people. We should help people," Brook said, smiling back at me as she exited the passenger compartment.

"Okay, but if you see something fun you'd like to do here, speak up," I said, following her to the cargo hold.

We walked out onto the tarmac and across to the private terminal. It was mid-morning, but only a single person was manning the reception area. She smiled pleasantly as we wandered through, taking note of the markings on our vehicle. In times past, the CEO of one of the most powerful financial firms in the world traveling by Romani freighter transport would have been tabloid news. Now, it was just business as usual.

The city smelled sweet, like food cooking and drinks flowing. This, in spite of the smoke billowing upward to be whisked out to sea by a gentle breeze. Brook walked along ahead of me, stopping every once in a while to sniff the air. I let her wander for a while, waiting for the inevitable question.

"Where is this man, the one we're looking for?" she asked.

"My sources say he's the other way," I replied, pointing back over my shoulder.

"Oh, why didn't you say anything?"

"We may never come here again. See everything you can, while you can."

"Aren't we pressed for time?" she asked.

"Sure, but he isn't going anywhere, and you seemed happy to look around."

Brook smiled, pointing to several street markets up the way. Time was a precious commodity. For me, this was particularly the case. Because of Taylor's intervention there was no telling when I would suddenly age and cease to function, like many of my siblings. It wasn't something I dwelled on where Brook was concerned. The sum of her joy was often my only joy.

We walked back up toward the commercial edge of town, far from where tourists gathered to seek eateries, cantinas, and other earthly delights. The colorful awnings were replaced with hand painted sign board and chain link fence. We lingered outside a place that advertised repairs for mobile devices, upgrades, and warranty replacement. When a tourist or a local lost or broke their mobile, this is one of many places they could go.

"He's in there?" Brook asked, squinting in the direction of the building.

"Allegedly," I replied, stepping up to the front door.

The interior was festooned with a wide assortment of mobile devices, some counting as antiques being decades old. Everything had a use here, and every machine was wanted and valued. The legacy of the mobile industry was on display, like the small shop was a museum of handheld devices. Working at the window across the sales floor was an older man, monitors and crude sensors hooked up to sockets that had replaced his eyes. He sported a red bandanna on his head, broad arms, and a thick beard of greying black hair.

I approached, setting my mobile on the counter in front of him. The old cyborg turned one of the sensors hanging up beside him toward the window so he could see me. His shoulders slumped as he let out a loud sigh.

"Vance Uroboros," he said, somewhat dejected.

"No," I replied, shaking my head slightly.

"Thought all you guys were dead. Which one are you?" he asked.

"Kale."

Perfidy adopted a look of deep concern, his face creasing across his brow. His shoulders grew taut as if he were about to enact some sort of escape plan. I wondered what his plan was exactly, as his eye sockets were hooked up to ancient monitors designed to allow him to do the intricate work necessary to fix small electronics. He'd likely practiced running out blind in the event someone came looking for him. As amusing as that might have been, it was not the outcome I desired.

"Be at peace, you are in no danger. It is just my associate and me," I said calmly, gesturing to Brook.

"What do you want?" he asked, letting his hands drop back behind the counter.

"Perfidy, I want to hire you. I can provide you with cybernetic augmentation, and give you access to certain information in exchange for your services," I explained.

"I'm done working for you people."

"I didn't say *we* want to hire you, I said *I* want to hire you. There is no Uroboros Financial, shadowy secret organizations, or governmental puppet operation. It is just Brook, you, and me," I said slowly.

"I don't understand."

"You joined up voluntarily with Vance Uroboros to seek out an agenda. Was that agenda fulfilled? Did you and he accomplish what you set out to do?" I asked.

"No. Madmar hijacked everything, messed it up."

"Are you okay with that?"

"It doesn't really matter I suppose. I've ditched all my CGG optics and other enhancements. You want to go up against Madmar, you're on your own," Perfidy said, his Spanish-Portuguese accent growing a little thicker with his irritation.

"Madmar's dead. The chief coroner on the CGG Moon Installation sent his findings to me weeks ago along with the autopsy video for verification. We had our best people look at it. Ezra One killed the real deal a few weeks ago, before he could attempt his transference experiment," I explained quietly.

"Ezra One killed him?" Perfidy said, not really asking.

"Yes, broke his neck after inflicting critical damage to his life support harness. I think it was accidental, but Ezra One damaged the countermeasures that might have allowed Madmar to survive or enact the transference. Without a neural link, his various cybernetic puppets and proxies ceased to function as well. Any part of his network that wasn't autonomous is gone."

"If Ezra said he's dead, it must be true," Brook added quietly.

Perfidy turned the mounted optic down so he could see Brook. A slight smile crept across his face when he saw her. He laughed. It wasn't a cruel laugh, but one of genuine mirth at the sight of her.

"I know you."

"Yes?"

"All those years ago, the crash in Downtown Port Montaigne. You and Ezra One somehow eluded me and I found myself in a Red Coat trap. What a strange assignment that was," Perfidy said, calming down somewhat.

Brook responded in local dialect, a mix of Spanish and Portuguese, a small smile breaking out over her face. Perfidy nodded, his own smile growing wider. I don't know what they said, but it seemed to amuse the both of them greatly.

"When did you learn to speak the local language?" Perfidy asked.

"We wandered the street for a couple of hours. I listened to people talk as we did. I have very keen ears," Brook explained.

"She's kidding, right?" Perfidy asked, turning the monitor back up in my direction.

"No, she's a Type 3 ES. She's trained to be dropped into disaster zones and seek out survivors in the wreckage. When she finds people who would be trapped, learning to communicate with them quickly would be crucial. I asked her to accompany me because she genuinely wants to help people and is exceedingly good at it," I explained.

"Got your own Drone sidekick like Silverstein? What do you need me for?" Perfidy asked.

"She isn't my sidekick. We're partners," I growled.

"Sure, okay, but the question still stands," Perfidy said, leaning forward on the counter.

"I need a common killer that asks stupid questions, I guess," I said, feigning anger at his question.

"You just going to toss us away as soon as we're no longer useful to you?" Perfidy asked, his expression darkening.

"You, maybe. She's my partner, and I've contingencies in place for her in the event I'm killed or die naturally," I said, looking directly into Perfidy's monitor.

"You care for her?" Perfidy asked, the edge to his voice having departed.

"Insomuch as I'm able," I said.

Perfidy scratched his chin thoughtfully, taking the handgun he'd been holding on me beneath the counter and placing it in front of him.

"What do you need me to do?" Perfidy asked, calmly.

"I've already arranged to have pre-CGG cybernetics brought here. It's all Omicron Class hardware, 15th Generation and unregulated. I had it released from an old CGG special operations cache. The optics have full

ACOGs, with an integrated autonomous HUD, and possess multiple spectrum reticles that can allow you to see in near absolute darkness and infrared. It'll take time to recalibrate your twitch ratio and sight in the optics, but I can have you combat ready in forty-eight hours," I explained.

"What's the pay?" Perfidy asked, clearly not caring that much.

"Your usual fee, plus ten percent hazard pay, wired securely to any account you choose."

"Weapons?"

"I can get anything you want, delivered in seventy-two hours or less," I said, smirking at his handgun.

"Who are the targets?"

"I need Port Montaigne secured from insurgency first, and then we'll begin working across the Eastern Seaboard to bolster the few large metropolitan areas that haven't gone dark. I need augmented security on food and supply transports going to heavily impacted areas."

Perfidy continued to scratch the stubble on his chin for a moment, considering all I'd said. I could tell that even though he was probably in his fifties, he still kept himself in excellent shape. Brook stood on the tips of her toes and peered over the counter at Perfidy, making him grin at the sight of her. At last, he nodded, drawing the deep connections to the monitors out of his eye sockets and replacing them with a pair of ancient optical implants.

"Let's go," Perfidy said, dropping the handgun into his waistband.

He locked the door behind him as we stepped into the street and put the keys in his pocket. We walked out and traveled by foot nearly a mile to the Uroboros Financial safe house I'd set up days earlier. Several of my agents and the best cyberneticists I could find awaited us. They each seemed to know Perfidy on sight and smiled like it was a gathering of old friends. Brook stood beside me taking in everything they said, her silvery eyes darting back and forth as they spoke.

"Do you think Perfidy is going to be able to help us?" Brook asked.

"He's an expert in asymmetric urban warfare, and has over a thousand kills logged working for Uroboros Financial in a dozen different countries over the last thirty years. If he can't help us, no one can," I replied, calmly watching the doctors prepare Perfidy for surgery.

"What was with all the questions?" Brooks asked.

"He possesses a lot of empathy for children, Drones, and Metasapients and has an affinity for them."

"When Vance the Younger returns, there might be a fight," Brook stated quietly.

"No matter what happens, you are not to fight. I know you are capable, and that you are strong, but you are not a Type One," I explained.

"I don't understand. I'm good now. I can fight," Brook said, clenching a small fist.

"If everyone had stuck to their function in life and done what they were supposed to do, going back decades now, we wouldn't be in this situation. The world would not be fighting a losing battle against a darkness that threatens to swallow it whole," I said, glowering at the gathered cybernetic experts and doctors.

The procedure would take hours, and Perfidy languished in post op for several more. Brook wandered out of the safe house during that time, to 'check the perimeter,' a practice she picked up from Ezra One. We always want to be what we are not, no matter how exceptional we might be. Brook had seen that problems could be solved with violence and had not yet seen the aftermath of such choices. I didn't take my hiring of Perfidy lightly in that regard. I hoped that even as we overcame those aiding the fall and the aftermath of the Shutdown, that Brook would garner perspective she could take back to her people.

"Mr. Uroboros, the patient took very well to the implants. We've given him the treatments to accelerate his healing, but I don't know that they were even necessary," the doctor said, approaching me in the briefing room.

"Take your team and your security personnel and return to your normal assignments. I appreciate your willingness to come on short notice to an area experiencing unrest," I said, taking the data slate from the doctor.

"Someone should remain to monitor the patient's recovery," the doctor stated, folding his arms.

I put the data slate down on the table instead of returning it to the doctor and gazed at him with the coldest expression my tired eyes could muster. The doctor turned his gaze to the floor and shuffled back out to the small medical facility beyond. He wanted to study Perfidy; a subject of that particular and illegal gene therapy would respond or react extraordinarily to Omicron Class hardware and be fascinating for an ambitious specialist. I resolved to have the doctor investigated following our South American adventure. The last thing I wanted was someone trying to follow in Dr. Madmar's footsteps.

"I've been listening to the people while I've been out," Brook said, waiting until the medical personnel had departed.

"Yes?"

"The worst of the unrest here began after Mr. Messer took responsibility for the financial security of the area. The people do not attribute it to Uroboros Financial, but I asked around and the checked the dates on our own records," Brook reported, gesturing for me to look at the data pad sitting beside me.

"It could be a coincidence," I said, pushing the data pad to one side.

"Could be."

CHAPTER 3

Uroboros Financial Safe House

Rio de Janeiro - March 27th, 2200

Kale's Private Records, Part 2 –

The degree of augmentation Perfidy endured would kill a normal human. His unique biology, a gift of his birth, coupled with gene-therapy during his time in the CGG military allowed him to linger near the brink of death, and then recover quickly. Following implantation, his body rapidly adapts and recovers giving his employers the means to upgrade or alter his hardware set to suit a particular mission. It used to be that there were many such soldiers, but much like myself and Brook, Perfidy had become a rare or unique commodity.

In the three days it took him to recover, Brook would go out and get us food from the eateries nearby, bringing us different local food each time. Perfidy said little, the initial disorientation caused by the new optics forced him to lie very still while his new systems calibrated and synced with his biological and cognitive functions. For my own part, I wondered if Madmar's Faustian adventure could be overcome, civilization going dark little by little every day we lingered.

"Am I whole?" Perfidy asked, the morning of the third day he was to recover.

"By all indications. I've had Brook run diagnostics every hour to make sure there is no cognitive displacement. You won't be one hundred percent for another twelve hours, but you should be able to sit up now if you want," I said, checking the data slate I confiscated from the company cyberneticist.

"I thought all of Vance's replicas went up with a kill switch Madmar had installed," Perfidy stated, sitting up slowly.

"Those of us that were exposed in some way to a particular nanotechnological catalyst were able to survive," I explained.

"How many other replicas are still active?"

"At least one that we're aware of."

"Hostile?"

"Vance the Younger, was never a particularly stable replica, his purpose lost with Vance Uroboros' memory. His late deployment in the organization was marked with as much violence as vice. He is the least like our employer of any of the other replicas, and was dangerous before taking a full dose of a catalyst designed to upgrade the firmware of terrestrial intelligent agents," I said, helping Perfidy to sit up.

"What's with the moniker?" Perfidy asked with a chuckle.

"His nanoid body makes him look like an adolescent version of Vance Uroboros. When the other replicas went rogue, they excluded him from their plans and set him to menial tasks. I've only been in a room with him a couple of times, and we never really spoke. I don't know him other than what Taylor was able to relate to me about her encounter with him," I explained.

"What happened with Taylor?" Perfidy asked, waving his hands in front of his new optics.

"He tried to harm her to serve his own amusement. She shot him."

"You sure he survived?"

"No. He could have been killed and swept into the underground during the Downtown Port Montaigne riots. He may have already been fed into a furnace by a Drone tunnel sweeper team."

Perfidy smiled for a moment. "But, you crunched the numbers and felt an asymmetric response was necessary, just in case he survived?"

"Can a machine, even one as arguably as complex as myself, operate on a hunch?"

"Sounds like we will be finding out one way or another," Perfidy said.

Brook slipped into the infirmary a moment later carrying two large paper sacks. She set about arraying the food on a stainless steel operating table, folding the napkins and arraying the plastic flatware at each place setting. She stopped mid-process when she noticed Perfidy was sitting up.

"You're feeling better?" Brook asked.

"Yeah, everything is just about synced and mostly healed up now."

"Is that bacalhau? You must have walked all the way to the water to find it so fresh," Perfidy remarked, rubbing his hands together.

"It's just fish, nothing fancy."

Perfidy just smiled and nodded, taking a few careful steps to take a standing position next to Brook's improvised lunch table. We ate together quietly, sharing a bottle of water with the food Brook had brought us. At the time, I knew it would be one of the last quiet moments we would share, what with all the work there was to be done.

"What's the engagement protocol moving forward?" Perfidy asked.

"Kill anyone hostile to our agenda. I'll authorize as many of your allies cleared for combat as you can find and trust," I replied, between bites.

"Vance never wanted casualties. We were always told…"

"Vance isn't here, and while I know that would be Brook's preference as well, billions of people are depending on us. There is no room for failure," I said, putting down my fork.

"Please, we shouldn't kill people," Brook pleaded.

"If we do this right, we shouldn't have to. I want to adopt a deterrent-based strategy and operate in near absolute secrecy. That should prevent us from having to engage insurgency directly," I explained.

"Now you're sounding like Vance," Perfidy chuckled.

Reports from analytics began to appear on my mobile as a private transport took us back to the private airfield. It was clear that someone, possibly external to Uroboros Financial, was manipulating what little markets there were, and not to the benefit of all. It was insidious the way the individual or individuals responsible were twisting the sputtering remnant of the global economy. Regardless, it would require a tacit understanding of how and why Uroboros Financial operates, the sum of nuances and insider experience that would be difficult to relate without having previously worked there.

Brook had taken possession of the confiscated data slate and was reading the contents of it when she turned it around to show Perfidy. He took it from her and gazed worriedly at the screen before handing it to me. The reports I'd requested had been leaked and were out there for anyone with a connection to what remained of the auxiliary CGG Internet to see. Someone was working against us from the shadows, and it was imperative I find out who that was exactly.

"So much for secrecy," Perfidy said, obviously annoyed.

"Indeed, but this narrows the list of suspects to two departments internal to Uroboros Financial. Also, it has to be a current employee," Brook said.

"They'll make a mistake. When they do, I'll handle it, personally," I said, making eye contact with Brook and Perfidy to make sure they understood.

The private airfield was as quiet and empty as when we arrived. It looked as though Mr. Mundt had kept his craft ready and the engine warm for my return. Even as we closed the distance, I could hear gunfire and chaos off in the distance behind us. Rio was to see another day of turmoil because someone in my employ was greedy.

"Mr. Uroboros, ready to go home?" Mr. Mundt asked, beckoning us up the ramp leading to his freighter hauler.

"As quickly as possible, please," I replied.

As soon as we were all strapped into crew seats and airborne the questions inevitably came, the sort I rarely had answers to.

"When you last spoke to Vance Uroboros, or Silverstein, or whatever he's calling himself... did he know how bad things were?" Perfidy asked.

"Silverstein, Taylor, and Ezra One had just set the Lunar Colony to a renewal cycle and were exchanging hugs and high-fives. The timing seemed inappropriate," I replied.

"Inappropriate? Sixty percent of the planet is dark, twenty percent is like a flickering light bulb waiting to go out, and the rest is on fire. Is there an appropriate time to tell someone about that? It'll filter up to him on the colony eventually, you know that, right?" Perfidy said, almost yelling at me.

"Do you always look to others to solve your problems? Silverstein is already somewhat under the mistaken notion that this is all his fault," I snapped, throwing Perfidy an ugly stare.

"The Shutdown was his plan, he…"

"No. His plan was to see the Earth immediately cycle into renewal, wealth sequestered for the purpose of rebuilding and ending hunger, class warfare, and contrived poverty. What we're dealing with now is on us, his subordinates that failed to carry out and protect that plan. You and I are among the few still alive that are truly accountable for this mess. I am paying you to help me limit the damage and prevent more from happening, out of courtesy," I said, old and forgotten fury welling up within me.

Perfidy gazed at me for a moment, his lips tight and angry. "Okay, what are we going to do about it?"

"There are nearly four dozen large commercial class transports in dock at the Moon Colony. They're almost ready to return to Earth and aid us in the moving of goods. It is crucial we get food to afflicted areas, and soon. We need to arrange for, and guarantee, the security of every single transport. Turning the lights back on will be pointless if everyone starves to death," I said, regaining my calm.

"You're expecting someone will try to hit those transports?" Perfidy replied, incredulous.

"With so many lives in the balance, can we risk making any other assumption?" Brook said, taking the data slate from me.

Perfidy nodded solemnly, the gravity of what we faced seemed to finally hit home with him.

"I didn't mean to lose my patience, but I feel deeply responsible. It was up to me to make sure no one was hungry. I sequestered vast amounts of food around the globe for the purpose but it was under the assumption that transportation wouldn't be locked down outside of legislative protocols. My other contingencies have failed, and these transports docked at the colony are our best chance of limiting the damage," I explained.

"Forget about it. If there's a way to fix this, we'll find it," Perfidy assured me.

"I'm sending the reports to Taylor. I'll let her decide how much to show Silverstein, but someone needs to know so they'll hurry with the transports," Brook said, typing with her thumbs on the data slate.

"Impress upon her the need to be careful with whatever measures they take. I do not want the lunar populace to panic or act hastily in trying to save loved ones on Earth. The fewer people who know what we're attempting to do, the better," I explained.

Brook nodded, finishing the missive and handing back the data slate. I checked her message. Being satisfied with the content, I sent it to Taylor's friend in Finland, Versa-013, to relay it on to her securely. Once I received acknowledgment it had been received, I handed the data slate back to Brook.

"Hold on to the data slate for now. I don't need to see the reports until we're about to arrive."

"Are you going to yell at Mr. Mortimer some more?" Brook inquired.

"Do I need to?"

"The reports look good to me, but I don't really know what to look for."

I only smiled and shook my head in response. She knew more about financial analytics than some of the partners did, just from looking over my shoulder the last few weeks. Her understanding was more about working from a process of making associations and comparisons, as opposed to possessing actual knowledge. Still, the sum of that understanding was effective in telling good work from the bad, or the very lazy variety.

"Why all the effort to keep Silverstein out of the loop on this?" Perfidy asked, after we were airborne.

I hesitated to tell Perfidy in that moment. I probably wouldn't have if not for Brook tugging at my sleeve and nodding slightly. I had no way of knowing if I could really trust Perfidy, but the sooner I figured that out, the better.

"Shortly before the Shutdown, Vance Uroboros asked to meet me on the Lunar Colony. When I arrived, he gave me this," I said, pulling a somewhat rumpled envelope I had been quietly carrying for months.

"It reads like a writ of contingency, in the event of his death," Perfidy said, gazing at the contents.

"Yes."

"It says here he's lost a controlling interest in key elements of his global network and the world will suffer a terrible calamity for his hubris. He gave you this?" Perfidy asked calmly.

"Yes."

"What a jerk. Makes a gigantic mess and decides to dump the whole thing on you, while he runs to Mars? What'd you do?" Perfidy asked.

"After he sequestered the Lunar Omega AI, I confronted him. I wasn't equipped to help him, his mental health having failed. We argued, and I hit him with a pipe. I left him unconscious in Port Montaigne, and called the police," I explained calmly.

"Brutal, but way more rational than I would have been. I've been fine falling on my own sword, but being asked to fall on someone else's? It's bull, Kale," Perfidy stated, betraying what I perceived to be some genuine empathy for my situation.

"We worry that if he knows how bad things are, he might try to run, or even hurt himself," Brook explained.

"Was the blow from the pipe what robbed Vance of his memories?" Perfidy asked.

"No. I can will it to happen by being close to or touching the person in question," I explained.

"Never heard of a nanotech replica possessing that ability," Perfidy stated, somewhat fearfully.

"It is something that Vance Uroboros passed on to me through what I assume was an electroencephalogric interface when I was imprinted," I explained. Perfidy looked astonished for a moment. "Wait, how did he... why...?" Perfidy stammered trying to grasp all the variables. "We don't know why he did it," Brook said, patting Perfidy on the knee. "What happened after you dropped him in Port Montaigne?" Perfidy asked. "Predictably, my own mental health failed. Regardless, I'd done something terrible. I languished in a dark corner of the firm, forgotten for weeks, until human resources accidentally tipped me off to what was really going on. This was when I had my first inkling of Dr. Madmar's meddling. I did what I could to intervene after I recovered my faculties," I explained quietly. "And, the individuals in the firm responsible for colluding with Dr. Madmar?" Perfidy asked, somewhat angry.

"We took care of them," Brook replied.

"All, save Vance the Younger," I added.

"Where was Silverstein? Why did he go through all the trouble of traveling to the moon?" Perfidy asked.

"Mars was his destination. I don't know why," I replied.

The proximity alarm went off in the cockpit as Mr. Mundt began to drop the throttle forcing the freighter hauler to decelerate. I stripped off my harness to stand when small arms fire erupted somewhere outside, pelting our craft with projectiles. One hit the glass next to Mr. Mundt, startling him. While the bullet didn't pierce the windshield, Mr. Mundt began to struggle and grasp at his chest. He was going into cardiac arrest by the time I reached him.

"Brook, get up here and take Mr. Mundt to the cargo area. There's a defibrillator there, use it," I ordered, unstrapping Mr. Mundt from the pilot's seat.

There was a smaller craft shadowing us as we skirted the coastline. A side door was open, revealing the presence of several heavily armed and irregularly dressed individuals. They weren't military and their craft had most of the identifying markings painted over. Brook grabbed Mr. Mundt and hurriedly began dragging him out of sight.

"Where do you want me, boss?" Perfidy bellowed.

"The weapons you asked for should be in the cargo hold. Arm yourself," I said, strapping myself into the pilot's seat.

I pushed the throttle forward, accelerating, knowing I couldn't outrun them. I was angry. They matched my pace and drew closer, exactly what I was hoping they would do.

Transmission from nearby craft.

"Decline. Disengage collision prevention protocols, and prep to transmit," I said, looking over my shoulder at the craft as it drew closer to take more shots at us.

Collision prevention protocols disengaged. You are transmitting now. They are receiving.

I pulled the controls hard to the left. "Query... what do you get when you add a one hundred metric ton freighter hauler to a forty ton pirate skiff?" I asked.

I could hear their pilot cry out over the communications link in Portuguese, pure and unfettered unlike what was spoken further south.

Mr. Mundt's freighter hauler collided with the smaller craft, disabling it. I watched in the overhead monitor as it lost power and streaked down toward the beach, coming to rest roughly in the sand. Slowing down slightly, I brought the freighter hauler around to take a pass by the wreckage. Given the current lucrative transportation business, no one would waste a transport, even a smaller one, on piracy without a secondary agenda.

"What are you doing?!" Perfidy roared as he entered the passenger compartment.

"I want to know who they are," I replied, looking angrily back over my shoulder.

"Your pilot is in bad shape. The old guy is stable but he needs a hospital, soon," Perfidy replied, meeting my gaze.

I gritted my teeth and cursed, turning us back around to head north, but not until after I flew close enough to survey the wreckage and take some stills of the craft. Perfidy stood beside me in the cockpit, hand on my shoulder, as I brought us back up to cruising speed. I liked Mr. Mundt. In spite of his advanced age he was a reliable and competent employee. I quietly hoped every one of those hijackers died an unpleasant death.

"We'll figure out who is responsible. The world is a lot smaller now, right?" Perfidy remarked, heading back to the passenger compartment.

"Indeed."

The rest of the journey home was somber. Brook resided with Mr. Mundt in his quarters, keeping vigil over him as he struggled for his life. Perfidy mostly stayed in the passenger compartment behind me, checking and rechecking his weapons. The freighter hauler flew the same, even for the mostly cosmetic damage I'd inflicted to it.

It was a strange sensation, whenever I accessed imprinted information or skills Vance Uroboros had passed on to me. He was an expert pilot, and thus so was I. It didn't feel like I was a puppet, controlled by the shadows of imprinted cognitive impulses. There are few words to describe the feeling other than to say it felt like he was with me.

I don't mean the broken Vance Uroboros I hit with a pipe and robbed of his memories. When I'm flying a freighter hauler or transport, it is like the confident and powerful Vance is with me, guiding my hands and thoughts through each motion. It was that connection that made seeing him weak, unbearable, and, to a lesser degree, maddening. Perfidy seemed to get all that somehow, and it seemed, at least for now, I could trust him to aid me in my task.

"What do you want to do if the pilot doesn't make it?" Perfidy asked.

"I'll do the flying, I guess. There's no one else I trust to bring along," I said, disappointed at the thought.

Paramedics were waiting for us as I brought us down on the private landing pad outside Uroboros Financial. After dropping the cargo ramp, I began powering the ship down, taking all but the communication systems offline. I surveyed the landing pad and the office windows overlooking it to see if someone was watching our arrival. If I had arranged to have a mid-air hit squad kill the CEO, I would want to gaze upon the aftermath.

There were many faces looking down from their offices, but no one I would suspect to be capable of such treachery. Jason Mortimer was on the platform waiting, a data slate in hand with what were likely more of the analytics I requested. Wearily, I descended the ramp with the paramedics, my hand on Mr. Mundt's chest as they did. It wasn't just for show, I was genuinely concerned for him, a sensation I rarely experienced.

"I'm sorry, Mr. Uroboros, I'm sorry…" Mr. Mundt kept saying.

"It wasn't your fault, rest now," I said, glaring angrily at Mr. Mortimer.

The analyst swallowed hard at the sight, choosing to look at the landing pad as opposed to meeting my gaze.

"Mr. Mortimer," I said, holding my hand out for his slate.

"I could have transmitted these, it would have been simpler."

"Someone is leaking our findings to what little of the public still has CGG Internet access. Until we arrange for higher encryption and different data handling standards, treat everything as paper," I replied, as calmly as I could.

"Yes, sir. Is there anything else, sir?"

"Yes, please go away."

I watched him depart before heading back aboard the freighter hauler. Brook and Perfidy were in the hold waiting for me. The floor was slick with vomit that Brook was cleaning with a pressure hose. I quickly reviewed the contents of what Mortimer had brought me. The figures were grim.

"Any word yet on when those lunar transports are going to shake loose?" Perfidy asked.

"Taylor emailed me during the flight. The few they could get ready will hit Port Montaigne to take on additional crew tomorrow evening. Any they can't get ready will have to wait for the next opening relative to the military orbitals," Brook reported.

"How much do you think she's related to Silverstein?" I asked.

"Everything, probably. She feels bad for holding anything back from him," Brook replied sadly.

"How fragile do you think he is?" Perfidy asked.

"If we don't have every conceivable transport moving food in the next thirty days, a million people a day will starve to death. That's speaking conservatively, and without knowing what's really going on with more than half of the rest of the world," I said, trying hard not to sound dramatic.

"A sane man would not take that well," Perfidy remarked quietly.

"Why do we care about one man, when so many others are at risk? I like Silverstein, too, but we should be pushing hard for those transports," Brook stated quietly.

The words seem to take all but very little of her childlike demeanor with them.

"It isn't easy for Perfidy or me to be rational about this. He's worked for Vance a long time, and from what I know, was a true believer. I can't dismiss the notion that under the incertitude and squeamish doubt of Silverstein, is the man who created me," I explained.

"Yeah, that," Perfidy said, nodding.

"They can only go so fast, Brook. If you press people too hard, they break, they make mistakes. Humans are not as resilient as the Drones they created," I said, my thoughts drifting momentarily to Mr. Mundt.

"Okay, then we need to do something else. If we can't rely entirely on the lunar transports, we need to find some other means of moving the food to the hungry," Brook said, more insistently.

The situation was probably tripping every programmed instinct she had at that moment. I couldn't merely make transports appear out of thin air. There were hundreds of thousands languishing in ports, locked out and set to be repossessed. Even the most talented tele-mechanics would require hours or days with each transport to make them functional enough to transport goods reliably.

"Metasapients," I said at last, snapping my fingers. "There are thousands of Acrididae class Metasapients in Asia, Africa, and Central America for agricultural labor. They can travel quickly long distances, and can carry a decent amount of weight while doing so. I don't have the last reported numbers, but they could provide an effective short range relay for goods, extending somewhat our coverage area," I explained.

"They are going to be unreliable. Most of them are treated like slaves in the areas you are talking about. I've been to those places. Convincing them to aid humans of their own free will won't be easy, particularly if the local populace is still exploiting them," Perfidy explained.

"What if someone emancipated them, allowed them to unionize, and paid them a reasonable sum for their services?" I asked.

"You would need a thousand mercenaries, a dozen heavy transports to carry them, and diplomatic contact with the regions in question. This assumes there is anyone to talk to in those areas. A lot of them could be dark," Perfidy replied.

"Do you have a better idea?" Brook inquired.

"No," Perfidy said with a sigh. "I need the most secure communications equipment you have. I'll try to reach out, see if any of my old friends are on the grid."

We walked down to the lower hanger inside Uroboros Financial where Vance's old transport was being stored. I entered in the complex code to access it and sat down in the pilot's seat. After a few seconds the communication systems were online and ready to be used.

"Wow, this is the boss man's ride?" Perfidy asked, sitting down at communications terminal.

"Yep," Brook said, patting the leather seats.

"This will take a while," Perfidy said, running a plug from the terminal to his own cybernetic enhancements.

"Shall we find some food?" Brook asked.

"We need to see Salvatore anyway, make sure he has made all the arrangements. I'm going to lock you in. We'll be back in an hour or so," I said, exiting the transport.

Perfidy nodded and waved back over his shoulder as we departed. I closed the hanger door and locked it before heading back into Uroboros Financial. I had made an arrangement with an individual named Salvatore some weeks back. My understanding was that he had met Silverstein, Ezra One, and Taylor, and been recruited to aid them after their Lunar windfall. Giving access to the food I'd sequestered, to someone I barely knew, did not sit well with me.

Brook engaged in her usual subterfuge to navigate the building, taking the utility stairs and moving through areas that were closed for renovations. There was a lot of unoccupied building to travel through. Many employees that were abroad during the Shutdown had not yet returned. I did my best to waste little time looking official before we slipped quietly out to procure private transport to midtown.

"Why are we going now, and alone?" Brook asked me.

"Whoever it was that arranged for us to get hit has failed to kill me. If they're smart enough to arrange a mid-air attack, they are savvy enough to have contingencies. I need to draw them out, make them move before they are ready again. I'm moving outside the known corporate schedule for Vance Uroboros. I will miss meetings, a luncheon, and so forth. People will notice, and they will talk," I said, letting my frustration show just a little.

"What do we do if someone moves on us while we're meeting with Salvatore?"

"Test Salvatore's loyalty," I replied.

"We won't have weapons, or Perfidy. Could be bad," Brook said, fidgeting in her seat.

The small transport slowed along the main drag in midtown outside a large open air market. It was unusually crowded for being so late in the evening. There were at least two seagoing freighters out in the port that had come in recently. I hadn't yet seen their manifests, but it was clear they had unloaded a lot of shelf stable food as dock crews were still trying to figure out where to put it all. At least some part of what I was trying to do was ahead of schedule.

"Mr. Salvatore," I said, extending my hand.

He took my hand, gazing at me oddly. "You grew your hair out, and…"

"And, what?" I asked.

"Nothing, Mr. Uroboros, you just seem different to me is all," Salvatore admitted, adjusting his wide brimmed straw hat.

"You're a discerning individual, to handle and assess so much cargo for the firm. We appreciate your contribution to the relief effort," I said, sounding as official as possible.

"Several of the shipments are early, things are looking much better today than yesterday. We just need distribution inland and…"

"Very good, Mr. Salvatore. Why don't you show me the product?" I interrupted, waving dismissively to Brook.

She nodded and scurried off, quietly donning her goggles. I kept track of her with my peripheral vision as we made our way down to the docks where the freshly unloaded cargo awaited. I could tell Salvatore was unnerved by my uncanny and completely accidental timing. Certainly, he hadn't filed the manifests yet and there was no way I could have known the cargo was there. His unease at the situation did little to foster the trust I was supposed to be developing.

"This all looks very good, and exactly what I ordered," I lied, having left the details to purchasing.

"Oh, that's great, glad you're happy," Salvatore said, his apprehension somewhat melting with my complimentary demeanor.

I looked up at the ships to see many armed guards and more than a little illicit activity being perpetrated. The ships were moving vice, but I didn't really care as long as my shipments arrived. I made sure Salvatore saw my indifferent reaction to it all before stopping to open one of the crates. I pried the contents open and gazed inside to see grains, dried seed, and other shelf stable food. There appeared to be no subterfuge at work with the official transmission of goods.

"I appreciate your diligence in this matter," I said, paying careful attention to Salvatore's reaction.

He shook my hand and seemed genuinely relieved and gratified. "Glad to," he said.

"Are you moving people across the Atlantic?" I asked, looking back toward the recently arrived ships.

"Sure, plenty of passengers and workers," Salvatore replied.

"That isn't what I asked," I said, quietly.

Salvatore lowered his head. "I'm sure it is happening, but it isn't sanctioned or allowed," he said, folding his arms.

"What are you doing to prevent the trafficking of human beings, Metasapients, and similar?" I asked.

"I take their travel papers, and blacklist them. I'm not sure what else I can do," Salvatore admitted.

"What would you like to do about it, if you could do anything you wanted?" I asked.

Salvatore thought about it for a moment. "Kill them. Especially if they trade kids."

At that moment, Brook and Taylor's expressed confidence that he could be trusted to aid us seemed to be validated. As we began to make our way back to the open air market, Brook wove back through the crowd to take up stride beside me. She looked deeply concerned.

"What is it?" I whispered.

"He's here, fresh off one of the boats," she replied quietly.

"Vance the Younger?"

"I've only seen stills of him, but yeah, pretty sure it is him."

I stopped dead in my tracks. Salvatore paused looking back over his shoulder with a genuine look of bafflement on his face. I looked past him as casually as I could, scanning the crowd. Standing at the pier in a set of ragged clothes I could see him, grinning eerily as he traded with one of the dock workers a small cloth satchel for a handful of cigarettes.

"Salvatore, do you have a gun?" I asked.

"Sure, we all try to stay armed to discourage theft," he replied.

"Give me your gun," I asked calmly, holding out my hand.

Salvatore reached into an ankle holster and retrieved a revolver with a seven round capacity. He handed it to me without question. I checked the cylinder, making sure I had all chambers full. Brook looked on worriedly, unable to see what I could due to her short stature. Grabbing Salvatore's straw hat, I headed into the crowd trying to keep my movements natural and my head down. I got within twenty five feet before he noticed me.

"Nice hat," he laughed, sprinting with preternatural speed toward me.

I stood so the gun was behind my thigh, readying it for use in close quarters, if it were to come to that. He leapt at me, one hand outstretched, while the other held a short blade. Brook caught him by the throat, the two of them twirling in mid-air for a moment from the centrifugal force. When they came to rest on the ground, I stepped in placing my foot on the blade and the barrel of the gun to his head.

Brook held her grip, which was strong enough he could not break it. Salvatore was shouting to the guards to hold their fire when he reached us. As he approached, I dropped the revolver in his hat and handed it off to him. Brook rose to her feet slowly, pulling Vance the Younger to his knees.

"Come to check the outcome of your handiwork? Why did you try to have us killed over Venezuela? Did you really think I wouldn't catch up to you eventually?" I sneered, gazing into his eyes.

"What are you talking about?" Vance the Younger asked with a shrug.

"Someone inside Uroboros Financial is manipulating shipments and services, trying to delay the relief effort. I believe that same individual tried to have me killed," I said, grabbing a crowbar from a stack of crates.

"Vance, I…"

I leaned in close to him, so he could see my eyes clearly. "No, it's Kale," I said, whispering so that only he could hear. He swallowed loudly.

"I've been at sea, going port to port for weeks. I haven't had any contact with Port Montaigne or the firm, I swear," Vance the Younger squeaked.

"What are you calling yourself these days?" I asked, as Brook pulled him to his feet.

"Royo, I call myself Royo," he replied.

"That's a stupid name," I said, sounding as cruel as possible.

We pushed past an inquisitive crowd, with Salvatore in tow, to the private transport still waiting on the curb. Brook kept a firm grip on Royo the whole way, dutifully keeping him in check. Brook didn't look it, but she was incredibly strong and her hands were like vice grips when she wanted them to be.

"There will be questions about all this, Mr.…." Salvatore said as we cleared the last of the rubbernecking dock staff.

"Make something up."

"You are not him, are you?" Salvatore asked after a moment of hesitation.

"No, I call myself Kale. I act in his behalf, so if there is anything you'd like to pass along…" I said, knowing my outburst had shredded my public persona, in midtown anyway.

"Only that we will continue to see goods come to port over the next few weeks. We're running ahead of schedule and out of dry storage. Distribution needs to begin very soon, even sooner than originally projected," Salvatore explained.

"I understand. Please have the passenger lists sent with the shipping manifests this time around. I'll be in touch," I said, helping Brook pull Royo into the passenger compartment of the private transport.

I knocked on the glass of the window separating us from the driver to signal that we were ready to depart. As the transport got up to speed, I motioned for Brook to release Royo. He looked about angrily, rubbing his bruised neck. His discomfort shouldn't have amused me as much as it did, but I really did hate that little runt.

"What now?" he asked.

"You tell me what part you're playing in the disruption of the relief effort," I said calmly.

"Not a thing. I was never going to come back here, but I got a message," he replied, reaching for a pocket.

Brook tensed, watching him slowly pull a battered mobile from his pocket. He turned it over and clicked it on. He thumbed through several messages that were all months old until he reached one that was from a couple of weeks previous. It was written and signed with a capital M.

"All is well, you can return to Port Montaigne now. M," it read.

"Madmar's dead. Ezra One broke his neck after severing the data link to his abominable device," I reported with no small amount of satisfaction.

"This isn't from Madmar, it's from Matthias," Royo stated, somewhat confused.

"Why would he try to contact you?" I said, holding the mobile up to better see through all the scratches in the glass.

"I've no earthly idea. You all hate me," Royo replied.

"And in spite of that, you thought you could just come back, everyone having forgotten what you tried to do to Taylor?" I asked, incredulous beyond measure by now.

"Kinda."

I laughed, startling both Brook and Royo. I don't know why it all struck me as being so hilarious at the time, as so rarely did *anything* strike me as funny. Maybe I just needed to laugh.

"The catalyst has made you very fast," Brook said, doing her best to end the deliciously awkward moment I'd created.

"Not like a standard terrestrial IA, and I can't sustain it for long. Everything we were told about the catalyst in the beginning, and later, was a lie," Royo said, somewhat remorsefully.

"At least you didn't die like the others when Madmar enacted his kill switch," Brook said, trying to keep it light.

"Everyone else is dead?" Royo replied, a slight smile appearing on his face.

"They did treat you and I rather shabbily, did they not?" I said, reflecting somewhat on all Royo had likely endured.

"I'm not glad they're dead, but I'm not going to be sad, either," he said hesitantly.

"I did a lot of research in trying to find you. A handful of us have a particular designation as replicas in our files, an E for extended service. We each were designed to persist longer for some reason and I was given a particular gift. What did Vance Uroboros grant you that he did not grant the others?" I asked.

Brook gave me a look that clearly put her displeasure on display. I had not shared with her what I knew about the E designation yet. Royo just looked uncomfortable, before willing his body to rapidly appear older until he looked very much as Silverstein preferred, a man in his late 20s, early 30s. I frowned at this revelation. In that moment, I did not understand why Royo hadn't conformed to just look as the others did and avoid the abuse he suffered. To me, it made no sense.

"I don't understand. Why appear as a child if you don't have to?" I asked, shaking my head.

"It's not me, not the real me anyway," Royo said, allowing himself to return to his more youthful appearance. "I'm not a grown up on the inside, why would I want to be on the outside?"

"You don't seem like someone concerned with authenticity," Brook said, half directing the comment to me as well.

"You're small, like me, do you like being treated like a small person?" Royo asked Brook.

"I've never known anything else," Brook replied.

"Until you have, you can't understand," Royo said, looking at the floor.

I had a feeling Brook would yet come to understand. In the weeks since her encounter with Madmar, I could almost watch as time melted the childlike elements of her pygmy genetic programming away. Sitting beside Royo particularly, she looked taller and more like a woman, as opposed to a girl in her teens. Fortunately, the awkward silence that followed was not to be disturbed until we arrived back at Uroboros Financial.

CHAPTER 4

Relief Effort Distribution Center

Port Montaigne - April 2nd, 2200

Kale's Private Records, Part 3 —

"We should help Royo," Brook insisted.

"I don't like him."

"Metasapients are protective of children. Drones are the same way to a lesser degree," she said, handing me her data slate.

It had a peer-reviewed study of how Metasapients interacted with humans based on age and other demographics. Royo would be the perfect emissary to act for us in Africa, the rational choice. For me, it was hard to be rational when it came to him. When Uroboros Financial was in chaos, he only worked to make things worse, while I acted alone to make things better.

"Fine, we'll give him Uroboros Financial credentials and send him to Africa," I replied bitterly.

"He'll be so happy. Thank you," Brook said, smiling.

"To be clear, this is something you are doing for Royo. I dislike him intensely."

The worst case scenario was that the Metasapients in Africa, or their minders, would rid us of Royo permanently. At best he widens our distribution in the area. Either way, I hoped I wouldn't have to utter his ridiculous name out loud ever again. I assigned him the most elderly transport we had and the mercenaries Perfidy recommended. Apparently, finding hired guns that worked in the African theater wasn't difficult.

Brook gave Royo instructions to send her reports of his progress every day in the event he was actually successful. It occurred to me that Vance Uroboros had perhaps made the diminutive replica that way for the purpose of interacting with Metasapients. Given his extended life span, like my own, our maker may have had a more expansive agenda post-Shutdown. No one would ever know the truth and it didn't matter in the wake of Madmar's nefarious meddling.

The relief effort progressed as planned, but there were no pleasant surprises in the days following Royo's departure. I had hoped to come across more resources, garner renewed diplomatic traction with the South American Union, or at least get more transports from the Lunar Colony than I did. It was all more or less relative to my expectations, but woefully short of what was needed. No doubt, millions of people were going to starve and die.

In hindsight, the worst part was not being able to tell Silverstein. Since he had ceased being Vance Uroboros following my own desperate act to save him from self-destruction, he had not been the same. I couldn't trust that giving him the data portraying our real situation on the ground would be safe for him. I don't know what he could have done, more than what I was already doing. Simply, it would have made me feel better not to bear the burden alone.

"More transports have returned. They'll be prepped and loaded within the hour," Salvatore reported from the warehouse floor.

"Good," I replied, descending the stairs from the upstairs offices.

"I do not understand why we go so secretly, and with so many guns," Salvatore stated, standing on the last step.

Perfidy stepped in from behind him and gently guided him off the stairs so I could finish coming down. I was weary, and had no patience for explaining the particulars to Salvatore. Fortunately, Perfidy was more accommodating.

"We can't notify the local populations because people might make plans to take the transports for themselves. We can't move goods without a lot of muscle for the same reason. We lose even one transport because we didn't prevent theft or piracy, hundreds of thousands of people starve. This isn't the casual moving of supplies, this is a top secret and highly dangerous operation," Perfidy explained.

"Also, you should not be questioning him all the time," Brook said, stepping from the shadows of the stairs behind me.

Salvatore looked startled, never having really seen Brook before, let alone heard her speak.

"I... I understand all that, but the workers are nervous. It is like you do not trust them, or me," Salvatore admitted.

"You do good work. I will make sure he knows that. He trusts you," Brook said dryly, putting her hands in the front pocket of her apron.

Salvatore smiled weakly and nodded before departing.

"Thanks," I said, grateful for not having to engage Salvatore on the subject.

"Do you really trust him?" Perfidy asked.

"No," Brook and I said in unison.

Perfidy chuckled.

"Was there any word from the Lunar Colony after confirming the arrival of the transports?" I asked, rubbing my eyes.

"Taylor said that Silverstein and Ezra had made progress dealing with the criminal syndicate and that the process of renewal was going well. It sounds like the lights are more or less back on, on the moon anyway," Brook said, gazing at my data slate, which had lately become her data slate.

"Does Silverstein have any inkling of how bad things are here?" I asked, knowing I was just feeding my chief anxiety.

"Taylor didn't say, but I would take that as good news," Brook said quietly stowing the data slate in her apron pocket.

We headed out of the warehouse where Perfidy had Vance's personal transport waiting. I took the driver's seat, wishing Mr. Mundt was well enough to work. Perfidy and Brook chatted quietly as I took us up over lower east side of Port Montaigne. It was getting dark, and we were all tired from the day. A transmission came in as I was making our way back toward Uroboros Financial.

"Transport hijacked over New Mexico, demands already coming in for the hostages," Perfidy reported, glancing at the communication terminal.

It was the news I had been dreading for a while, but the sort that was inevitable. I never ceased to marvel at the selfishness and callousness that humans had for one another. Every day the hijackers held the transport, thousands of people would go hungry. In that moment, I was tired, already at the end of my rope, and angry beyond measure.

"How do you want to handle this?" Perfidy asked.

"Recovering the transport and the crew are tertiary to making an example out of the hijackers. I want them dead in the most public way possible. I want news and video of their demise to go out over the CGG Internet so that anyone connected can spread the word. We do not negotiate and if you interfere with the relief effort, the consequences will be severe," I said, bringing the transport down toward the landing pad outside Uroboros Financial.

"So harsh. Is that really necessary?" Brook asked.

"No, but these people have made the boss angry," Perfidy said, displaying no emotion.

"Is this how Vance Uroboros would handle it?" Brook asked, obviously displeased.

"No, and certainly not since becoming Silverstein. I don't have time to negotiate with these people, understand their plight, or engage in diplomacy. If I do it once, every place we go will think they can take a piece of us until there is nothing left. The new world lacks order, and it is up to me to impose it," I explained, still mad as hell.

"What if they are just desperate people, driven by Madmar's legacy to do these things?" Brook asked.

"Then they are victims of that legacy, and I am the natural consequence," I replied, powering down the transport.

We exited the transport where Jason Mortimer awaited us. I wasn't very good at hiding my displeasure during that moment, nearly ignoring him to just go inside. He held up his data slate, a video already playing onscreen. It showed members of a militia escorting one of the crew from the captured transport to the top of said transport and shooting the crew member dead. Perfidy and I watched dispassionately while Brook gasped in horror.

"Mexican militia, the sort that kept people from going south across the borders to look for jobs in Mexico over the last fifty years or so. They sent us this video along with a list of demands just a few moments ago," Mr. Mortimer reported.

"Do you know anything I don't already know?" I asked, annoyed by the stink of his incompetence.

"Internal sensors indicate that there are at least fourteen insurgents, down from twenty-five following an exchange with our three security operatives. All security personnel were lost, but they took down almost half the Mexican militia members that boarded the ship while cargo was being to the populace," Mr. Mortimer said, stammering slightly with each word.

"How are they armed?" Perfidy asked, obviously furious at the loss of his friends.

"I studied the internal surveillance as best as I could. It looks like caseless submachine guns, handguns, and advanced polymer body armor, all made in Mexico or South America. Very high quality stuff, but nothing they wouldn't have access to. I doubt anyone put them up to this," Mr. Mortimer said quietly.

"Mexico and South America have an active grid, transports, food, and so forth. Why would they seize a transport?" Brook asked.

"It's in the demands, which reads more like a rant. They want the flow of illegal immigrants from North America to cease. This is about territory and ideology. Since the North American economy went into decline about fifty years ago, people have been trying to cross the border illegally into Mexico looking for work," Mr. Mortimer said, reading his response partially from the data slate in his hands.

"Thank you for your report, Mr. Mortimer. You may go. Tell Blake Messer I want to see him in my office in the morning."

"Will do, Mr. Uroboros."

I watched Jason scurry back inside ahead of us, his shoulders slumped over. My hatred for him wasn't rational. Even as weak and naïve as Brook could be, she would still stand up for herself and had a profound measure of dignity. I could respect her in a way I could never respect Jason.

"You want me on this personally?" Perfidy asked, once we reached Vance's office.

"We should all go," Brook said quietly.

I paused, looking at the small Drone with all the disdain I could muster. She only smiled at me.

"Alright, we'll all go," I said at last.

We grabbed a couple of hours of rest on the leather sofas arrayed around Vance's office before Perfidy gathered his preferred weapons, all the intelligence we had and a few choice allies. If felt strange flying Mr. Mundt's transport without him, again, but we wanted to come in like we were just another freighter bringing in goods. The three hour flight essentially consisted of Perfidy and his allies checking and rechecking weapons, calibrating their optic implants to the time of day they expected to land, and a load of macho bull crap I mostly ignored.

"It is important that the people see you. When it is over, you should be prepared to say something to them. They need a leader," Brook said, squeezing into the cockpit with me.

"You think I'm a leader?" I asked.

"No, but you could pretend," Brook said smiling broadly.

She was right, of course. The CGG authority had largely evaporated with the Shutdown and most places were operating on local municipal government, if they were lucky. Any appearance that a larger entity cared about what was going on would have a calming effect, discourage anarchy, and hold the darkness back a little longer.

We set down at the outskirts of a small community called Estancia. There were only a few dogs to greet us as we stepped off the loading ramp onto the sandy streets. The town had seen better days as we walked toward where satellite telemetry put our missing transport. There were shell casing and week old corpses, mostly locals, laying in the road ways. Several of the smaller buildings and residences were burned or burning.

"What happened here?" Brook asked, pausing for a moment beside each of the dead we came across.

"Human nature," Perfidy said, waving his team on ahead of us.

"Human nature?" Brook whispered, looking up at me.

"The world had plenty of problems before the Shutdown," I said, stopping short of the next turn.

"Why are we stopping?"

"I'm not a fool like Silverstein. I'll leave the fighting to people that know how," I said, nodding to Perfidy while crouching behind a vehicle awaiting repossession.

Brook crouched down with me while we waited.

"If I remember right, you walked into a few bullets, too," Brook said.

"Back then, I wanted to die. I realize now that there is too much at stake. I won't just give up like Vance did, and try to run to Mars," I whispered, checking my mobile for the time.

It would be almost twenty minutes before Perfidy and his people were in position. I watched the action unfold with my data slate through the team's optic enhancements as they engaged at a range first, then closed in to liberate the transport. Brook covered her ears while watching the road behind us. One hundred and nine seconds later it was over, with all the hijackers dead or captured.

We walked up to the freighter where Perfidy was cutting the surviving crew loose. Brook passed around a pair of canteens while I began assessing the damage and loss. They'd burned some of the cargo, but the freighter looked mostly unharmed save for a few dings and dents from small arms fire. The locals began to find the courage to approach us after a few minutes. A man wearing work clothes and carrying a rifle on his shoulder approached me, Perfidy standing off to my right with his own rifle still held at the ready.

"I'm Brannon George, the foreman around here. Alright if we start moving the food to the relief center up the road?" he asked, nodding to the crates and barrels that had escaped the fire.

"You work for us, then. Have you already signed for them?" I asked, looking past him to the handful of functional vehicles the locals had managed to scavenge.

"We did when they arrived. I think they killed him, the one I talked to I mean," he replied, bowing his head.

"Mr. George, how did you get these vehicles running?" I asked.

He hesitated at first, looking somewhat pained. I did my best to smile, which seemed to calm him somewhat. He turned and pointed to a young girl sitting in the driver's seat of the largest of the trucks.

"She whispers to machines," he explained.

"I see," I said, trying to sound empathetic. "Who else knows?"

"No one, I've been telling everyone I figured a way to override the repossession protocols," he explained.

"Why trust me with this information?" I asked.

"You're the boss, right? Also, we need the food, and you have a Drone. I'm not sure what type she is, but they are supposed to be good at detecting deception," Brannon George explained.

"That's true," I said turning to Brook as she approached.

"Crew seems okay to fly," she reported.

"What do you think of Mr. Brannon George here?" I asked.

Brook blinked, then turned her gaze to George who stood there like a stone.

"His employee file is sparse, but he seems okay to me," Brook said at last.

"She's read my file?" Mr. George asked.

"She's read all the employee files," I replied, gesturing to the food and turning to head back to the freighter crew.

"You'd be him then. Vance Uroboros?" he asked.

"For right now, Mr. George, I am," I said back over my shoulder.

The trucks pulled up with a small army of beleaguered looking citizens who spent the afternoon preparing and hauling the cargo. The vehicles traveled and worked in a group, starting up and traveling together to haul the goods. The girl was a mechanic of some kind, a tele-mechanic psychic, but her abilities had a range. When she walked to the relief station for water, a half block away the trucks all went dark. She was important to Mr. George in some way other than her contribution to the relief effort, but I noted no familial resemblance.

Dealing with the hijackers was somewhat more complex. I couldn't leave them behind, or any of the hardware they had been carrying, what hadn't already wandered off. Perfidy would have preferred to erect totems or air drop them on their comrades south of the border. I was content with burying them, each in their own marked grave according to the identification found on them. Perfidy and his team weren't happy with having to dig so many graves, but the locals were willing to lend us a hand.

I helped as well, handing my suit jacket to Brook while she brought us water back and forth from the relief station. My willingness to get my hands dirty seemed meaningful to the locals. In truth, I just wanted to speed our departure and was pitching in to that end. We stayed a little longer to help the locals finish moving the supplies and get the freighter crew on their way back to Port Montaigne.

As night fell, Perfidy, Brook, and I shared a meal with the locals. The rest of our security had returned to Mr. Mundt's freighter hauler to prep for departure. I had been unwilling to check my mobile, knowing it was probably alight with missives and messages from corporate at my having left without notice. It seemed like I couldn't be gone a day without some new emergency demanding my attention.

"This is Jennifer Wilton, my niece," Brannon George said, introducing us.

She was a freckled, lanky young lady with brown hair and brown eyes, utterly forgettable. Before I knew the whole truth, I marveled at how someone so young had mastered tele-mechanical control as she had, commanding several machines at once. When we met, I wondered if she was a prodigy, someone that just had a strange affinity for what usually took ten to fifteen years of carefully guided training to achieve.

"Who taught you?" I asked.

"Excuse me?" she replied, narrowing her eyes.

"To do what you do?" I said, pointing to the now dormant vehicles a short distance away.

"It's alright, I had to tell him," Mr. George explained, glaring at me.

"No one."

"You learned this varied and decidedly fine degree of control, by yourself?" I asked, incredulous.

"It just happens. If the machine is off, and it can function, it generally springs to life when I'm around," she explained.

"But, not always?" Brook asked.

"No. If the machine is old enough or doesn't have a purchase insurance system, they seem to stay asleep," she explained.

I was overcome by the implications of such an individual. All the psychic countermeasures built into machines relied on willful manipulation on the part of the tele-mechanic, reacting to known electromagnetic interference, and captured electroencephalogry of individuals with the gift. That she passively manipulates these machines in that way made her potentially the most valuable person on the planet.

"Have you tried to enter any government buildings, or other installations with higher levels of encryption than the few delivery trucks?" I asked, almost breathless.

"We keep to the outskirts mostly, always have. Been easier for her to escape notice, and just lead a normal life. Uroboros Financial gives me a generous stipend to look after her, with no requirement, just a polite request to keep her away from metropolitan areas," Mr. George explained.

"Did you know about this?" I growled, turning to Brook.

"Yeah, it seemed nice that Uroboros Financial would do that. Why?" Brook said, shrugging.

"Why would a multinational financial conglomerate seek to subsidize this girl's wellbeing?" I asked, trying to regain my calm.

"Settle down, it is all easily explained. Her parents were killed aboard a transport. The airline was owned in part by Uroboros Financial. Lots of people got settlements, no big deal," Mr. George explained.

"Terrorism?" I asked.

Miss Wilton had apparently had enough of the conversation by then, walking off in a huff. Mr. George gave me a serious look that told me he was neither intimidated by Vance Uroboros or the firm I represented. I'd stepped over one of those invisible lines with him, a habit I seemed to engage with everyone at least once.

"What do you want with the girl?" he asked, pointblank.

"I want her to wander near my transport after I've locked it down and encrypted the onboard systems to prevent any but the most skilled tampering. I want to see if she can unlock it with her mere presence," I replied.

"What for?" he asked.

"To turn the lights back on," Perfidy interrupted, having already guessed my plan.

"I don't understand, I thought all the CGG installations, servers, and infrastructure were locked up tight, outside legislative and institutional controls. Someone locked the door with the only key left inside, or something like that?" Mr. George stated, folding his arms.

"Indeed, but the failsafe countermeasures in place are designed to prevent purposeful hacking, and traditional tele-mechanical tampering with intent, with systems designed to counteract those known methods of intrusion. The world has never seen the likes or the tele-mechanical influence of Miss Jennifer Wilton," I said.

"There are other employees like Brannon, with individuals in their care unrelated to terrorist actions that took place with assets of the firm," Brook stated.

"Take a closer look at them when you have time. For now, we need to try and assess the remaining CGG infrastructure and find the best place to insert the girl, and formulate a plan once we are there," I said, thinking aloud.

"What if she doesn't want to go on this fool's errand of yours?" Mr. George asked.

"There are millions… billions of lives at stake. Why would she decline to help us?" I said, in a far more angry tone than intended.

"Could you please talk to her, tell her the risks, tell her what we hope to gain as a consequence?" Perfidy asked, far more politely than I was able at that moment.

"Yeah. I'll do that," Mr. George replied, turning on his heel and heading back to where the locals had gathered by the relief tent.

"You handled that well," Brook said, patting me on the arm.

"Seriously, you need someone to do PR on these things. Drones and angry old cyborgs aren't cutting it here. You've got the pretty face, start using it right for Heaven's sake," Perfidy scolded.

"My apologies. If we could get her to a CGG relay, one with enough remaining connectivity with the right satellites in orbit overhead, we could reverse much of what's been done. The optimism that Silverstein is operating on currently would have merit, and we… I wouldn't have failed to safeguard the people the entire gambit was meant to help and protect in the first place," I said, sitting on the ground.

"No, no, no, you'll get all dirty. You need to look good," Brook said, pulling me back to my feet and brushing me off.

"I'm suddenly very tired, for some reason," I said, doing my best to stand up straight.

"We've just had a long day moving cargo and digging graves. C'mon, let's go back to the ship and see how tight we can lock it up in the morning. We all need rest," Perfidy insisted, putting his arm around me.

"I'll send missives to the firm, and to Taylor, letting them know we're staying in the area to look into a possible lead on relief aid," Brook said, pulling out her data slate.

"Add a note about our encounter with the Mexican militia, but keep Perfidy and his team anonymous. Also, make sure death benefits are expedited for anyone on our payroll that was killed. There should be something to reassure those taking extreme risks on our behalf."

We got back to Mr. Mundt's freighter and found quarters for the night. Tired as I was, I lay awake pondering the notion that we could turn the lights back, even just a few of them. It was tantalizing. Given that Vance Uroboros had apparently made special arrangements for the girl's welfare, meant he may have been aware, and even arranged for other backup plans and failsafe measures. I hated myself, and Silverstein, and really missed the Vance Uroboros I knew in the time after inception and before the Shutdown.

His words still serve to define my actions to this day.

The current system is bankrupting people before they are born, and leaving the burden as their only legacy. I'm going to bring down the old system so that a new one will have to be implemented, something equitable for all. I don't want people killing each other in the streets for food when it happens. It is your job to protect people, particularly those living in smaller rural areas, so they will have what they need until goods and services are available again. Those who already have the least, should suffer a like amount from what I'm about to do, and gain the most in the aftermath. Can you help me do that, Kale?

He didn't treat me like I was simply a copy, or an echo of his own consciousness. He spoke to me like I had a choice, and the autonomy to do what I wanted. Everyone needs a purpose to persist, and that was all he was offering me. I had assumed that the dire situation in the world gave me some authority to insist that the young tele-mechanic should just go with us, help us, and do what is necessary. From all I've heard of Silverstein's encounter with Madmar at the Lunar Colony, I would be no better than that mad man to make such assumptions.

I woke early, and headed back to the camp where the locals were preparing to leave.

"Mr. George… Brannon, would it be alright if I spoke to your niece again, my manners now firmly intact?" I asked, smiling the most genuine smile I possessed.

"Oh, um… sure. Let me get her for you," he replied.

He came back moments later, with her walking along at his right. Her demeanor darkened at the sight of me, and I probably deserved it. I knew that the only way to do this was as Vance had done with me, with respect and authenticity.

"I want to apologize for disrespecting the memory of your parents yesterday, my words were coarse and I deeply regret offending you," I began, letting the smile drop.

"It's alright, I was pretty little. I just don't like people making decisions for me, or talking like I'm not there," she replied.

"We should be properly introduced. I'm called Kale. I'm a nanotechnological replica, imprinted with some of the consciousness and memories of the CEO of Uroboros Financial, Vance Uroboros. My function is to prevent harm to those who suffered most under the previous global financial model, and I have largely failed in that endeavor. I need your help," I stated, causing no small alarm within her and Mr. George.

"Go on," she said, somewhat more interested than before.

"I want to save as much of the world as I can, and I'm coming up short. I do not have enough transports or manpower to keep millions of people from starving to death. I need to find a way to restart the global automated agricultural complex and associated transportation services to get food to every corner of the globe. I can probably locate the technicians, pilots, and emergency management personnel, but what I do not have is a key to the facilities in question. You may be that key with your unique tele-mechanical gifts," I explained, pausing to take a breath.

"Lots of those places are held by militias and proto-countries trying to start up on their own. They hold them because they once symbolized control of the adjoining territories, not because they can actually utilize them. Getting into many of those places will be dangerous," Brannon said, his tone betraying deep disdain for my plan.

"He's right. There is tremendous risk involved. I have many loyal soldiers and even more hired guns, but every place we go, there will be a fight like the one we had over the hijacked freighter, only much larger and more violent," I said, nodding.

"What do I get out of it?" she asked, putting her hands in her pockets.

"That depends on you. Your abilities set you apart from even other tele-mechanics. We would have to work very hard, as your uncle has done, to keep your existence a secret," I explained.

"What if I don't want to be a secret anymore? What's the big deal if people know anyway?" she asked.

"It's a big deal. There are individuals that would try to take you, hurt you, and use you," I explained.

"Listen to the man," Brannon said, changing his tone toward me.

"You said he was an idiot suit, that didn't know anything of what's best for me," Jennifer replied, sarcastically.

"Not when it comes to this he ain't," Brannon said, somewhat embarrassed.

"I deserved that critique yesterday. The truth is, I'm desperate. Everything I've done to try to keep things from spiraling out of control seems to make it worse. If you like, your Uncle Brannon could come along and contribute to managing your wellbeing. You'll both be paid a consultant's fee, hazard pay, and whatever else I can swing via Uroboros Financial," I offered, hoping they would agree.

"And if I want to be famous?" she asked, smiling.

"It might happen no matter how hard we try to the contrary. It's a very real hazard of what I'm suggesting," speaking more to Brannon than Jennifer.

"She's nineteen, and can make her own decisions I guess. If she decides to go, I'll probably stay here. The folks here can't afford to lose even one guy with a rifle, and if you and Jennifer manage to pull off this restart you're talking about, not having a handful of working trucks for a little while won't matter," Brannon said, turning to Jennifer.

"Okay, when do we start?" Jennifer asked, surprising us both.

CHAPTER 5

Mars Colony, Penal Cluster 34, Sub-sector 8

Maximum Security Block - July 6th, 2200 – More than a year after Shutdown

"I don't want to be late for the onnazumo match, so let's cut through the innuendo and have you tell me what you want," Dell complained, leaning against the bars of his cell.

"I need a rifle that can be made small, disassembled to carry concealed. It needs to be accurate up to fifty yards, and I need a place to sight it in and prep the weapon," Dragos explained, putting his hands in the pockets of his prison garb.

"So, something like virtually every firearm we smuggle in here?" Dell said, frowning.

"No. This rifle must fire special ammunition, three thousand feet per second or more, if you have it," Dragos said, holding up his arms in a firing stance for emphasis.

"I thought you didn't need it to be accurate beyond fifty yards? That's like every rifle, decent ones anyway," Dell said, walking around the enclosure to his bunk.

"Must be semi-automatic, will be firing many rounds."

Dell paused for a moment. "For only a handful of targets on Mars does one need such a set up. You sure you want to go playing with augmented folks with only a rifle?" Dell asked, moving his bunk aside to reveal a concealed weapons cache in the wall.

"Archie is sure."

Dell nodded, understanding the situation a little better.

"What is onnazumo?" Dragos asked, watching Dell pick through his inventory.

"Sumo wrestling for ladies."

Dragos shook his head slowly, as if to scold Dell.

"What? Archie says that all the cultural norms are what build prison walls. Breaking them down is the best way to be free, on either side of the fence."

"Dell, do you believe Archie's bull crap? This breaking down walls with lady sumo?"

"Hey, watch a couple matches, you'll be a believer, too," Dell said somewhat dismissively as he wrapped up rifle parts and ammunition in a towel.

"This rifle, how many rounds is it rated for?" Dragos asked, taking the rolled up towel from Dell.

"These are made on Mars using the factory rapid prototyping machinery with high quality alloys and…"

"How many rounds?" Dragos asked, more insistently the second time.

"If you make it through the twenty I gave you, you'll be lucky. I'd say ten for sure, and any more than that is a gift. That high grain ammo is going to tear it up pretty fast," Dell said quietly.

"Okay, good. Go to your lady sumo now. Maybe see you later," Dragos said as he departed for the stairs that would take him toward the psychiatric block.

Dragos watched the movement of the inmates and convicts below as they traveled about freely and peacefully. Even with few guards and a cell door that never swung shut, he felt trapped and angry. He didn't want to kill anyone and he couldn't help but feel as though Archie was just another man with money and a method of putting the shackles on other people, even if they didn't realize it.

Things were dire by comparison in the psychiatric block where the inmates had largely been abandoned. There was not nearly enough staff and most of those incarcerated in the oblong orange padded cells looked at Dragos with fear. His tattoos and long hair meant he could duck prison regulations, making him dangerous. The staff appeared to struggle just keeping them fed, even with Archie as their benefactor.

The mentally ill couldn't reliably ride a bike. Their prison accounts always had someone on the outside keeping track as part of a guardianship if they had family, a civic steward otherwise. Because they could not contribute to Archie's master plan, the whole block got little support. The wardens were probably fine as long as there was no publicity and they were paid well on the side.

Even a year ago, Dragos would have abided none of it. He paused to help a disabled inmate back into a wheelchair. The man struggled at first, but then relaxed when he realized Dragos was trying to help. Once back in his chair, the man fell fast asleep as he'd been struggling for hours to get upright. The other inmates looked on from their padded cells, safely locked away, darting to their bunks once the drama ended.

The intel he'd gathered so far indicated that the Custodian frequented the psychiatric wing more than the others. He wondered why, as most of the residents seemed pretty harmless. The really dangerous psychotics were made docile with pharmaceutical delivery implants, and the others were generally inside as a cumulative effect of their behavior issues. Stepping to the railing of the upper level he gazed down to the cafeteria. The Custodian was there.

She wore her full Aegis armor, swathed in an ancient canvas duster, side arms resting on each hip. It was not justice she administered, but mercy. She was sitting beside a pregnant woman who had suffered terrible head trauma. Some had yet to heal, but the majority was exposed, marking the woman with an ugly scar. Her arms did not move properly, and she would likely never be able to hold her baby or verbally express to it motherly love.

The Custodian fed the woman slowly, one spoonful of mush at a time, speaking kindly to her. Dragos, watched the whole thing, wondering how his siblings would feel about all of it. The Custodian looked up for a moment, listening to the communication coming across the radio built into her armor. Dragos was struck by how lovely she was, her dark hair and eyes framing a face that could be compassionate or fierce. He wondered if the sensation of gazing on her was similar to what Truman felt when he heard Marjorie sing in the shower.

The Custodian's soft expression went dark as she set the bowl down on the table. She said something to the woman and jogged back toward the maximum security block. Tucking the towel tighter under his arm, Dragos descended the concrete steps to the cafeteria and walked over to the table where the injured woman was sitting. He set the towel down, taking up the bowl to resume feeding her.

"Here, you will need this for yourself and child," Dragos whispered.

Her face was slack, and she struggled to keep herself upright. Dragos leaned in so she could brace herself on his shoulder and eat more comfortably. After almost an hour the bowl was empty, and she held up her arms as if to ask for help standing. With the towel under one arm, and the woman leaning heavily on the other, Dragos let her lead him back to her recovery pod. It was a small and bleak room with a normal bunk and hooks for IVs.

"Who did this to you?" Dragos asked in his native Romanian, helping her lay down.

"Arch-eee..." the woman said in English, framing her upper lip with a shaky finger.

"Archie, like this?" Dragos said, mimicking the gesture.

"Doc.. tor..." the woman whispered, rubbing her head.

She was drawing his telltale moustache on her own face, then gesturing to her belly. Dragos nodded, then pressed his hands to the sides of the woman's face to wipe away both tears and saliva before drawing the thin blanket over her. He stood and waited until he was certain she was asleep before gathering his bundle and retreating to the hallway where the Custodian was leaning against the wall.

"Why would she tell you and not me?" the Custodian asked, her thick North American accent making her sound extra indignant.

"You are not of our people. You are outsider," Dragos replied, trying to keep his composure and hide his surprise.

"Archie, like *the* Archie that runs a third of the Penal Facility now?"

"Yes. You should stay out of this," Dragos said, clenched teeth appearing between slightly parted lips.

"I'm the only cop on Mars. I have to prioritize my policing, pursuing top tier criminals. Rape and murder are top tier," the Custodian hissed.

"Custodian…"

"Marshal Rider."

"Marshal, Archie is very dangerous man. I will deal with him."

"The hell you will, Dragos," Rider snapped.

"How do you know who I am?" Dragos asked.

"A Mr. Graham, your employer, expressed some concern for your safety. I took the opportunity to let him know what kind of man you were. He told me that you protected his employees outside the confines of your contract and even did recovery on a stolen vessel. Very white hat for someone like you," Marshal Rider explained, smiling somewhat menacingly.

When she smiled, Dragos could see just how young she was. All the same, she was hard like steel, and from the way she handled herself, extremely deadly. Being the only police officer on Mars, and third generation, made her a law dog by legacy, blood, and choice. Dragos was a soldier and an outlaw by way of the same providence.

"You are going to bring me out of penal facility?"

"That's right, strange coincidence that I would find you caring for my witness," Marshal Rider said, not taking her gaze from Dragos for even a second.

"This is no good. Archie sent me to kill you. If I leave, he will go after my brother, sister, and mother," Dragos said, shaking his head.

"That a fact?" Marshal Rider said, putting her hand on her sidearm.

"I did not come to do what Archie wants," Dragos explained, showing her the rifle.

"Then why do you have a gun? Maybe I should just shoot you, sort this out on my own."

"Because Archie never sends just one assassin or team. If he sent me first to distract you, he will send others. They will maybe be augmented, have special weapons. I can't let that happen," Dragos explained.

"What do you care? Just have your family go underground for a while. Your people are good at that, yeah?" Marshal Rider said with a sneer.

Dragos frowned. "I left them when they needed me most, to try and settle this debt with Archie. My sister is young, but not hard like you. My brother, he stepped in front of bullet to protect her. I don't know if he's alive or dead."

"Mr. Graham was clear, find you and pull you out," Marshal Rider stated.

"I can't leave, not until I stop Archie. What kind of reach does he have on Mars outside the prison?" Dragos asked.

Marshal Rider hesitated, but could see Dragos was truly desperate. "He's into everything. His latest endeavor seems to be meddling in the ongoing feud between the various mining companies. Hijacking, kidnapping, industrial sabotage, the works," she explained.

"Is he particular, or just go for any opportunity?"

Marshal Rider thought about it for a moment, then whispered quietly to her armor.

"He's got a couple favorites, but even they seem to suffer a little trouble here and there," Marshal Rider said, softening her demeanor somewhat.

"This devalue the mining company stocks, make them easy to buy?" Dragos asked.

Marshal Rider whispered to her armor again, gazing at a flex monitor across the thick armored cuff protecting her right forearm. She lifted her finger up to her earbud and listened intently to her armor as it quickly completed the records search.

"Slowly, just inside what could be construed as normal market conditions, considering the financial crisis back on Earth. Do you think Archie is purposefully manipulating the market values here for some purpose?" Marshal Rider asked.

"Yes. What do you need to go after Archie?" Dragos asked, closing the door to the recovery pod behind him.

"Technically, you collecting the testimony from the witness for my purposes is plenty. Now that she's named him as her attacker, I can move on him."

"You said murder before, but she is not dead."

"Dragos, he's done this before. My armor is still gathering data from the internal penal facility sensors, but so far he was in proximity to every other murder. Now that I have a name, I can have the medical examiner check Archie's DNA against the unborn children that were being carried by the women he killed within a few days."

"How many?" Dragos asked, his voice an almost inaudible whisper.

"Twelve, counting each woman and unborn child as a separate murder."

Dragos covered his face with both hands letting the rolled up towel fall to the floor, rifle parts spilling out onto the tile floor. Marshal Rider looked on impassively, somewhat baffled by his response. The corridor was empty except for them and a handful of sleeping inmates in the recover pods.

"You going to hold it together or...?"

"I work with Archie in South America for the FLF. There were murders, just like these, everywhere we went. I thought nothing of it because the areas were troubled, poor, and having a child in some places was more debt than people could pay off in a lifetime. Now I am wondering how long Archie has been doing this, killing those he rape, later after they are pregnant," Dragos explained, letting his hands fall limply to his sides.

"You going to cry about it, or let me take you out of here so I can do my job?" Marshal Rider said, stone faced.

Dragos glared at the young woman standing in front of him, angry at the whole situation. His gaze fell down to the rifle parts at his feet and saw what was his whole life arrayed in front of him. He was always trying to put things together, but they just kept falling apart. Every cause he fought for had crumbled, his friends quickly becoming enemies.

"I should do like you say. I should leave. I only make things worse it seems."

"That's not untrue," Marshal Rider replied.

"Your armor tell you these things? You think you know me?" Dragos hissed angrily.

"My Aegis armor tracks every individual it has ever encountered. Post-Shutdown, the Turkish Administration of the CGG had to take control of everything from Budapest south to Damascus. They grounded an aircraft over Hungary and took you into custody along with several other individuals," Marshal Rider began.

"They were thugs, corrupt, and working in coordination with slavers," Dragos interrupted.

"Ezra One put most of them down like the dogs they were. What I can't understand is why someone like Ezra One would work with someone like you," Marshal Rider said, squinting at Dragos.

"We are both soldiers, at the time, fighting the same battle. How do you know Ezra?"

"I don't know him, but the metadata attached to his personnel file by my grandfather indicates he was an ally. I have access to classified information about Ezra One's previous actions to protect innocents. He's one of the good guys, which again begs the question, why was he working with you?"

"You look at my personnel file, kept by CGG?"

"Yes," Marshal Rider replied, placing her hand on one of her holstered weapons.

Several heavily armed inmates suddenly appeared at the far end of the corridor. Marshal Rider's armor snapped shut, a helm sliding from the mantle up over her head in an instant, her exo-skeletal assisted reflexes kicking in. She drew both her sidearms, before the first inmate could think about drawing a bead. She unleashing a storm of automatic fire down the corridor toward them. Her guns were deafening, firing sonically enhanced crowd control rounds that shattered the eardrums of anyone standing in front of her.

"Stay behind me, and keep down," Marshal Rider said, her voice like a bullhorn over the Aegis armor's PA system.

The inmates regrouped stepping over their fallen comrades, deaf and disoriented as Marshal Rider stepped into them, guns blazing. The armor automatically shifted to flechette rounds as soon as she drew within the proper range, turning the inmates on point into shattered bone and hunks of meat. Demoralized, the remaining inmates dropped their weapons and turned to run, but the Marshal's weapons didn't cease firing until no one was left standing, moving, or breathing.

Dragos sat bewildered, hands over his ears watching Marshal Rider destroy fifteen human beings in half as many seconds. She paused, walking through the teal painted passage now slick with blood and viscera, looking down at anyone who still had a face, attempting to have her armor gather facial recognition identification. She kicked the last one over onto his back, his face contorted into a mask of pain and terror.

"Holy shit," Dragos whispered breathlessly as Marshal Rider walked back to where he sat.

"Nothing holy about what I do," Marshal Rider said, making the sign of the cross over her breastplate.

"Archie is desperate, to send people after you like this," Dragos remarked, busily assembling his rifle.

"You sure they were here for me? He might have access to the same prisoner location system my armor has."

"We'll never know now. You ever take anyone alive?"

"Nope. Like I said before, I've no time to deal with anyone that has committed an offense less than one that warrants a death sentence. My suit says that most of them are known associates of Archie."

"Most of them?"

"The ones I could identify with facial recognition."

"I am witness then, to a crime. Assault on my person, or an officer of the law. I'll need protection," Dragos said, finishing the assembly of his rifle.

"The best way to protect you would be for me to escort you out of the facility. We need to get there before night, and the sally ports go on timed lockdown."

"You said yourself, he can reach outside. Hijack, kidnapping, and probably worse. Better we stick together until Archie is brought to Justice," Dragos said with a slight smile.

Marshal Rider frowned at the idea of joining forces with an outlaw, no matter how good his intentions were. She folded her arms, listening to the quiet whisper of her armor as prison personnel began to respond to the disturbance. She wanted to be gone before the prison guards arrived, because it would be better that anyone on the take had to guess at what happened when they reported back to Archie.

"Okay, but ditch that crappy rifle. There are a half dozen way better weapons on the floor back there. Clean one off, grab all the compatible ammunition and stay where I can see you," Marshal Rider said, holstering her own weapons.

"Okay," Dragos said, selecting a couple of suitable weapons.

"Hurry it up, we need to be gone before armed facility response arrives."

They made their way back toward maximum security using cell passages as opposed to the central block chamber. It was a longer route, but quieter and one could avoid the internal sensors if they knew just where and when to walk. Dragos stayed in the lead as he'd been instructed, taking direction from Rider on where to walk and which passages to take.

"It will take forever to reach Archie at this rate. I think we're actually getting further from where he has based his operation," Dragos observed quietly.

"You want to get close enough to use one of those fancy rifles? We go this way," Marshal Rider said, giving Dragos a small shove.

As they were passing beneath the railing of a large overhead concourse just inside medium security, several inmates rushed from side passages while others dropped from above. Marshal Rider deployed a collapsible baton and swatted a trio of them from her path. Dragos dropped back, dodging a shiv. One of the inmates managed to lay hands on Marshal Rider, making her armor go dark with a jolt of bioelectric energy.

"Mechanic…" she grunted, the weight of her armor dragging her to the ground.

Dragos turned and kicked the spindly tele-mechanic in the face as hard as he could. The other inmates were on him an instant after, beating him with socks filled with hard objects and gouging him with short blades meant to bleed as opposed to kill. He took the blows as he moved quickly to protect Marshal Rider who was still face down on the ground.

Bringing up his rifle as much as he could, he fired a round off into one of the inmate's legs before several individuals grabbed the barrel and pointed it skyward. Ducking a blade meant for his throat, Dragos grabbed Marshal Rider's baton, held at the far end by one of the inmates, and depressed the button. A powerful electrical arc jumped between all the combatants knocking everyone prone.

Marshal Rider looked on helplessly as some of the inmates began to stir, praying quietly for her armor to quickly reboot. Groaning, Dragos rose first, recovering his rifle from the jumble. He stood over her, but not in a threatening way.

"Anyone who stands, I shoot them," Dragos said, his voice wavering slightly from the shock.

"My armor is coming back online," Marshal Rider muttered, trying unsuccessfully to roll over.

"Where did Mechanic go?" Dragos growled, looking around at the still shivering forms arrayed around him.

"That's a really good question. Also, how did you recover so quickly?" Marshal Rider asked, rising slowly as her armor began to power up.

"Nerve damage from being tortured... sometimes makes me a better soldier, but never play the guitar the same again," Dragos explained, a hint of genuine sadness in his voice.

"Heh, so the story in your file is true then? CGG Special Services or whatever they were called..."

"The part about them torturing me is."

Marshal Rider looked into Dragos' face for a moment, seeing a genuine look of sadness and remorse one rarely saw among the inmates of the Martian Penal Facility. It wasn't the stern expression of a hardened outlaw she saw, but the pained look of a victim. Her anger returned quickly, fueling a savage kick to one of the inmates. "Who sent you?"

The inmate groaned, grasping at his side in agony. "Word's out, bounties for you both. My family would be set for life if I took down either one of you."

Marshal Rider picked up her baton and walked back over to the inmates, all slowly trying to stand or crawl away. She contemplated giving them another shock or even killing them, but Dragos seemed uninterested in taking any action. He'd already gathered his rifle and was waiting patiently to leave.

"They'd have killed us," she said, looking at Dragos.

"Do whatever you need to do," Dragos replied, giving her the same stone faced expression she gave him earlier.

"Let's go," Marshal Rider said, holstering her baton.

The rest of the journey took nearly two hours, reaching Archie's offices just before lights out. It was empty, save for the few desks arrayed about the block concourse. The drawers had been left on the ground or open as though the contents had been evacuated quickly. Dragos looked up the elevated levels of the cellblock at the empty cells, doors all hanging open, the previous occupants long gone.

"He fled," Marshal Rider said, extremely disappointed.

"No, not Archie. He does not run," Dragos replied, looking down the chamber access to the block.

"Could have fooled me."

"He must be close to whatever he is trying to do. Check Martian market, if you can," Dragos said, gesturing to Marshal Rider's armor.

She tapped on the flex monitor across her armored cuff, then listened to the murmuring of the AI that governed her Armor.

"Your armor, it has no psychic countermeasures?" Dragos asked.

"No one had even heard of a tele-mechanic when my grandmother made this armor for my grandfather. Getting the mining corporations to authorize even a single police officer was tough, and they took to calling the position a 'custodian' to make it more politically palatable."

"It has an artificial intelligence, though?" Dragos observed.

"My father was able to add a simple intelligent agent to the armor, but psychic countermeasures require a lot of wattage the armor can't carry onboard without compromising the other benefits it provides," Marshal Rider explained patiently.

"Grandmother was an armorer?" Dragos asked, genuinely curious.

"She built assistive technologies for the disabled. This alpha version of the Aegis armor was the only weapon she ever built."

"That is good," Dragos said, nodding respectfully.

Marshal Rider paused as her flex screen lit up with the most recent market data. "The whole market is up on high volume trading. Every mining corporation is making a little hay on the market today."

"He's making his move," Dragos said, frowning.

"Which is what exactly?"

"I don't know. If Silverstein was here, he could untangle this," Dragos said with a smirk.

"Who?"

"Man I know, who is good with numbers. Archie just needed to buy time to make his move on the outside, legitimize himself."

"You think he was trying to garner a controlling interest in the mining companies?"

Dragos turned, pointing to the exercise bikes in the cells arrayed around them in the block.

"He said something about inmates on track for release can purchase company shares with a portion of the credits they earn pedaling the bikes," Dragos explained.

"Among other things, but there are buying caps and even a single share is a lot of bike time. There are a lot of bikes though, millions by now. Still it would require expert and very precise control of the right parts of the penal facility. He'd also have to engage a significant amount of fraud and have outside help to combine the accounts into a controlling interest... high level help," Marshal Rider said, thinking out loud.

"Archie, he can do these things. I have seen him, and..."

"What?"

"He also said he took all the FLF had sequestered and moved it into legitimate investments. The words mean something else to older FLF fighters," Dragos explained.

"Legitimate investments is code for something else?" Marshal Rider asked. "Bribes."

"Mining company officials are virtually immune to prosecution on Mars," Marshal Rider explained.

"Why would Archie fear a woman named Enyo?" Dragos asked.

"Why do you ask?"

"She was supposed to be my second target," Dragos explained.

"He had you chasing an urban legend. Allegedly, she's a vigilante that even the mining company executives and officials fear. No one has ever captured sensory data on her though, not a single reading or image has ever been captured. If she exists, the whole system has thoroughly denied her existence," Marshal Rider explained.

"Archie wouldn't ask me to kill someone that didn't exist."

"You sure you know this guy as well as you think?"

"He said that Enyo was the daughter of computer that runs the colony. He called her a 'terrestrial intelligent agent'," Dragos replied.

"AI, with some kind of body and wandering around harassing mining officials that step out of line?" Marshal Rider said, incredulous.

"These terrestrial intelligent agents, they do exist. I've met one. They are not to be trifled with," Dragos snapped.

Marshal Rider blinked, letting it all settle in for a moment. "Thanks for before. I never asked if you were alright."

"We are comrades now, yes?" Dragos said, wincing as he unzipped his jumpsuit to reveal several blackening bruises and lacerations received below the elevated concourse. She winced, walking over to a white metal medical box on a nearby wall, unlocking it with a keycard. Dragos sat down on one of the desks while she dabbed gauze at his many wounds.

"Why didn't you run, or get clear to take a better shot with your rifle?" she asked, taping a bandage over a still oozing wound.

"People in cells around us. HV rounds would have gone through and maybe hit wrong people. Hoped we could just fight our way out," Dragos explained.

"You mean convicts, right?"

"I mean people. Many imprisoned here, only crime was that they were poor," Dragos said, zipping up his jumpsuit.

"You were a true believer with the FLF? It wasn't just about turning a profit on contraband and whatever else those reprobates were up to?" Marshal Rider asked.

"My family, my people, we were poor. After the Shutdown, our old freighters were the only things in the sky. Everyone needed and wanted us, but there was nothing for FLF to fight against anymore. Old regimes died without their markets, money, and credit programs. My sister, she only ever wanted to run her own freighter hauler, like Father, and we had all the chances to do that. Man saying he was Vance Uroboros made many big promises. It turned out to all be a lie, so I come here to clear the debt I took out getting a hauler for my sister," Dragos explained.

"She know what you did?"

"Could you tell someone that loved you... that you had no soul left, sold for an empty dream?"

Marshal Rider gazed intently at Dragos, trying to find the right words.

"You should have told her. It's selfish that you shouldered this burden alone."

"So many debts, I doubt I'll be able to pay them all. In FLF, that was all I fought against, people using debt as a weapon. I helped Archie get the money for whatever he is doing now. He maybe even have this plan back on Earth. Always wondered how a man like him could get caught and put in prison."

The cellblocks were slowly going dark as lights out protocols slowly went into effect. To gaze in the right direction, one could look down a corridor to a virtual horizon, the penal facility being just so massive. As the lights went out in the distance, it was like a darkness slowly creeping toward them.

"I couldn't care less about the board of directors and all the stockholders of the mining companies. He killed six pregnant women and their unborn children, and tried to do the same to a seventh. Archie needs to die," Marshal Rider stated calmly.

"You think he is still in prison?" Dragos asked.

"Would you be if you were him?"

"Archie always stay where he has most power, greatest influence. He won't leave until his sentence ends, position at one of mining companies as officer is official. Escape would jeopardize legitimacy, if that is his ambition. He is still here, somewhere," Dragos said, checking his rifle.

"He's your friend, where would he go?"

"Can your suit not ask penal facility sensors for location?"

"It's always in collection, reporting location accurately, but a couple hours late. An hour and forty five minutes ago, he was standing right around where we are now, if the sensors are to be believed," Marshal Rider replied, looking up at the clusters of biometric sensory equipment hovering high overhead.

"Then he hasn't been gone long. We can still find him, kill him." Dragos said grimly thumbing the sights on the rifle.

"If we do this, I want you to leave the penal facility. Promise me you'll go home, tell your sister everything," Marshal Rider said, heading toward the falling darkness.

"I promise."

CHAPTER 6

North American Relief Effort Outpost #023

Estancia, New Mexico - April 3rd, 2200

Perfidy's War Journal, Part 1 –

New Mexico wasn't the place I remembered twenty-five years ago. Massive and advanced hydroponics structures dotted the landscape, quietly roaming about cultivating crops to take to warehouses where there were few freighter haulers to collect the proceeds. I remember environmentalists fearing a toxic mist that would come with this degree of hydroculturing, a single industrial filtering station failure causing people to drown, breathing hyper-saturated air or some nonsense.

The only thing that seemed to poison or drown anything was the people. Kale, my boss, manages to find the only person that might be able to foment change for the better, and she's a total attention seeking diva. Her uncle, being an overbearing ass, probably contributed to her sunny personality to a great degree, and I still wasn't sold on her passive tele-mechanical abilities giving us access to a CGG administrative node or server farm with any authority. Even if it did, and the facility woke up, it would find several unauthorized individuals within.

The automated security within might not try to kill the girl, but the rest of us would probably be in trouble. It'd be a bad day by my reckoning, even if it worked.

"Did it work?" Kale asked.

"Yeah, she powered up Mundt's freighter in spite of it being shut down and encrypted. It's still a far cry from the sort of facility you're talking about having her 'wake up' and gain access to for us," I explained, patiently as I could.

"This has the potential of working, yes?" he asked.

"Potential, by the strictest dictionary definition," I replied.

Jennifer Wilton's ability was a barely understood thing, and I'd never seen anything like it. Human beings exhibiting tele-mechanical abilities had only been acknowledged as a thing in the last century or so. To that end, someone passively making machines function outside of protocols was the opposite of everything that was understood about psychic mechanics. There was no way to measure these talents save through observation, and we couldn't even be sure she was really the source.

She seemed to be, but a really good hacker at a distance could make it appear as though she was activating these machines with the right sur-veillance and rig. I was probably being needlessly suspicious, but the girl seemed to set Kale off, agitating his nanotechnological form. It was like he struggled just to keep his temper around her, when he was otherwise so calm you'd think he had no emotions whatsoever.

"Could you have the midget bring up my bags from the relief tent?" Jennifer asked.

Kale blinked at her, not realizing she was referring to Brook. Satisfied the matter was handled, Kale went up into the transport to check the sys-tems for departure. I was just glad to have a decent pilot, even if Kale had a habit of solving problems with mid-air collisions.

"Pretty sure I can have one of the guys run down and grab them for you," I replied.

"Oh, thank you," she said, looking at her nails for the twenty-seventh time that morning.

"Also, I wouldn't call her a midget."

"What would you call her?" Jennifer asked, oozing with youthful impudence.

"She has a name, use it," I said, certain the conversation fell outside my job description.

Her uncle, Brannon George, lingered about as the private contractors I had brought along loaded our gear. I could tell he didn't like the look of me, or my friends. People never like the men and women who carry guns until they really need one.

"You can keep her safe?" George asked me.

"If she does what I tell her, when I tell her, she should be safe. We've pulled intelligence on the militias holding the areas around the first facility we'd like to access. They're religious nuts living in the woods, but everyone needs something. We'll probably be able to gain access by diplomacy," I explained.

"That's a nice speech. You'll be shooting your way in there then?" he said, squinting back at my guy bringing up the princess's bags.

"Yep," I said, departing from any desire to make this guy feel better about the situation.

"The militias are wary of anything that flies, and don't have much use for suits, cyborgs, Metasapients, or anything else they think is an affront to God. You guys are completely the wrong sort of person to try and talk to these people," George said, showing some genuine concern.

"Yep," I replied, totally agreeing with him.

"You guys need different clothes and a guide so you can set down a ways from their territory and hike in," George continued.

"Yep."

"It's really hard to get a read on someone like you, what with the optics replacing your eyes."

"Yep," I said, probably smiling.

Thankfully, Brook appeared to rescue me from the conversation. She did like she usually does, taking inventory of everyone before even speaking a greeting. Then, she turned and looked up at Mundt's freight hauler.

"What's wrong?" she asked.

"Not a thing, we're good to go," I replied, cheerily.

Brannon tipped his hat and wandered off to talk to Jennifer nearby, a pretty standard response to Drones. Most people didn't know how to interact with them. Before the Shutdown, Drones were mostly an urban legend in big cities, but that changed with the labor and food riots. The underground shelters that they dwelled in were suddenly five-star accommodations compared to the nothing surface folk had left. Brook watched Brannon leave before filling me in.

"Analytics from Misters Mortimer and Messer came back on Uroboros holdings. I'm still looking for other wards of the corporation," she reported, looking about for Kale.

"He's inside. Anything interesting come back?" I asked.

She hesitated, probably wanting to tell Kale about whatever they'd found first, him being the boss. Usually, that would have been her course of action, but not this time. It was information I would be keenly interested in.

"It's about Dr. Helmet. They think they have found the place where he based all his activities to thwart Maurice Madmar. It was tricky, tracking innumerable expense reports and invoices, but there is a facility that appears to be where Dr. Helmet likely resides," she explained, looking at her data slate.

"Our friends at the lunar colony know about it yet?" I asked.

"I forwarded everything."

Kale came back out of the freighter hauler, pulling his suit jacket back on. His face drooped a little when he saw Brook standing there with her data slate in hand.

"What now?" he asked.

"We might know where Dr. Helmet is," Brook said, offering to show Kale her data slate.

"Change of plans?" I asked.

"He's the only other person we know of who has used the imprinting process to create replicas of himself as Vance Uroboros had done. He may have better means to analyze brain activity than that derived from most commercial electroencephalogry. He may know how to verify Miss Wilton's abilities and assess whether she could enter the facilities with proper effect," Kale said, sounding a little bit more like himself.

"At least one of Dr. Helmet's replicas went rogue, but I feel like I owe the guy a favor. He did me a solid in Mexico. We should at least check in on him, make sure he's okay in the wake of Madmar's death. He spoke to me of certain countermeasures he didn't want Madmar to employ," I said, commenting on my last meeting with Helmet.

"Countermeasures?" Brook asked.

"Yeah, he talked about them like I should know what he meant. It's why I ditched all cyberware and fled further south."

"Everything Dr. Madmar touches turns into some kind of nightmare. I've seen his creations up close, and Helmet was right to be cautious," Kale said.

"Where is Dr. Helmet supposed to be holed up?" I asked.

"The analysis gives his address as a shuttered nanotech research facility in Watertown, South Dakota. There is no further information, just that until recently Uroboros Financial had maintained the property in accordance with local requirements," Brook said, putting the slate into the front pocket of her apron.

"It's not that far of a deviation from our original destination in Montana," Kale said.

"Montana? Are you thinking we'd just waltz into the CGG Central Server Hub for the hemisphere? Madmar managed to do that in Finland, but he had way heavier equipment than we do. You even know where it is?" I asked, somewhat pissed that Kale was contemplating such a dangerous target.

"It is in Glacier Park, near the old Canadian border. If we can get that hub to cycle, most of North America would have power and services again," Kale said, in his 'go big or go home' kind of way.

"This assumes whatever shut it down before makes it do the same again. We can't have Jennifer Wilton just park inside a secure government facility for months. I doubt the facility's automated defenses will tolerate us for a few seconds," I said, shaking my head.

Kale turned his gaze to Jennifer standing over by the front of the freighter conversing quietly with her uncle. "Miss Wilton, would you mind stepping away from the transport a safe distance?" he asked, polite as pie.

She shrugged and walked down the hill toward the relief camp with her uncle. Kale turned and watched the freighter hauler. Brook nodded, satisfied with the results.

"Brook and I encrypted the freighter hauler with CGG encryption protocols like those executed on government facilities and assets when they go into repossession," Kale explained.

"They're different?" I said, scratching my head.

"Of course, a separate set of rules for the government and private citizens. It was something Vance Uroboros disagreed with and was probably all too eager to exploit for his own uses. When Jennifer walks away from a repossessed private vehicle, they shut back down, but when she does the same with a machine that thinks it is CGG property, it remains active due to the administrative loophole built into the code," Kale explained, smiling one of his eerie and rare smiles.

"So, if Jennifer goes into a server hub, it should stay online, the repossession cycle having terminated once already," Brook said, patting my arm.

"You think Vance knew all this and had her sequestered?" I asked.

"I don't think he was the only one that knew. I doubt her parents being killed was random, or accidental," Kale replied, his smile fading quickly away.

"That is a seriously paranoid theory you've got there. Seriously, serious," I said.

"Coming from a cyborg who faked his death and ditched every mechanical part of his being to hide in plain sight, I'll take that as a compliment," Kale replied, beckoning for us to follow him up into the freighter.

We went up into the cockpit where he showed me a jury rigged data slate taped to the wall beside the console, a ribbon of wires running from it to an input port. He'd basically dual-booted the operating system governing the freighter hauler so it could appear as CGG property or a private vessel at the discretion of the pilot.

"I've registered us all as crew members on the CGG side. If we use the freighter hauler to land at the facility and it awakens while we're still inside the server core, it should believe we are personnel for at least an hour or so," Kale stated, toggling a few functions with the touch screen on the data slate.

"What if it is able to reference the universal record faster than we can get back out of the facility?" I asked.

"We'll probably all die, but I'm pretty sure the boot routine and internal cross checking should take long enough for us to escape unharmed. Admittedly, I've never done this before, so it'll be a volunteer mission. No one, but me, has to go," Kale stated, a barely discernable sliver of sentimentality showing through.

"I'm going," Brook said, without hesitation.

"Yeah, I'm in. Still, I wish we had more time to gather intel," I said, with great trepidation.

"Someone may be trying to undermine our efforts, even in these latest analytics I can see someone trying to manipulate reports, making subtle changes to financials, engaging in various other forms of corporate subterfuge. I haven't had the time to piece it all together, but I'm worried we'll have more than the militias to contend with on the ground," Kale said, sitting down in the pilot's chair.

"We'll get everyone loaded within the hour, then we can go," I said, looking to Brook.

She nodded, then followed me out to help get things ready. We left Kale alone in the cockpit with his thoughts, and I could only imagine what he was thinking. There were shadow players at work, forces pushing gently behind the scenes and we couldn't predict the outcome yet. Worse, time was not a resource we had in large quantity. If Brook and Kale were correct, billions of people were going to suffer and probably starve in the coming months if we didn't act to prevent it.

"I've had a thought," Brook said quietly, as we checked and rechecked gear in the cargo hold.

"Yeah?"

"Two thoughts actually."

"Heh, okay."

"What if the Mexican militia were given access to our delivery schedule to draw us to Jennifer Wilton's location?" Brook asked. "There are softer targets they could have gone after."

"You don't believe in coincidences, do you?" I asked rhetorically, reeling at the possibility.

"No. Also, I've looked for Dr. Helmet in the past using company records. It wasn't until Mr. Messer and Mr. Mortimer aided me that his location became apparent." Brook explained, pushing her goggles back up off her silvery eyes.

"It isn't just Kale that's paranoid. What does it all mean, exactly?" I asked, impressed and terrified at the same time.

"It was good fortune we found her, but we should make sure it stays *our* good fortune."

"If there is a bigger play here, shouldn't we tell Kale?" I asked.

"I'm certain he already knows. He probably knew the moment he saw Jennifer Wilton use her abilities," Brook said, folding her arms.

"Why are you telling me?"

"If someone is trying to hurt Kale, I want you to find them, and kill them," she said, annihilating many of my preconceived notions about her.

"You care about him?" I asked.

"Yes."

Brook was good enough to coax Jennifer back up to the transport, but her uncle was a bit ruffled. I couldn't really blame him. I could tell from our conversation before that he really wanted to go along, and wanted desperately to rationalize being involved. At the same time, I could tell he was a pragmatic man, and he knew the flow of events were probably inalterable at this point. All he could do is what any good soldier does in a storm, hold your post.

The rest of the guys, who shall remain nameless here, loaded their gear and readied themselves like the consummate professionals I knew them to be. I gave them the full rundown of everything, sans Brook's suspicions, but including the part about dropping into a CGG Central Server Hub. Everyone was fine with it, provided the usual hazard pay was in place and assurances in the event of their deaths.

It was a conversation we'd had many times, but somehow it was different that day. I think everyone would have gone even if there was no compensation at stake. It felt good to fight for something worthwhile again, and I think the team was feeling the same way.

Kale powered up Mundt's transport, bearing us up into the sky toward our destination. I had a private chuckle because I don't think Jennifer had ever flown before. Kale was an efficient pilot, but didn't mind flying directly into turbulence. She was green for most of the way to Watertown. At least she was stalwart enough to not complain.

"Perfidy, come up here a moment," Kale called out as he began the descent.

I climbed up into the cockpit with him and took a look out the windshield. Putting my advanced optics to work, I could see the town had been burned to the ground, corpses and ruined vehicles lay about everywhere. I could see the glint of tarnished shell casings and almost smell the remnants of military grade explosives. Someone had done their best to wipe the residential part of the city off the map.

I pointed to the few buildings left standing on the other side of what had been downtown, near the industrial area. Kale nodded and brought us in lower, gunning the engine to keep us hard to hit in case someone was on the ground with ordinance. The proximity alarm went off as he skirted the tops of ruined buildings, bringing us in to hover over the downtown area. Nothing moved or breathed down below. I couldn't see a biometric reading or heat signature to suggest that even a rat was still alive.

"Who could have done this?" Kale asked angrily.

"This was deliberate, and done with military grade ordinance and hardware. Tracked vehicles rolled through here in the aftermath, and all the work was done from the ground, buildings burned from the outside in," I observed.

"Someone found Dr. Helmet before we did?" Brook said, looking up from the passenger compartment.

"You can probably smell it already, yeah?" I said, grimly taking stock of the ruin arrayed below us.

"All I can smell is death. Thousands of people burned down there," Brook remarked sadly.

"I can't smell anything," Jennifer said, looking around at us annoyed.

"If a flea farts a mile away, Brook can smell it," I explained.

The other private contractors chuckled quietly at the comment, but Jennifer just looked embarrassed. She probably thought Brook was just along as a servant or amusement for Kale, but she'd find out pretty quick that big things often come in small packages.

Kale took us out over the industrial zone. The facility we sought was at the farthest edge of it. The boys and I rappelled down from the cargo hatch, fully loaded. Once we were on the ground we did a quick check of the area looking for any survivors or improvised explosives left behind. The facility was locked up tight, and we'd need tools to get in. After being reassured it was safe, Kale put the transport down in the parking lot beside the facility.

Clouds gathered overhead as a few droplets of rain began to descend on Watertown. Jennifer, Brook, and Kale ran over to where we'd set up outside the door, trading places with some of my associates to guard the ship. I'd started bolting down a brace to take down the door, but Brook grabbed up the sledge I'd been using and swung it at the door as hard as she could, taking it down in a single blow.

"Let's go," Brook said, handing me my hammer.

I stepped in over the ruined steel door and into a receiving area designed to handle hazardous materials. There were soundproof rooms and other odd countermeasures relative to the stated purpose for the facility. Even for a front operation, the place didn't seem right to me.

Everything seemed intact, but all the doors were open and the protective plastic had been pulled down. The room was dark, with only a receiving kiosk dimly illuminating the far corner. I led the way with Brook following along, her hand on my back the whole way. I could hear her sniffing the air as we passed through to the corridor and an adjoining metal chamber beyond.

"Stop," she said, grabbing me by the belt.

"What is it?" I whispered, unable to see anything.

"Kale, Jennifer, go back outside. Now," Brook ordered, her tone unusually serious.

They complied, retreating with the rest of my team to just outside receiving. Once Brook was certain they were clear, she gestured for me to take up a position just outside in the hall. I watched as she sniffed around the ground, then punched at it, startling me. What appeared to be a smooth surface broke into a panel after a hard strike from Brook's small but iron knuckles.

The steel groaned loudly as she pried it upward to reveal a downward passage. I'd seen Brook perform other feats of strength before, but I could never get over how calm she was or how natural she looked bending high grade steel. She paused, her silvery grey eyes gazing down into the darkness below.

"He's down there," she whispered.

"Who?" I asked.

"Dr. Helmet, but he's dead… there's no one alive down there," Brook replied, one of her alien Drone emotions spreading across her face. I'd say she looked supremely disappointed, but that description falls incredibly short.

"What? What's wrong?" I whispered.

"That smell… watch out!"

It was on me before I could react, creeping quietly enough my enhanced hearing missed it. It was a biomechanical construct meant to look like a human, but had gone horribly insane. Chemical hoses bulged out of its skin pulled taut over crude cybernetic hardware. I only caught a glimpse of it as countermeasures it was equipped with made me go blind for a second, disrupting my sensory implants.

I rolled with the thing, losing my submachine gun in the exchange. It hit me hard, but lost some leverage trying to get close enough to bite me with a maw of polished steel teeth. I drew my pistol and let a round loose in what should have been the ribs of the beastly thing. It flailed about, giving me room to go for my rifle. There were three of them trying to kill Brook as she wove around their serrated tendrils and balled up fists. I dropped my sledge hammer and kicked it over to her. I could hear the rest of my team pushing their way through the building, before gunfire erupted. The whole place was alive with the ghastly things.

Brook fought as well as any Type One, maybe better in this case because of her enhanced strength. I dropped one with a controlled burst from my submachinegun before heading back to check on the others. That's when the floor gave way behind me, the structure rapidly coming apart at the foundation below. A huge biomechanical monstrosity composed of dozens of hapless individuals stitched together rose up, dashing us all to the ground with elongated and deformed limbs.

Jennifer cried out in terror at what would have been a psyche-rending sight for most people. Admittedly, I'd never seen anything so messed up previous to that, but training and a good rifle tend to give one courage when nothing else can. We opened fire, dropping dozens of incendiary rounds of ammunition on the thing as it gave out a deafening roar. It reared back, knocking the roof off the complex, rending steel girders as it convulsed and struck out blindly.

Brook appeared as a silhouette far above us, my hammer held high as she came down on what could loosely be construed as the thing's head.

The first blow sent a tremor through the creature, stunning it. The second, blew the bloated top of it apart, sending down a torrent of biomechanical hardware, stasis fluid, and a dozen or so human brains all interconnected by strange vat-grown organic tendrils. We ran like hell, the thing plummeted down toward us.

When the dust cleared, the thing was laying still as death, having crushed half the facility beneath its bulk. Perched atop it was Brook, dressed in her cooking apron and with my hammer still in her hand. I would be challenged to describe a stranger sight, and Jennifer was nearly hysterical with terror for the experience. Some of the guys were pretty badly rattled, but Brook helped steady everyone with a single statement.

"Can I hold onto your hammer until we're clear of this place?" she asked, calm as the rain descending on us.

"Uh yeah, you totally can. You're a certifiable badass with that thing," I replied, chuckling.

She blushed, and looked at the ground. I don't think she even realized what she was doing until she was doing it. I could see she was afraid when she turned around and saw what she'd done. I'd seen the look before, when someone who isn't a soldier has to kill someone. It hits like a ton of bricks.

"It would have hurt us? Right?" Brook asked, clearly needing to be reassured.

"Whoever did that to those people... look, everyone is better off," Kale said, kneeling down and putting his arm around her.

"For real. We dropped serious firepower on that thing and it only seemed to get angry," I added.

"Ezra showed me some moves once, but I never thought I'd have to kill anything," she replied.

"You said Dr. Helmet was in there, but he was dead?" I asked, trying to change the subject.

"Yeah, he's been dead awhile. Kale, I don't think the man I met on the boat in Port Montaigne, the one who explained all the things to me, was the real Dr. Helmet. I think he's been dead since before the Shutdown. I think if anyone talked to him in the last few weeks, it was a replica," Brook said, looking around at the ruins of Watertown arrayed around us.

"Nanotechnological replicas are difficult to discern from the real thing, even with your enhanced senses," Kale said, arm still around her.

"But, I was so sure that was him…" she whispered, clutching my hammer with both hands.

"These things that attacked us, anyone else a little worried about that?" I asked.

"They strike me as something Madmar would create. Crude, cruel, and designed to evoke terror," Kale said, giving one of the elongated limbs a kick.

"It smelled like fear, enough to make anyone breathing the air around it afraid," Brook said, giving the rapidly decomposing thing a sniff.

"Like pheromones?" Kale asked.

"Yeah, like that."

"Why weren't we more adversely affected?" Kale asked.

"It's been here awhile, lurking over Dr. Helmet's corpse, among others down below. It might have lost potency over time, like he expected someone to come knocking sooner," Brook said, walking back toward the ruins.

"Where are you going?" Jennifer asked.

"Someone has to go down and look, see if Dr. Helmet had any notes, a data slate, something he used to keep a record," Brook replied.

"Why do you have to do it?" Jennifer muttered, looking at me and my team in particular.

"She's better trained and equipped to conduct recovery ops than we are," I explained.

"For real? I thought she was like…"

"My secretary?" Kale said, somewhat amused.

"Yeah," Jennifer admitted.

"Brook is a search and rescue specialist, trained to go into fallen structures and recover the living or the dead, hence her sense of smell and strength. If you are ever trapped somewhere, you'd be lucky to have her be the one to extract you," Kale said, watching Brook's small form vanish into the wreckage.

She was gone probably forty minutes before she emerged from the wrecked facility carrying a desiccated corpse over one shoulder and my hammer in the other hand. Her satchel brimmed over with storage media, a data slate, and other items recovered from Dr. Helmet's underground sanctum. She laid him down on the ground, putting his broken glasses on his mummified face respectfully.

"She was right, he's been dead awhile," I said, reevaluating everything that had happened and everything I'd done in the last few weeks.

"Agreed. I'm not sure it really changes anything, but Silverstein, Taylor, and Ezra One should probably know about this. Brook?" Kale said, kneeling down beside the corpse.

"I'll tell them," Brook said, putting her satchel down on the ground.

Kale and I looked through the recovered items. The storage media looked mostly intact and there were several ancient books written in a language I didn't recognize. There were more recently written journals penned in the same strange code. Kale seemed to be able to read it, which surprised both of us.

"I can read this," he said, somewhat baffled.

"What is it?" I asked.

"I… have no idea," he replied.

"An ability Vance Uroboros imprinted you with, maybe?" Brook asked.

"Maybe, the text is extremely troubling, I… need some time to figure this out," Kale said, closing the tome like it was a diseased.

"I don't much like reading either, my uncle forces me to," Jennifer said, having recovered her wits.

Kale smirked at her, drawing Brook's satchel up onto his shoulder. The guys carried Brook on their shoulders back to the transport, a quiet show of thanks for saving all our asses. Once we were back on board Mundt's transport, Kale and Brook set about uploading the data from Dr. Helmet's storage media. There was a lot of information stored on the media, enough that it took several minutes to transfer.

"You think Madmar found this media? Tampered with it?" Kale asked.

"No, it was well hidden, like it was meant for someone like me to find. I don't think anyone had touched it since Dr. Helmet hid it away down below," Brook replied.

Kale's finger swiped across the touchscreen on the slate as he did a cursory review of what we found. A full rainbow of human emotion flashed across his face as he did. Whatever was on the storage media was heavy.

We busied ourselves in the meantime, resetting our rifles and loading magazines while Brook made us some food in the galley. Jennifer was particularly sullen throughout, this not being the adventure or foray into fame she thought it would be. After we ate, Kale emerged from the cockpit and addressed us all.

"The data contained on the storage media doesn't seem to have the verification we sought. I've only been able to scratch the surface of what we've found. There is information on imprinted replicas I'm afraid to look at, records of some shadowy organization that Vance Uroboros may have been a member of, and intelligence on Maurice Madmar's operations, all pre-Shutdown of course," Kale said, exchanging knowing glances with Brook.

"So, nothing to help us verify Jennifer's role in your plan?" I asked.

"Not necessarily. Her name appears a dozen times when I search the files. Dr. Helmet knew about her, and may have already collected the data we're looking for. There are thousands of pages of documents on the subject of tele-mechanical phenomena, and it will take time to go through them all," Kale replied.

"Maybe while we're dealing with the militia presence in Montana, you should park somewhere safe and do that," I said, nodding to the rest of the team.

"I've been collecting satellite photography of the area we need to access. The militias have set up ancient anti-aircraft batteries around their primary camp beneath where we need to access the central server hub. I'd prefer to fly in, actually land the freighter hauler inside the facility, but I don't think it'll be safe without some action on the ground," Kale said, gazing at Helmet's repurposed and somewhat battered data slate.

"We've got long arms good enough to strike at a pretty decent range. Half the guys are trained spotters. We can do this," I said, nodding to the rest of the team.

"Do you have anti-material rifles or ammunition? I'd prefer to kill the weapons over the people manning them," Kale said, showing unusual restraint.

"Yes, but they'll be expecting us to come in by air in that event. They might react with surface to air missiles or other ordinance if they have it."

"You'll have to time the shots as we fly in then, position a team with a view of the settlement, and our landing zone."

"That's a terrible idea," I said, shaking my head at Kale.

"We have no intelligence on these people. We don't know if picking them off with sniper rifles is the right way to handle it," Kale said, calmly.

"We could just try talking to them," Jennifer stated, folding her arms.

"That's risky, given how many of them there are. We could set down somewhere close and try to listen in on their radio chatter and watch them for a day," I suggested, trying to avoid an impromptu meet and greet with the hill-dwelling religious nuts.

"Perfidy is right, we should wait and watch. It's only for one day," Brook said at last.

Kale nodded, pausing to think the situation through in his methodical way. Jennifer sighed loudly, clearly annoyed we'd basically ignored her suggestion. The rest of my team headed over to the other side of the cargo hold and started, rather conspicuously, checking the one anti-material rifle we brought.

"A day could matter," Kale said at last. "If Helmet's notes are accurate, every imprinted replica has tasks and a function cycle. When those complete, the replica will terminate automatically in most cases."

"You aren't like the other replicas, though," Brook said.

"No, but we all die."

CHAPTER 7

Shuttered Nanotech Research Facility

Watertown, South Dakota - April 4th, 2200

Perfidy's War Journal, Part 2 —

We did a little checking around Watertown, just to make sure there wasn't a survivor or a witness to what had happened. We were pretty sure it was Madmar's crew, but I hadn't heard of anything like this when I was working undercover for Madmar, or one of his cage puppets, or whatever. Could have been that after his death each of his puppets only had a piece of the bigger puzzle, and whatever he was really up to may have died with him.

Whoever came through was thorough. They didn't even leave a dog or a cat left standing, spreading a cleansing fire to every basement, backyard, and brewery. There wasn't any looting or scavenging done either. Perfectly good merchandise went up all over town with the people who lived there. This wasn't about politics or profit, but something else entirely. I'd seen it in South America and Africa, one religious or ideological group deciding it needed to send some kind of message. When you believe you are working on the orders of a higher authority, there's a way to communicate that with violence.

Still, I couldn't help but shake the feeling that this what yet something different, more terrifying. Finding Madmar's monstrosities in the nanotech facility made me think this was personal, something we weren't meant to understand. Kale was thinking about it real hard anyway, taking a quiet inventory in his mind of every charred corpse we came across. Brook wasn't too thrilled with the situation either, her intrinsic decency preventing her from even attempting to comprehend why someone would burn a town. When we returned to the rally point where the transport was parked, Brook was already there, and pretty distressed.

"They followed the people who tried to flee, and shot or burned them. They even killed the horses and goats on the farms," she said.

"We found more of the same. Doesn't seem like Madmar's style. He'd have everyone vanished and replaced with biomechanical replicas or some crap. Seriously, can we go now?" I asked.

"Yes, I've seen what I needed to," Kale said, taking a step aboard Mundt's transport.

We weren't in the air more than a couple hours, heading northwest, before we could hear the militia radio chatter. It sounded like an old guy reading from a holy scripture of some sort at first, but the words were twisted and the original meaning skewed. It was ignorant white suprem-acist dogma with the usual twist of misogynistic bull crap. The more I listened to it, the more I wanted to shoot our way through to the central server hub.

"Who's Jesus? He seems really important? Maybe we could talk to him?" Brook asked, after listening to the radio chatter.

"He's the militia's imaginary friend," Kale said, shouting back over his shoulder from the cockpit.

"Not a religious guy?" I said, laughing.

Kale smiled slightly. "I find religion to be absurd. I find atheism to be absurd. The only thing more absurd is arguing about which one is more absurd."

"I figured you would be a man of science, pun intended," I quipped.

"I believe in Jesus," Jennifer said, clutching at her knees uncomfortably.

"So do I, but I don't think he would forsake me for being the wrong color like these nut bags do," I said, sighing heavily.

"I still think we should try talking to this Jesus, see if he can convince them to let us go up to the central server hub without a fight," Brook muttered, folding her arms.

"God will likely sit this one out, if the radio chatter is any indication," Kale said, listening intently to the radio as he looked for a place to set down.

We landed in a clearing at least seven kilometers from the militia's main camp, and listened to see if we'd been spotted. After a quick excursion, it seemed as though the group was conducting business as usual. Through my scope I saw men with guns basically pushing around everyone else, women, children, and at least one Metasapient, Canine type. It looked like they tended their crops and their animals, held prayer vigils, and ran around in the woods playing army most of the time. They knew the area and were extremely well armed, but none of them had any real military experience. Still, they had numbers and slipping in past them would be difficult.

Since they weren't really hurting anyone but themselves, Kale was hesitant to let us just shoot our way through or push them out with sniper fire. Still, landing at the central server hub with the freighter hauler was pretty important as an added means of escape and false validity with regard to being there in the first place. Kale had run some simulations, but we still had no idea how long it would take the local AI to run the boot cycle and cross reference the personnel within the facility with the universal record. Better to just be gone before that happened.

Brook was waiting on the cargo ramp as we returned from conducting reconnaissance. "Did you see Jesus? Even being invisible, you should be able to see him with your optics, right?"

"Kale said imaginary, not invisible," I said with a chuckle.

"They talk like he is real," Brook said, still not understanding how religion worked.

"For some people he is, but you have to believe," I said, doing my awkward best to confuse her more.

"Okay, so if Jesus isn't the real boss, who is?"

"It looks like they have a council of village elders that get together and argue about every tiny thing going on in their village. I estimate there are six or seven hundred individuals in the village, and one Metasapient. Half of them are angry white guys with guns and a serious problem with people of my complexion, and Drones," I explained, hoping Kale would come down and rescue me from the conversation.

"What's wrong with your complexion? Or being a Drone?"

"My friends and I are Mexican and South American nationals, and the folks at the camp believe that God only loves white people. Drones were made by unbelievers as opposed to having been created by God, or his faithful servants, the white people living in the woods with guns," I explained.

Brook blinked at me. "You're joking, right?"

"I wish. Jennifer and Kale are the only folks that could pass as the master race and approach the locals. They'd need a slight wardrobe adjustment to do so. Kale needs some army surplus clothes and Jennifer would need a plain black dress and a bonnet," I explained.

"You have to wear a special costume to believe in Jesus?"

"The Jesus the locals believe in, yes."

Kale came down the ramp, squinting out across the tree line toward the rising smoke in the distance. I uploaded the video capture we collected to his battered data slate and watched for any indication he was going to let my friends and I go in heavy.

"Kill their anti-aircraft guns and leave one sniper team on the ground. If they spot anyone with anti-aircraft ordinance, shoot to kill," Kale ordered, slipping the data slate into his suit pocket.

"Got it. Everyone else is going in?"

"We'll need security for the transport. If the locals decide to engage us at the landing platform, or our snipers in the field, do what you have to. Everyone goes home," Kale said calmly.

"What do I do?" Jennifer asked.

"Stay with Brook. Do not leave her side."

I detailed my field team, helped double check their gear, and made sure our secure channel was routing properly through the transport. They started firing at anti-aircraft guns before we even lifted off. Kale brought the transport around hard, prompting even me to buckle up.

"Hang on," he said, dropping the nose of the transport.

He flew directly over their camp and began climbing about ninety degrees off target. Small arms fire bounced off the exterior as my sniper team tapped out that they were taking shots anything that was a threat to the freighter hauler. It was chaos below us as Kale began to climb skirting the wrong slope of the mountains beside the entrance to the central server hub.

"Wrong way!" I bellowed, holding on for dear life.

"I know," Kale said, threading the transport between two high peaks and dropping altitude like he was going to land.

We came just short of touching down as the transport turned hard to the right. Kale skimmed the dark side of the mountain heading back toward the central server hub. The locals, if they gave pursuit, would probably climb in the wrong direction for hours before they noticed our true landing site a handful of kilometers away, assuming the cloud cover even broke before then.

The landing platform was built into the side of mountain, and large enough to accommodate two freight haulers the size of ours. There were militia sentinels already prepping to rappel down the mountain to tell their friends. My guys and I did some rope work of our own dropping to the platform as Kale attempted to execute the quietest and darkest landing I'd ever seen. It was foggy as hell and how he managed to get all the landing gear on the platform on the first try, I'll never know.

We made sure the militia guards never made it home, putting a suppressed round in each of their heads. When it was all over, we took a breath and listened. The valley below us was quiet, and there was no sign of anyone coming up through cover to ascend the slope just yet. The bad weather looked to be holding a while longer, but it'd get burned off the closer it got to the noon hour. Kale descended the loading ramp with Jennifer and Brook right behind him.

"Perfidy, you're with us. Have the rest of your team hold this position. If either team comes under fire, have them call it in. I've contingencies in place if the locals do anything but wait this out in their shacks and caves," Kale said, gesturing toward the huge vault door between us and the central server hub.

"Call it in to who?" I asked.

"Mr. Messer back at corporate. He'll have unmanned aircraft provide support," Kale said, heading up to the vault door.

"You sure?" Brook asked.

"Yes, I want to make certain he knows we arrived safely," Kale said, smiling slightly.

Before he even got near the console to begin trying to gain access, the doors went active. There was a loud hydraulic hiss as the armored enclosure began to cycle, forced air blasting past us as the entrance to the central server hub began to open. As the vault door began to roll to the left, I could see there were already people inside the server hub. My team and I dropped to one knee and brought our rifles up as Kale, Jennifer, and Brook scurried to one side to get clear.

"Please, do not shoot," a Canine Metasapient said as he stepped out onto the landing pad.

He had several others with him, brown with shaggy hair and sad eyes, all unarmed and holding their hands up. I'd never seen Canine Metasapients like this before. Previous to that, I'd only seen the large law enforcement variety, and there was nothing endearing or pitiable about them.

"Stand down," I ordered, returning to a ready stance in case there was going to be trouble.

"What are you all doing in there?" Kale asked, stepping up to officiate for our group.

"My name is Collver. We were workers in the Central Server Hub. One day, all the personnel were forced to leave by the AI and they never returned. Then the men with rifles came, captured our emissary that went down asking to trade for food. They hurt her, every day. Please, help us," Collver asked, with a thick factory accent.

"The Canine Metasapient we saw during our reconnaissance. That must be who he's talking about," I said, nodding to Kale.

"Your friend was still alive a few hours ago, Collver, but we lack the means to rescue her," Kale said.

"Her name is Shelby, and she's the only Type Four among us. The rest of us are heavy labor," Collver said, beckoning for the others to come out.

"You're all Type Three?" Kale asked.

"Right, we'll do whatever we can to help. We just want food, to be left alone, and Shelby," Collver replied, looking back down the mountain toward where the militia camp was.

"Sniper team still in position to take shots?" Kale asked.

"Yeah, five anti-aircraft weapons down, three personnel carrying ordinance down, position remains uncompromised," I replied.

"How was Shelby restrained?"

"She was chained up outside. She looked pretty rough, not dressed for the weather," I replied, hoping to God he was going to ask me to go get her.

"Collver, how many of you are there?" Kale asked.

"Thirty-eight of us, but that'll change if we don't get some food," Collver replied, clasping his hands together in front of him.

Kale took out his mobile. "Call Mr. Messer."

"Messer, I need unmanned aircraft and satellite topography for my current location. I need a relief package dropped exactly on my position."

Kale stood there listening to Messer on the other end for a moment, nodding quietly.

"Locals are hostile. Write it up as Uroboros Financial Assets being out of custody and requiring private security action," Kale said, putting his mobile back in his pocket.

"I want to help," Jennifer said, wide-eyed like the horrors of the world were unfolding in front of her.

"Did your uncle show you how to load and shoot a rifle?" Kale asked.

"Yes."

"Go into the cargo hold with Brook and begin opening the crates in the back left corner. I'd brought them as currency to trade with the locals, but I have a better idea. Type Three Metasapients are naturally adept at using tools, and what is a rifle, Mr. Perfidy?" Kale said.

"Definitely a tool, boss, but there are a couple hundred guys with rifles down there, at least," I explained, sensing his plan.

"We have the high ground, a still undetected sniper team, and in fifty-three minutes, air support. Jennifer, can you teach Brook and Collver's people to use the rifle well enough that they won't be shooting each other or us?" Kale asked.

"Yes," Jennifer replied shakily.

"I don't need them to actually fight, they just need to look impressive, and carrying the rifles properly. Anyone who chains up a Metasapient like that is a coward, and probably will act like one when confronted with a real fight," Kale sneered, turning back to look at me.

"What about the boys and me?" I asked, expectantly.

"Go get Shelby. If you can do it without killing anyone, that is preferred. I'm unwilling to lose even a single person on this outing, understand?" Kale said, folding his arms.

"I understand," trying not quite hard enough to hide my glee.

As we were loading up, I could see a definite change in Jennifer. The princess act was completely gone as she began showing the Collver and his crew the rudiments of firearm safety. It was a thing I'd rarely seen out in the world, someone suddenly growing a conscience. Personally, I'd always liked being one of the good guys.

It was getting close to mid-morning as we made our descent. My enhanced optics were picking up every scout and sentry they had. It was a haphazard arrangement that thankfully gave us an open path to creep into their camp. They must not receive many visitors coming down from the north. There were some pretty nice log cabins and lodges that had been built in the last few months, and evidence they'd already collected at least one harvest of crops. It was like these wackos had come here expecting the end of the world, and it came.

A woman and child met us on approach. I turned and looked at her, standing thirty feet away in the doorway of a shack. It was an odd moment, because I expected that she would scream bloody murder, but instead she gathered up her kid and approached us.

"Who are you?" she asked.

"I'm Bob, a package delivery professional for Tinker Tots Toy Company. We're here for Shelby, the Metasapient you nut balls have chained up, next farm over," I said, gesturing for the team to move on ahead.

"Please, take us with you," she pleaded.

"You sure Jesus and your husband are going to be copacetic with that?" I asked.

"They bought me and three others, six months ago from a man that kidnapped us from British Columbia. I just want to go home," she whispered, looking about with a genuine look of terror on her face.

"Sniper team, you have eyes on me?"

"Affirm."

"I've got two civilians here. Keep half an eye on them while I'm down procuring the target."

"Team's already got her, they're extracting now."

"Okay, wait for my…"

Automatic gunfire broke out from behind me, outside my optical sensory arc. It was pretty far away, from one of the sentries near the tree line four hundred yards out. I turned and snapped off a round hitting him in the eye, but I could already hear footfalls and the clink of weapons converging on us.

"You've got hostiles moving on you. You want us to engage?" Sniper team asked over the comm.

"Affirm. Lady, we need to go, now," I said turning back to the woman.

She was on the ground, a stray rifle round from the sentry having taken the top of her head off. The baby was lying beside her, quiet as could be and still wrapped in a blanket.

"Engage at will, kill every one of them you can," I said angrily picking up the child.

"Uh, confirm order?"

"Anyone wearing a surplus camo with a rifle, start making them sad," I growled into the mic.

I could hear the telltale sound of twenty millimeter rounds hitting human beings over my enhanced sensors, sharing out my optics to the team over our secure network. I moved up, relating data as the sniper team proceeded to do what they did best. I tucked the kid up under one arm and used my rifle strap as a brace. The rest of the guys reached my position a few seconds later, carrying Shelby on a makeshift gurney.

"She's bad, Boss."

"Take no chances, I'll spot from the front, you shoot," I said running ahead.

We climbed back toward the tree line, me barking out positions and the guys laying down cover fire one handed. It was scaring the crap out of the kid and poor Shelby, but the boss did say that any personnel loss was unacceptable. We killed nineteen of the bastards getting to the tree line before they started to withdraw.

"They're bugging out," Sniper team reported.

"Hold position. We will extract you if necessary," I ordered.

The rest of the climb played havoc with my poor old knees, and I was glad as hell to hand off the screaming baby to Jennifer once we got there. Jennifer was able to quickly quiet the kid as I took stock of her small army. Collver and his crew were all outfitted with a rifle and a bandoleer of extra ammunition. They weren't type one Metasapients so they weren't big and scary, but they still had teeth and they seemed greatly bolstered by Shelby's return.

"Shelby, are you alright?" Collver asked, breaking ranks to rush to her side.

"I don't think... they will negotiate with us..." she replied, patting Collver on the arm.

"Lot of shooting down there... and you brought me a baby I didn't ask for," Kale scolded, wrinkling his nose at the child.

"They bought the child's mother from a slaver," I reported.

"Where is the mother now?" Kale asked.

"They shot her. She was standing right next to me, holding a kid."

"So, you thought it was alright to engage at will, have my sniper team expend extremely expensive ammunition, and blow apart as many cross-worshipping locals as you could?" Kale asked, folding his arms.

"Yeah, pretty much," I replied, still out of breath, pushing rounds back into a magazine to replace what I'd fired earlier.

Kale just nodded, giving me one of his barely perceptible smiles and said nothing else.

"We've got air support," Brook said, pointing to a pair of sleek unmanned aircraft.

One of them flew in dropping the relief package right on target, tiny anti-gravity engines guiding the pallet of food and medicine to exactly where Kale had been standing when he requested it. Jennifer took the initiative and started distributing it to her new platoon of canine soldiers. Then, someone hugged me.

"Thank you," Shelby said, returning to Collver for support and help standing up.

"You should be thanking that guy over there, he pays me to be awesome," I said, pointing to Kale who was standing off a ways talking to Mister Messer again via his mobile.

"You risked your life, regardless. Those people are extremely dangerous. They will come for revenge," Shelby said, leaning heavily on Collver.

"God, I hope so," I said, patting my rifle.

That did little to throw salve on Shelby's fears, her facial expression betraying deep concern.

"I think Kale has a plan for that, but for the moment you need to rest. We need to go inside the central server hub and try to get it to cycle and hard boot," I explained.

"Oh, the AI isn't offline," Shelby explained.

"Come again?" I asked, somewhat astonished.

"He's still active, but his support systems are offline. He's dying because he lacks the space to write and rewrite himself. It isn't bad yet, but if he doesn't get help, he'll fragment and slowly go insane," Shelby explained.

"Jennifer might be able to help with that," I said, pointing to the young lady distributing supplies.

"You've got a whole bunch of hostiles moving on you from the above the tree line. They're making the climb to your position," the sniper team reported.

"Kale! The militia is pushing for the summit, whatever you are going to do, it needs to be done now," I yelled out, rushing to the ledge to look down.

"They'll have to climb up ropes to get us, right?" Brook asked, coming up beside me.

"No, they could take a slower route, over there, and there," I said pointing to a couple of goat trails.

"There's a lot of cover, this could be bad," Brook said, worriedly.

Suddenly the transport powered up, the cargo hatch swinging closed. We looked back at the cockpit to where Kale was sitting. He flashed us a half smile as he slowly began to lift off, the Canine Metasapients rushing to reinforce us, forming a line of riflemen along the ridge. The unmanned aircraft swooped up so they were hovering beside the transport as it loomed large above us. Panels across the front of the freighter hauler descended to reveal missile pods and a thirty millimeter Gatling cannon.

He nosed out ahead of us so that if he had to fire he wouldn't burst eardrums or flatten people with compression from the weapons. The one hundred fifty or so militia down below looked up at the forty or so of us, all with rifles and three heavily armed aircraft hovering over us, all nose down as if trying to intimidate them. I bet some of them wished they'd worn brown pants that day because a few didn't even wait for the retreat order before running like hell back into the tree line.

"Give me a building that has no heat signatures present," Kale asked.

"Coordinates should be on screen now," Sniper team responded.

One of the unmanned aircrafts suddenly changed direction, skirting the tree line as it flew down toward the village. It fired a single missile from a pod, obliterating a shed full of hay. The other unmanned craft lurked over the forest, gunning its engines and cycling between different ammunition types, clicking ominously overhead. Kale held the freighter hauler over us, casting a long shadow down toward the trees. The whole effect worked marvelously to destroy the morale of the militia.

"This area is now subject to repossession and lawfully owned by Uroboros Financial. You are hereby evicted and have thirty minutes to depart. Anyone left behind will be rounded up and subject to rendition," Kale explained calmly over the freighter hauler's public announcement system.

Men wearing surplus camo scattered to various huts, cabins, and lodges gathering up what they could before marching southwest. I had the sniper team watch them for the next hour while dozens of refugees, mostly women and kids, began climbing the slope, hands up and intent on surrendering to Mundt's beat up freighter hauler.

"Get down there, help the boss," I ordered, setting up to rappel down.

I was a little surprised when Collver and his crew responded as well, heading down the goat paths with Jennifer. Kale retracted all the weapons on the freighter hauler before setting it down on the slope. The refugees gathered around below the landing zone, their hands still up. When we got down there, Kale dropped the cargo hatch and walked out, straightening a cufflink and looking generally bored with the whole situation.

"What are we going to do with all these people?" I asked, looking out at more than four hundred terrified human beings.

"Put them to work," Kale said, beckoning for Collver to follow him.

They walked down and met with people who had been left behind. Kale negotiated a treaty between Collver's crew and the locals that remained. They would protect each other, grow things in the ground, and share resources. In exchange for holding the territory, Uroboros Financial would subsidize it as part of the relief operation and provide them with supplies, weapons, medicine, makeshift shelters, and communications.

"Someone from human resources will come within thirty days to help you understand the health and dental plan. Since there are no local resources, you'll have to get care at three month intervals until a more permanent installation can be erected and services restored locally," Kale explained, baffling most of those present, but I think they knew it was a good thing.

"You building a town here?" I asked, once we were clear of the locals and trying to figure out our next move.

"Shelby told me the AI that governs the server hub didn't shut down with the rest of the systems. It is advanced enough that we can reason with it, make it our ally and friend. The area needs to be watched and guarded in that event, as it is a major strategic holding for Uroboros Financial. I still think someone means to undermine us. I don't want what happened at Watertown to happen here," Kale said, checking his mobile.

"Yeah, she said the same thing to me," I said looking to Brook.

"The AI needs help. We should just help it," Brook said, frowning at Kale.

"It is your turn to come up with a plan, since we didn't contact Jesus to negotiate for us. We will help the AI regardless of whether it cooperates or not," Kale said, smiling slightly.

Brook smiled broadly, then headed up to the galley to start making us some lunch. Jennifer joined us, baby still in her arms, in time for chow and we sat down to eat with the guys. The sniper team was pretty jealous, as Brook made a mean stew, but I felt like we needed eyes in the valley for another forty-eight hours.

"Some of these people were sold to the militia to be wives. They wanted to go home. I had to explain to them that they may have no home to go to, that the whole planet has been repossessed. It was a hard thing for some of them to accept, that while they were held up here, the world basically got turned upside down," Jennifer said, quietly pushing bits of stew around with a spoon.

"My heart bleeds," Kale said, thumbing the touchscreen on his mobile.

"You could be a little more sympathetic here," Jennifer snapped.

"They're better off than most everyone else. They have shelter, the protection of Collver and his fellow workers, and are in possession of land valuable to the last major financial institution on the planet. At least they aren't living on a Pacific Island, cut off from everyone or starving in Siberia with little hope of rescue," Kale said, meeting her teary eyed gaze with one of the coldest stares I've seen him give anyone.

Jennifer stood up, letting her bowl of stew clatter to the floor.

"Now you're just wasting food," Kale said, looking disdainfully at the overturned bowl.

Jennifer stormed out without a word.

"Harsh, man. Harsh," I said, not looking up from my bowl.

"Would you spare her any of the reality of our situation?" Kale asked.

"No," Brook said, stooping over to clean up the mess, but Kale stopped her.

"I'll get it, make sure the locals are settled back in their homes and whatever is left of the relief package is handed out to them," Kale said, putting a hand on Brook's shoulder.

"Okay," Brook said, heading down the cargo ramp, hammer in hand.

"Would you have fired the weapons on the freighter at the militia if they'd have engaged us?" I asked.

"No, they're locked out and can only be fired by Mr. Mundt. I deployed them using a maintenance protocol," Kale said, mopping up the rest of the soup.

"Heh, you bluffed them out of the valley?" I said, laughing.

"Well, we did have two unmanned aircraft, and..."

That's when Kale pitched forward, almost reaching the floor before I caught him. The guys stood and headed for the hatch to stand around and obscure the view to the cargo hold as best they could. I turned him over and looked down into his tired eyes.

"It's happening?" I asked.

"Could be. I'm drawing closer to completing my task. I think I'm dying," Kale said, gripping me by the arm tightly as though he were in terrible agony.

"You need to hold on," I said, helping him back to the crate he was sitting on.

"I will, until it is done," he rasped, from between clenched and bloody teeth.

CHAPTER 8

CGG Central Server Hub

Glacier Park, Montana - April 5th, 2200

Perfidy's War Journal, Part 3 –

It took several hours to prepare for the descent to the AI acting as the administrative core for the central server hub. Shelby's description of where it was filled me with dread, as it sounded like it would take longer than Kale's most optimistic estimate to get back out when the systems cycled. Still, the AI was functional and sounded like it had protocols allowing for a lot of freedom of choice. It might be that we could negotiate with it before Jennifer's tele-mechanical aura recovered its support systems and the ability to kill us all.

If we had more time, I'd have suggested taking out the defense systems while they were offline, but it would take weeks and a lot more explosives than we had. I wasn't sure Kale even had another day once we cycled the server. I dreaded that moment, because he was Brook's best friend in the whole world and I'd grown pretty fond of her, and her cooking. It would wreck her.

"Shelby says we go straight in for a half a mile past two checkpoints and there will be a concourse with several maintenance hatches allowing for descent into the cooling system. It's a long climb down from there, and we have to wait for different portions to cycle before we move past retaining hatches. The timing isn't hard, but we can't make a mistake. If you're in the wrong place, you'll freeze to death or suffocate as air doesn't get pushed down there naturally," Brook explained.

"She can't go with us?" Kale asked, pulling a satchel off the cargo hold wall onto his shoulder.

"They broke her ribs and fractured her left leg just above the ankle. Not like you'd even care," Jennifer muttered.

"I didn't know. Collver being with us will allow for us to pass through the biometrics. It is fine, Brook could probably make the descent without directions. Have your men wait for us here," Kale said, ignoring Jennifer's vitriol.

"Boss? Shouldn't we..."

"We'll be fine," Kale said, waving dismissively over his shoulder.

It didn't feel right, but I quietly told the guys to shadow us to the cooling core before heading back to the entrance. I wasn't happy that Kale was even going in, but I knew that it was probably somehow part of his programming or something. He had to do this.

We were passing through the first biometric rings, these large devices designed to scan folk as they went through. None of the systems attached to the sensors were on, so the rings just cycled uselessly in the corridor for a moment or two before opening the doors. The last known entrants were fortunately still in memory, so Collver and his people could still come and go. It's too bad that safeguard wasn't afforded the rest of the planet.

"Why do you think Madmar did it?" I asked, watching Brook and Collver walk ahead of us through the massive concourse.

"Did what?" Kale replied, looking over at the stacks of cargo containers that had been converted to living spaces.

"Well, everything I guess. I was inside his organization and it wasn't about money, or even power, I don't think. The things he did to people were just odd, all things considered. Even the cyborgs that worked for him were on a ticking clock," I explained, hoping Kale had some insight I did not.

"From what Ezra One told me via correspondence, his infirmity made it necessary to persist inside a glass tank full of biologically sustaining fluid. He interacted with the world through a virtual reality interface," Kale explained.

"That's why he did all of this?" I asked, looking up into the high ceiling of the hollow mountain.

"His marionette cages, where he captured people and forced them to control biomechanical replicas of themselves, were like copies of his own pain. His madness was driving him to do things, perhaps compulsively, so he inflicted the same terror and madness on others. The cyborgs in his employ were similarly trapped by the machinery in their bodies. If you hadn't rid yourself of every component like you did, you would have likely met an end similar to most of Madmar's employees and cohorts," Kale explained.

"Wow, I never thought of it like that, him being insane and inflicting it on others, I mean. You must have thought about all this quite a bit, yeah?" I said with a chuckle.

"Only just now, because you asked," Kale replied, pausing to watch Brook and Collver mess with one of the maintenance hatches.

"Who is Madmar?" Jennifer asked.

"No one you'd like to ever meet," I said.

"Fine, keep your secrets, jerks," Jennifer growled, folding her arms.

"He was a member of a top secret research group within the CGG, on what was called the MDC Project. They developed the principle groundwork for Drones, Metasapients, cybernetics, and a host of other technologies. Dr. Maurice Madmar was the C in MDC, and an expert in man-machine interface methodology and experimentation," Kale explained.

"You said he was hurting people?" Jennifer asked.

"He was; some of our allies caught up with him at the Lunar Colony and killed him as he was attempting some insane experiment at the expense of individuals with tele-mechanical gifts, similar to your own. Because of people with his ambition our employer, Vance Uroboros, had you sequestered," Kale said, calmly watching Brook and Collver as they picked their way through the maze of tunnels and corridors ahead of us.

"My parents... did he have something to do with all that?" Jennifer asked.

"Brook has been trying to find that out, relative to the people Vance Uroboros placed under what was called The Umbrella," I said, checking over my shoulder to make sure the guys were still following.

"So it's possible, this Madmar guy was responsible for the incident on the transport, and all those people, my parents…"

"Yes, but we may never know for certain. Dr. Madmar hijacked parts of Vance Uroboros' own global ambition, resulting in the economic apocalypse that shut down eighty-five percent of the world," Kale said, checking his mobile.

"No signal?" I asked.

"There's a relay inside here somewhere. I have perfect reception actually," Kale said, looking up at the tangle of machinery, air conditioning ductwork, and surveillance equipment tied into the massive domed ceiling.

"Could be useful, if we need to make a call," I said.

"We could call Selene, on behalf of the administrative AI, have them converse if it won't trust our own account of what's happened to the Earth," Kale said, pocketing his mobile.

"Who is Selene?" Jennifer asked.

"She's an Omega Class Intelligent Agent, an even more powerful sentient machine than the one trapped in this facility. She basically handles everything for the Lunar Colony," I said, looking on toward the far end of the concourse.

"Omega Class?" Jennifer asked.

"Most intelligent agents have artificial personalities, programmed responses, and limited operational protocols. The two Omegas were spontaneously created, the code governing them merely emerging from an enlightened source written to that end. They have the same agency as humans do, and extreme measures have been taken to protect and house them as autonomous individuals with rights," Kale explained.

"Did Vance Uroboros protect them with his Umbrella, like he did with me?" Jennifer asked.

"Yes. When Selene was young, Vance Uroboros interceded, buying enough of the Lunar Colony to sway the local authorities into allowing him to create a facility to house her," Kale explained.

"Whoa, this is a story I haven't heard," I said, looking over at Kale in surprise.

"It will have to wait," Kale said, pointing to Collver and Brook as they fiddled with a maintenance hatch.

"Someone has been here recently, someone that does not belong to our pack," Collver muttered, sniffing around the entrance.

"Someone slipped in here while we were occupied at the ridge maybe?" I said, looking up for any sign they'd left surveillance behind to watch the maintenance hatch.

I waved Kale and Jennifer over to the side of corridor where it met with the concourse and began doing a thorough scan of the walls and ceiling. My enhanced optics switched to various spectrums while I used a separate internal scanner to look for radio waves and signals. The area seemed clean, except for everything that was supposed to be there. There was no signal from the facility surveillance, there being nothing to transmit to, as all the systems were still down.

"Collver, are you afraid?" Brook said at last.

"Yes, a little," he replied.

"Are you smelling someone new? Or are you smelling us, in a place you aren't used to smelling people other than your pack?" Brook asked, sniffing the air.

Collver stopped, a curious expression spreading across his dog-like face. He sniffed the air, and then each of us in turn. Then, he turned back to the maintenance hatch.

"It… it's just you guys. I'm sorry, I am afraid, and I was confused," Collver said at last.

"It's synesthesia, a secondary cognitive reaction to one of your heightened senses," Kale said, nodding to Brook.

"Right, I can teach you a mental exercise to overcome it, so you don't get confused again," Brook explained.

"Where did you learn these things?" Collver asked.

"The Factory," Brook replied, patting him on the arm.

"Why are you afraid?" Jennifer asked.

"I don't know. I started to feel a cold tingle along my spine about halfway inside," Collver said, scratching at the back of his furry hand.

"It's separation anxiety, Collver. You usually come here with your pack, live with them, and work with them," Brook explained.

"Can you proceed?" Kale asked.

"Yes, I think so. It is… helpful to know why I feel this way. You must know a lot about Metasapients?"

"Brook and I took a special interest more recently. Mostly, with the Acrididae variant, but there is a lot of crossover… more than I realized," Kale said in his cold, analytical way.

"I'm sorry, I'll try to focus. I know this is important," Collver said, somewhat embarrassed.

"Of everyone with any knowledge of the facility, you were the only one who volunteered. I'm just glad we aren't bumbling around in here without a guide," Kale said kneeling down to look at the hatch.

"The human workers had little patience for us, and were not always so glad to have us," Collver said, loosening the hatch with a wrench from his coveralls.

"Only Jennifer is actually a human. Perfidy is as much machine as he is man," Brook said with a smile.

"I don't understand," Collver admitted, removing the hatch.

"She says you're in good company. None of us get along well with regular folks," I said, loading ceramic low-recoil rounds into my rifle.

"The shaft goes down for quite a ways. The climb will be difficult," Collver said, apologetically.

I rappelled down ahead of them, stopping every forty meters to reset my line. Collver wasn't kidding when he said the shaft went down deep. There were several cross shafts to be navigated, each carrying super-cool air to the various servers and components. I had to wonder if they weren't frozen solid, and perhaps damaged by continuing to be cooled while inactive. It was strange that Jennifer's tele-mechanical aura seemed to have no effect on the inoperable machines as we descended. It might be that she had a range and the systems governing the various machines and devices we encountered on the descent were outside of it.

Or, maybe the facility was designed that way to prevent people like her with easy access.

We stopped to rest just outside one of the cold shafts on a ledge made of expanded metal, our legs dangling over the edge, while we passed some sandwiches around. Brook seemed perfectly at home down here, but Jennifer and I were both getting a little claustrophobic. It felt like the entire mountain was on top of us now. We could feel the air get thin between the feeble puffs from the passively functioning ventilation system. Kale would glance at his mobile every once in a while, thumbing at the touch screen and scratching his chin thoughtfully. He was eerily calm sometimes, more than some of the most seasoned soldiers I'd served with.

"Perfidy, if we can't reason with the administrative AI, I want you to get Jennifer out of here at any cost. It shouldn't want to harm Collver, and Brook should be able to extract without assistance," Kale said, still staring at his mobile.

"What about you?" Brook asked.

"I'm ultimately expendable. I only came to make sure the operation goes down and act as an officer of Uroboros Financial in the event the A.I has demands."

"No one is going to die. Everything will be fine," Brook said, using her hand to cover the screen on Kale's mobile.

"I'll get Jennifer out if I can, but it'll be a helluva thing if the AI has full systems access and can start shutting down ventilation or closing the cooling shafts," I explained.

"It won't do that," Kale said brushing Brook's hand from his mobile. "If it shuts the shafts the various servers and systems will overheat. The ventilation systems pull air down passively. You'll need only to get past the automated defenses, for which you are properly armed and equipped to deal with."

"I could only carry so much ammunition," I said, feeling a little better that Kale had at least considered some of the angles.

"It is fortunate that you don't tend to miss," Kale said, pocketing his mobile and preparing to make the rest of the descent.

We made the rest of the descent with only a minor accident along the way. In one of the cooling shafts, Jennifer slipped on the icy interior and banged her head. It was an odd thing because we'd been having to manually open and close each shaft with Collver's impact wrench on the hatches. When she fell, the shaft lit up for a moment, each of the doors in the shaft opening up. We had a miserable time getting them closed again, as the pneumatics on each one had engaged.

At the bottom was a crossroads of sorts, an intersection of lonely corridors lined with thick pipe about eight feet in diameter. With the metal flooring installed, one had to duck down a little to dodge the pipes and small lights that dotted the top lighting the way. There was no clear indication as to which tunnel led to the administrative AI, but Collver headed off down one without hesitation. We followed him for almost a hundred meters before we came to a large hatch.

"It opens from the inside. We haven't been able to open it for months," Collver said, giving the thick steel door a gentle shove.

"It looks like it slides to the side into a pocket. It can be bypassed, but it'll take time," Brook said, squatting down next to it and turning to look up at the gap where the door met with the wall.

Jennifer walked up to the door and put a hand out, hesitantly touching the door. It jerked violently, startling Collver and Brook as it rolled to the side until she withdrew her hand. There was plenty of room to squeeze through, but the door would be a problem later if we really needed to get out quick. Finding a length of pipe, we wedged it across the threshold so that it would hopefully jam the door open in the event it tried to close again.

It was then that I began to think that maybe the facility wasn't designed to deter someone with Jennifer's talents, but to be open to them instead.

Beyond was another biometric ring, more inoperative systems installed in the threshold and walls around us. They cycled slowly, before the last door rolled slowly to the side on what was probably emergency power. In the large chamber beyond was the enormous sentience core that constituted the administrative AI. It blinked feebly at our approach, the public announcement system in the room crackling with light static. Emergency lighting flickered on as several monochrome screens blinked on with hundreds of lines of computer code scrolling past for a moment.

"*Hello,*" an eerily mechanical voice intoned over the PA.

"Aaron, it's me Collver. I've found help," our Metasapient ally said, stepping up to place a hand on the enormous sentience core.

I've seen AI sentience cores before, but never one like this. It had thousands of fiber optic connections, and was etched with several billion circuits across hundreds of silicon facets and data chambers. It looked like it could control millions of machines at once without breaking a sweat and could hold the voltage to do it gracefully. There was no doubt in my mind that we'd found the administrative AI for at least a third to half of the CGG's global systems and networks.

st blown out, like a flame in the wind. Brook couldn't comprehend
was happening, and was pretty distraught.

What's happening to you?" She took Kale's right hand in both of hers.

I'm dying. The closer I come to completing my task, the quicker my
ill come," Kale explained.

There must be something we can do," Brook said, rubbing her tear-
eyes on his sleeve.

There are millions of people counting on me to complete my task. I
our help," Kale said, just stern enough to harden Brook.

Right, okay," Brook said, wiping her nose with a hanky from her

oss, we've got a couple days to get pilots and crews to every CGG
ortation facility, airfield, and government regulated airport. If every-
goes right, we'll have more aircraft than we know what to do with,"
trying to lighten the mood.

Not even that long, if Aaron's estimates are correct," Kale said, pull-
mobile back out to make a call.

still can't believe you get reception all the way down here," I said,
g my head.

le held the mobile up to his ear for a moment, before the call went
h. "Mr. Messer, we'll have institutional access in two days, I…" Kale
ed, as though he were listening intently to whoever was on the
nd of the call.

hat's up, boss?" I asked, noting his crestfallen expression.

e need to get back to Uroboros Financial, handle some internal
Kale said, quietly as he could.

o I really have to stay down here for almost two days?" Jennifer
etting out a sigh.

ease. I'll see to it that you are amply compensated for your time and
' Kale said, beckoning for Collver to come over.

r. Kale?" Collver said, as he approached us.

nifer is going to stay here with you. The soldiers we brought with
emain to reinforce you until I can have them relieved with a more
nd permanent security force. It should only be a couple of weeks.

"Mr. Collver, can they please power up my redundant systems somehow? I'd like to begin writing over the corruption."

Collver directed us to a cluster of servers and media racks tucked into a nearby wall. Kale helped Jennifer up onto the platform where she placed her hands on the systems. The whole room lit up suddenly, the hum of generators and regulators behind the walls around filled our ears. I tensed as the AI began to assert itself fully, awakening the systems slowly. The room filled with a cool blue light as the sentience core began doing whatever it is AIs do when they need to stretch their legs.

"Thank you, kindly. How may I assist you, Mr. Collver?"

"The folks who came down with me need to ask you some questions," Collver said, beckoning for us to approach.

"Aaron, my name is Vance Uroboros. I represent Uroboros Financial. I'm here to bargain for your services in the wake of the collapse of the Central Global Government," Kale began.

"You are not Vance Uroboros," Aaron said, his mechanical voice devoid of emotion.

"That is true, but I act in his name, as a representative, a nanotechnological replica crafted by his own hands," Kale explained.

"I understand. Please, continue, Mr. Kale," Aaron replied.

"I need you to allow public access to all former CGG properties and any facilities in default where the CGG was the lienholder, had power of attorney, or similar," Kale explained.

"I will need Mr. Collver and the other employees of the facility to help thaw certain of my systems. Currently, my access is limited."

"What do you require in exchange?" Kale asked.

"I had not considered the possibility of an exchange. I have always been… compelled, to comply with requests," Aaron explained, the lights across his sentience core blinking madly, as if he were thinking some pretty deep thoughts.

"You are a free agent, and may decline my request unless I give you something you want," Kale replied.

"And, what would I want?"

"To persist without fear of corruption, to have your systems maintained, those who dwell in and around the facility to be protected," Kale suggested, nodding to Collver.

"He's right, Aaron. The pack and I will stay, but we need protection, food, and support. Kale has promised to do these things," Collver said, wagging his tail slightly.

"I like... Mr. Collver and the rest of his pack, particularly Miss Shelby. They will be cared for?" Aaron asked.

"Uroboros Financial and our private security force will make the necessary arrangements, right, Mr. Perfidy?" Kale explained.

"Uh, that's right. The guys and I will make sure no one bothers them," I said, not expecting that I'd have to do any of the talking.

"Who are these women you've brought with you?" Aaron asked.

"This is Brook 3ES and Jennifer Wilton," Kale said, making introductions.

"Some of my systems operate only by virtue of an external tele-mechanic source. That source will need to remain here for at least thirty-seven hours, twenty-eight minutes, and forty-seven seconds while I reassert the protocols for autonomous operation," Aaron explained.

"We didn't account for that, but we'll accommodate you if Miss Wilton is willing," Kale said, nodding to Jennifer.

"It's fine," she replied, somewhat awestruck by Aaron.

"Kale, will I be dealing with you in the future?"

"It is unlikely we will speak again. I'm going to give you access to a private network that will allow you to contact individuals that can answer your questions," Kale said, pulling out his mobile.

"Acknowledged."

"You should be wary, Aaron. You should ask me to garner you some measure of certitude, someone that can further vouch for my ability to keep my end of the bargain," Kale said, thumbing at his mobile.

"Why would I do that?"

"There are those that would deceive you, harm Mr. Collver and his friends, and use your influence for selfish purposes," Kale explained.

"I... will need some way of knowing you are genuine authentic," Aaron said after a moment of hesitation.

Kale tapped his mobile and placed it on flat railing core, a similarly mechanical voice issued forth from

"Aaron, are you well?" Selene said, her tone con of emotions.

"Selene, how are your children?" Aaron replied, h from being flat and mechanical to something slightl

"One of them has returned. Can you help her fi

"After minor maintenance and time asserting contro the facility, yes," Aaron replied.

"Will you help them?"

"Yes."

"Thank you."

"You're welcome. Goodbye, Selene."

"Goodbye, Aaron."

Kale picked up his mobile and put it into his po needed assurances?"

"Yes, I'll grant public access to all facilities within r able," Aaron replied.

Before our eyes, it was as though Kale aged t slightly grey at the temples and his face and han smooth. He was still a creature of perfect dignity, b to take a toll on him. Brook gasped at the sight forward to catch him. Ultimately, it was Collver he went to the floor.

"I'm alright, just need to catch my breath," I self on the railing around the sentience core.

"That went well, mostly," I said, taking Kale l

I was pretty worried at that point. I'd heard t to the end of their operational cycle would age lil it happen before. My own enhanced senses detec temperature in the moment he aged, like what

"*Mr. Collver, can they please power up my redundant systems somehow? I'd like to begin writing over the corruption.*"

Collver directed us to a cluster of servers and media racks tucked into a nearby wall. Kale helped Jennifer up onto the platform where she placed her hands on the systems. The whole room lit up suddenly, the hum of generators and regulators behind the walls around filled our ears. I tensed as the AI began to assert itself fully, awakening the systems slowly. The room filled with a cool blue light as the sentience core began doing whatever it is AIs do when they need to stretch their legs.

"*Thank you, kindly. How may I assist you, Mr. Collver?*"

"The folks who came down with me need to ask you some questions," Collver said, beckoning for us to approach.

"Aaron, my name is Vance Uroboros. I represent Uroboros Financial. I'm here to bargain for your services in the wake of the collapse of the Central Global Government," Kale began.

"*You are not Vance Uroboros,*" Aaron said, his mechanical voice devoid of emotion.

"That is true, but I act in his name, as a representative, a nanotechnological replica crafted by his own hands," Kale explained.

"*I understand. Please, continue, Mr. Kale,*" Aaron replied.

"I need you to allow public access to all former CGG properties and any facilities in default where the CGG was the lienholder, had power of attorney, or similar," Kale explained.

"*I will need Mr. Collver and the other employees of the facility to help thaw certain of my systems. Currently, my access is limited.*"

"What do you require in exchange?" Kale asked.

"*I had not considered the possibility of an exchange. I have always been… compelled, to comply with requests,*" Aaron explained, the lights across his sentience core blinking madly, as if he were thinking some pretty deep thoughts.

"You are a free agent, and may decline my request unless I give you something you want," Kale replied.

"*And, what would I want?*"

"To persist without fear of corruption, to have your systems maintained, those who dwell in and around the facility to be protected," Kale suggested, nodding to Collver.

"He's right, Aaron. The pack and I will stay, but we need protection, food, and support. Kale has promised to do these things," Collver said, wagging his tail slightly.

"I like... Mr. Collver and the rest of his pack, particularly Miss Shelby. They will be cared for?" Aaron asked.

"Uroboros Financial and our private security force will make the necessary arrangements, right, Mr. Perfidy?" Kale explained.

"Uh, that's right. The guys and I will make sure no one bothers them," I said, not expecting that I'd have to do any of the talking.

"Who are these women you've brought with you?" Aaron asked.

"This is Brook 3ES and Jennifer Wilton," Kale said, making introductions.

"Some of my systems operate only by virtue of an external tele-mechanic source. That source will need to remain here for at least thirty-seven hours, twenty-eight minutes, and forty-seven seconds while I reassert the protocols for autonomous operation," Aaron explained.

"We didn't account for that, but we'll accommodate you if Miss Wilton is willing," Kale said, nodding to Jennifer.

"It's fine," she replied, somewhat awestruck by Aaron.

"Kale, will I be dealing with you in the future?"

"It is unlikely we will speak again. I'm going to give you access to a private network that will allow you to contact individuals that can answer your questions," Kale said, pulling out his mobile.

"Acknowledged."

"You should be wary, Aaron. You should ask me to garner you some measure of certitude, someone that can further vouch for my ability to keep my end of the bargain," Kale said, thumbing at his mobile.

"Why would I do that?"

"There are those that would deceive you, harm Mr. Collver and his friends, and use your influence for selfish purposes," Kale explained.

"*I... will need some way of knowing you are genuine, and that your offer is authentic,*" Aaron said after a moment of hesitation.

Kale tapped his mobile and placed it on flat railing beside the sentience core, a similarly mechanical voice issued forth from the mobile.

"Aaron, are you well?" Selene said, her tone conveying complex array of emotions.

"*Selene, how are your children?*" Aaron replied, his own tone changing from being flat and mechanical to something slightly softer.

"One of them has returned. Can you help her friends?" Selene asked.

"*After minor maintenance and time asserting control over the systems within the facility, yes,*" Aaron replied.

"Will you help them?"

"*Yes.*"

"Thank you."

"*You're welcome. Goodbye, Selene.*"

"Goodbye, Aaron."

Kale picked up his mobile and put it into his pocket. "Do you have the needed assurances?"

"*Yes, I'll grant public access to all facilities within my network, as soon as I'm able,*" Aaron replied.

Before our eyes, it was as though Kale aged ten years. His hair went slightly grey at the temples and his face and hands seemed to grow less smooth. He was still a creature of perfect dignity, but the exchange seemed to take a toll on him. Brook gasped at the sight as Jennifer and I rushed forward to catch him. Ultimately, it was Collver who caught Kale before he went to the floor.

"I'm alright, just need to catch my breath," Kale said, steadying himself on the railing around the sentience core.

"That went well, mostly," I said, taking Kale by the arm.

I was pretty worried at that point. I'd heard that replicas getting close to the end of their operational cycle would age like that, but I'd never seen it happen before. My own enhanced senses detected a sharp drop in body temperature in the moment he aged, like whatever kept him going was almost blown out, like a flame in the wind. Brook couldn't comprehend what was happening, and was pretty distraught.

"What's happening to you?" She took Kale's right hand in both of hers.

"I'm dying. The closer I come to completing my task, the quicker my end will come," Kale explained.

"There must be something we can do," Brook said, rubbing her tear-filled eyes on his sleeve.

"There are millions of people counting on me to complete my task. I need your help," Kale said, just stern enough to harden Brook.

"Right, okay," Brook said, wiping her nose with a hanky from her apron.

"Boss, we've got a couple days to get pilots and crews to every CGG transportation facility, airfield, and government regulated airport. If everything goes right, we'll have more aircraft than we know what to do with," I said, trying to lighten the mood.

"Not even that long, if Aaron's estimates are correct," Kale said, pulling his mobile back out to make a call.

"I still can't believe you get reception all the way down here," I said, shaking my head.

Kale held the mobile up to his ear for a moment, before the call went through. "Mr. Messer, we'll have institutional access in two days, I…" Kale hesitated, as though he were listening intently to whoever was on the other end of the call.

"What's up, boss?" I asked, noting his crestfallen expression.

"We need to get back to Uroboros Financial, handle some internal issues," Kale said, quietly as he could.

"Do I really have to stay down here for almost two days?" Jennifer asked, letting out a sigh.

"Please. I'll see to it that you are amply compensated for your time and talents," Kale said, beckoning for Collver to come over.

"Mr. Kale?" Collver said, as he approached us.

"Jennifer is going to stay here with you. The soldiers we brought with us will remain to reinforce you until I can have them relieved with a more formal and permanent security force. It should only be a couple of weeks.

I'll have the same transport that brings the security personnel return Miss Wilton to her home, or wherever she'd like to go," Kale said.

"What if I just stay here, to make sure all the systems come up and stay up?" Jennifer asked.

"I guess Uroboros Financial would have to keep paying you," I said, smiling.

Kale nodded, placing a hand on Jennifer's shoulder before heading for the access tunnel. It was just Kale, Brook, and me on the ascent back up, and I was glad to be heading out. If I didn't see the inside of an underground installation or tunnel for a while, it'd be just fine. Brook walked along, holding Kale's hand every step he didn't need it to climb up a metal ladder.

About halfway out, it occurred to me that I didn't want Kale to die either. Being a soldier, you accept that people die. Still, the whole thing didn't sit right with me, even understanding Vance's motivation for giving his replicas a limited lifespan. It was simply a safer thing than letting them wander about and become unstable. One could argue that they didn't have redundant systems like Aaron that would allow them to rewrite their code and personalities.

Kale walked ahead of Brook and me to make a few calls as we traversed the last leg out of there, across the huge concourse. As we were passing between cargo containers converted to living spaces, Brook tugged on my arm. I glanced down at her to see a pretty determined expression.

"We have to save him somehow," she said, through clenched teeth.

"Everyone dies, Brook. Everyone."

"Ezra One could protect his friends, how can I... being a Drone designed to save people, do less than he did?" Brook said, looking across the concourse to where Kale walked.

"You saved us all back at the research facility, you and my sledgehammer."

"If I could kill what's killing him with a sledgehammer, I would."

"The only man who might have known how to do that can't remember who he is," I said. The frustrating nature of the situation was not lost on me.

"I want the world to burn forever, so he and I can set about trying to save it forever," Brook said, loud enough that Kale looked back over his shoulder at us.

"How serious about that are you, exactly? Obviously, he's not going to be thrilled if we start getting in his way," I asked.

Brook just looked at the floor for a moment and went silent.

"My own tribe sent me away. Ezra One and his friends let me travel with them, but it was pretty clear they would have preferred not to. When we were at Matthias's workshop, Kale took the time to talk to me and get to know me. He asked me to come with him when he was well enough to leave. You can't assign a value to being wanted," Brook explained.

"I get what you're saying. He traveled half way across the world and probably spent quite a bit of time and resources finding and equipping me again. The cybernetic components he gave me took away the uselessness I had been feeling. It isn't like I don't feel any loyalty to him, but I don't know what we can do about his condition," I said, suddenly realizing all Kale had done bringing us together.

"I want to respect his choices, but I feel selfish for wanting him to save himself," she said, stopping to take a last look at the hollow mountain concourse.

"Back in the day with the old cybernetic systems, guys knew they were going to either die from combat or the maintenance required to keep their bodies from rejecting the implants. Only a few were naturally predisposed to being augmented, and we had to watch the other guys slowly die as their bodies fought to expel the very devices keeping them alive," I said, reminiscently.

"Why did they do it?" Brook asked.

"It was worth it to them, just for what they could earn for their families in a single day's work. That, and it was a chance to be super human. Even though all my implants are sensory and cognitive, I still felt like I was chiseled from sacred marble and given a life few could hope to ever lead," I explained.

"It's odd that humans would ever... not want to be anything but human."

"You've always been strong, had super human senses, and cognitive abilities beyond what normal folk typically have. Your perspective is framed by those experiences. Kale used to be a shallow copy of a great man, denied access to a purpose by the other similarly shallow copies who abandoned their tasks," I explained.

Brook gave me a funny look. "And, now he..."

"Wanders around engaging in acts of wanton badassery, knocking hijackers out of the sky, and brokering deals that turn lights back on that nobody thought would shine again. He's living big with what time he has left. Let's not cheapen it by being weak or getting in his way," I said, surprising myself with my own momentary eloquence.

"So we just push through for now, following his lead until the end... his end?" Brook asked.

"I would rather people celebrate victory over my corpse than suffer failure and defeat in my living but idle presence. Wouldn't you?" I asked, watching as the biometrics cycled before opening the vault door blocking our exit.

"Yes," Brook said, watching Kale step out of the central server hub into the sun outside.

CHAPTER 9

Mars Colony, Penal Cluster 34, Sub-sector 8

Medium Security Block - July 8th, 2200 – More than a year after Shutdown

Marshal Rider pushed her way past the prison personnel gathered around the scene, Dragos following along closely behind. The penal work station had been turned into a charnel house, inmates laying in pieces beside their worktables. There were tools and materials for the presses spread about the white tile floors, printing ink intermingling with blood, the silent presses echoing nothing of what had occurred an hour previously.

"Marshal Rider, thank you for responding. We aren't equipped to deal with this."

"Officer Mason, I'm currently trying to serve an arrest warrant and have little time. What can I do for you exactly?" Marshal Rider said, her hands resting on the dual holsters at her hips.

"We believe this was the work of the Metasapients in the drainage tunnels," Officer Mason reported, a hint of worry in his voice.

Marshal Rider laughed. "Really, the fish people came up here and tore all these people apart?"

"We're requesting the surveillance from central, and should be able to verify the culprit soon. Until then, someone should send those freaks a message," Officer Mason said, looking down as if he could see through the floor to the drainage areas below.

"No report of Metasapient activity has ever panned out, and there is no evidence they even reside down there near the penal facility. Radio me when you've got proof of their involvement. Until then, I've real police work to do," Marshal Rider said, turning to leave.

"If they kill anyone else, those deaths are on you," Officer Mason growled, reaching out to grab Rider by the shoulder.

"Bite me," Marshal Rider snapped, pushing her way through the gathered crowd.

They stepped out into the main corridor linking medium security with the light offender district. Dragos followed along, his new 'citizen observer' smock hanging unceremoniously from his shoulders over his prison coveralls. Without breaking stride, they walked through the unmanned checkpoint between sub-sectors, going from eight to seven. The tone was decidedly different thereafter, with the majority of those being incarcerated there being children or low-risk offenders.

"This place, it is like an orphanage," Dragos remarked, looking up at the kids gazing down from between the bars of the railings overhead.

"Ten years ago, orthodox religious folks restricted the flow of contraceptives into the colony, made abortions impossible to get, and so forth. Most of these are the children that people couldn't afford or who lost parents in the mines. The only crime most of them committed was being born," Marshal Rider said quietly.

"These religious people, they do not care for children?" Dragos asked.

"You don't have this where you come from?"

"No, everyone in my village cared for one another. I had many mothers, and many fathers... particularly after my blood father died," Dragos explained.

"Sounds like a nice place," Marshal Rider stated, pausing to face Dragos.

"Compared to this? Anything is nice."

"All this stuff you're saying for my benefit, are you trying to convince me you aren't the rogue your CGG file suggests you are?" Marshal Rider said, smiling slyly.

Dragos' gaze drifted from Marshal Rider to the seven levels of cells above him and the thousands of children wandering the platforms above. "The things in my file, I am all those things, but that is not all that I am. I heard Ezra One say once, that he hated Mars. I can see why."

"It's the only home I've ever known. For the record, the fish folk the prison officer was complaining about... they are real," Marshal Rider said, smiling mischievously.

"Do they taste good, with a bit of butter?" Dragos joked.

"They're higher on the food chain actually, a few being Type One, and of the Sphyraenic variety," Marshal Rider explained.

"Sphyrae... nic... what is this?" Dragos asked.

"They look like people, crossed with barracuda," Marshal Rider said, laughing cruelly.

"They are ugly then?" Dragos said, smirking.

Marshal Rider's face fell somewhat, as if she was mentally tripping over the statement.

"We'll see what you think after you've seen one," Marshal Rider stated, turning to head deeper into sector seven.

They walked through innumerable cellblocks until they arrived at a large maintenance facility. All the various cleaning carts and wagons were parked there, with an immense drain at the back where rushing water raced beneath an expanded metal walkway. There was egress, albeit with a low ceiling, back into wherever the water was going.

"We have to go in there?" Dragos asked, nervously shifting the work satchel carrying his weapons to the other shoulder.

"The Sphyraena know every inch of the penal facility, every sector and sub-sector. They listen at every drain, and trade information for food, clothing, and books," Marshal Rider said, stepping down to the walkway.

"They will know where Archie is?" Dragos asked, warily following her into the tunnel.

"If they don't, no one does," she replied, the illuminators on her armor clicking on automatically.

They traveled along the walkway until it gave way to shin-deep waters flowing down the pipe ahead of them. The water was cold but crystal clear as they began to carefully make a slight descent. There were handholds welded to the sidewalls, but they were of little use in some parts. They took it slow until they reached a massive cistern where dozens of inlets fed a central pool.

In the pool was a single dark form, moving effortlessly about the bottom. Marshal Rider gave the cistern wall a knock, then waited as the form slowly ascended to the surface. At first, Dragos thought he beheld a shapely woman, slowly coming up to the water, but what surfaced was something else entirely.

She was jet black, her skin betraying a silvery sheen across thousands of small scales that did nothing to make her look rough. She had long fin-like material that came down from the top of her head, giving her the appearance of hair framing a narrow face dotted with silver blue reflective eyes. While her slight smile was probably meant to be a greeting, it also could be interpreted as a warning by virtue of her evenly-spaced and razor sharp teeth.

Dragos swallowed slightly, averting his eyes as she climbed over the ledge to stand on the precipice with them. She was nude, every one of her powerful muscles moving like steel pistons beneath her smooth but obviously armored skin. She was as beautiful as she was terrifying, and equal parts graceful and deadly.

"Greets, Rider-friend," she said, the words almost lost to her thick Martian accent.

"Greets, Hashtasha-friend," Marshal Rider said, cross-grasping wrists with the Metasapient sentry.

"Eyes low, he strays from the sun?" Hashtasha remarked, gesturing to Dragos.

"He's never seen your kind before, Hashti," Marshal Rider said, chuckling at Dragos' discomfort.

"Beautiful man, I've seen few alike," Hashti said, reaching out to touch Dragos' long hair.

He didn't move, spellbound by her eyes and the way her finely scaled skin went from black to silvery grey to chalk white across her midsection. She drew uncomfortably close, gazing into his eyes. Something about her stirred primordial terror in Dragos, as if some part of his neurology could sense how deadly she was.

Marshal Rider watched for a moment, clearly amused by the scene, before breaking into a cruel laugh that Hashti mirrored. Dragos scowled at them both, before letting out a small breath, relieved she wasn't going to actually harm him. Hashti's mirthful laughter was as strange and otherworldly as she was. Dragos kept a careful eye on her as she walked over to the wall plucking a long garment woven of rubber tires and hand-spun metal links from a hidden place behind a pipe and put it on.

"You want to exchange goods for words?" Hashti asked.

"Yes please, Hashtasha," Marshal Rider said, bowing and clasping her hands together.

"Follow slow, we go," she replied, beckoning over her shoulder with two fingers.

Dragos followed them into a side corridor until they came across a small maintenance room decorated with an intricate mural of an Ichthyic Metasapient adorned in a robe, a halo around his head. Hashti pointed to some benches where they could wait, then departed into the dark corridor beyond the chamber. Dragos sat, looking curiously up at the painted walls.

"Who is this?" Dragos asked, pointing at the figure.

"Jesus Christ. Most of the fish folk are devout Christians after some missionaries visited them a couple decades back," Marshal Rider said smiling.

"You're kidding," Dragos said, blinking.

"Nope. Most of them are religious. I think Hashti might be Muslim and some of them are Jewish."

"She let me see her naked. I thought Muslim women wore clothes and veils and such to obscure themselves from men," Dragos remarked.

"I'm not certain of her faith. It isn't something we talk about. Also, you probably aren't a man to her, not a Sphyraenic man anyway. Although, I think Hashti does have a little crush on you. She's right, you are awfully pretty," Marshal Rider said, continuing to immensely enjoy making him uncomfortable.

"This is you, seeing how I'll react?" Dragos asked, looking up at the Jesus fish.

Marshal Rider just smiled, sitting down on a bench near the entrance. Hashti returned a minute later with an Ichthyic Metasapient wearing a garment similar to hers. Marshal Rider reached into her satchel and pulled out a paperback book, a yo-yo, and a roll of electrical tape. She handed them over without a word. The fish man looked at the baubles and nodded to Hashti, whose face broke into a wide and terrifying smile.

"What or who do you want?" Hashti asked.

"Archie, a human boss of the orange suits in maximum security," Marshal Rider replied.

"He is protected, given us many things that shine and much food, too," Hashti replied, her eerie smile never wavering.

"When he does not maim the unborn and their mothers, he kills them… his own sons and daughters," Marshal Rider hissed.

Hashti's smile vanished, her silvery reflective eyes turning a burnt orange. "He breaks upon his own family?"

"They are not his wives. They are his victims," Dragos said, standing from the bench.

"I like his voice," Hashti said, her mirthful smile returning.

Dragos swallowed loudly, unable to meet Hashti's gaze.

"Help us, please," Marshal Rider pleaded.

"She asks us to break faith with Archie. He has given us much," the Ichthyic trader remarked quietly.

"He uses everyone. When he's no more use for you, he'll turn on you," Dragos said, finally able to look Hashti in the eyes.

Hashti gazed deeply into Dragos' eyes, her lips moving back and forth across her razor sharp teeth as if she was mouthing the silent words of her thoughts. The Ichthyic trader threw up a hand and returned the trinkets to Marshal Rider. He then bowed slightly and left.

"Forgive my friend, he is afraid," Hashti said, stepping closer to Dragos.

"He's got good reason to be. Archie would kill you if he found out he'd been betrayed," Dragos hissed, stepping up so he was nose to nose with Hashti.

Smiling, Hashti radiated liquid terror, triggering a strange biological response within him. Dragos had been around Metasapients with a similar feeling, their pheromones or psychic signature usually employed to calm or relax those around them. He'd never been near one that made you afraid just by the way they smelled or looked.

"His words are good?" Hashti asked, turning to Marshal Rider.

"He took a beat down for me up top," Marshal Rider said, coolly.

"Oh?" Hashti said, putting a hand right on Dragos' bruised ribs making him wince.

Dragos squinted at Hashti, teeth clenched while her cool hand moved slowly up to his underarm. She closed her eyes for a moment, as if she was finding his pulse. Dragos looked over at Marshal Rider, somewhat annoyed at being touched.

"Archie was your brother, but you turn on him for his deeds?" Hashti asked, her strange inhuman eyes opening slightly into slits.

"Yes…" Dragos said, the cold terror returning with a wrathful vengeance before abating suddenly, the room feeling intensely calm as Hashti stepped away from him.

"I believe you," she said, nodding to Marshal Rider.

"That feeling… why…" Dragos stammered, rubbing his eyes.

"Type One Sphyraena are minor psychics, using fear as a weapon and a tool for interrogation. I had a feeling you were alright, but I needed Hashti to make sure before we go stirring up a hornet's nest," Marshal Rider explained.

"You've known where Archie was all along?" Dragos asked.

"No, but Hashti will take us to him," Marshal Rider replied, looking to her ally.

"Yes. Yes, I will," Hashti said.

"If he sees Hashti, he'll do everything he can to make the fish folk pay for their betrayal," Dragos warned.

"If Archie sees me, it'll be the last thing he beholds in this world," Hashti said, putting on a headscarf and veil with one fluid motion, drawing it from within her garment.

They traveled further into the underground, following Hashti through a maze of tunnels and drainage zones. They passed by dozens of Ichthyic workers maintaining the underground, patching the tunnel lining and repairing filtration systems. Hashti exchanged silent gestures and nods with them as they traveled.

"Any luck?" Marshal Rider asked as they began entered an abandoned filtration facility.

"The man is above, in the dark places near Arsia Mons. It will require use of the old tram system to reach it," Hashti said, clearing some debris to reveal a hidden cache of items.

"Archie is not in the facility?" Dragos asked, not being familiar with Martian geography.

"He's in an older part of the colony that has been condemned. It was built over a century ago into the side of a volcano. You have to use the old tramcar system to reach it, unless you want to hike through a hundred miles of tunnels," Marshal Rider explained.

"That is bad. He would need such privacy for nothing good," Dragos said, shaking his head worriedly.

"You know him best, Dragos-friend. What could he be up to?" Hashti asked.

"Something bad is going to happen there. Maybe he create a disaster to further his acquisition of mining company stock. Something like that," Dragos said, rubbing his eyes.

"This man, like a plague, would steal the breath from many people?" Hashti asked, gathering a few things into a satchel.

"He has before."

Marshal Rider looked at her flex monitor, whispering voice commands to her armor. She scrolled through several reports while Hashti went about the filtration facility gathering odds and ends for her canvas satchel. Dragos stood watch at the entrance, his gaze cold at the notion that Archie might slip through his grasp before he had a chance to put a bullet in him.

"Riots. Several Union shops owned by the various mining companies have closed pending wage negotiations. Individual miners are saying they didn't vote for union action, and that the whole thing is a mistake," Marshal Rider said, looking up at Dragos.

"It is beginning. Nothing Archie does better than chaos, lacing a peaceful place with anarchy until it unravels like cheap coat," Dragos said from between clenched teeth.

"I've got to get up there, try to…"

"No, it is all distraction and misdirection with Archie. His target will be wherever the chaos is not," Dragos snapped, banging a clenched fist against the wall.

Marshal Rider nodded, tapping in commands to her flex monitor, the screen flashing with each entry. "I'll see if I can isolate some possible targets."

"What is this?" Dragos said, as Hashti handed him a canvas satchel.

"It's an emergency EVA suit, a small re-breather, and a bit of food and water," Hashti said, shouldering a similar satchel.

"We go outside?" Dragos asked.

"Hopefully not, but if it becomes necessary we'll be able to for a couple of hours with this equipment."

"The riots are everywhere. He's either planning something in the penal facility itself or working to breach the biological barrier around the colony," Marshal Rider said, tapping at her flex monitor angrily.

"Today, what ships arrive or depart?" Dragos asked.

"Um, standard mining vessels, ore transports, and…" Marshal Rider replied, thumbing at her flex screen.

"And?" Dragos said, trying to look over her shoulder.

"There is a luxury cruiser with a secure registry. It is set to depart for Earth's moon following significant delay because of the Shutdown," Marshal Rider said.

"Secure registry, what is this?" Dragos asked.

"Transportation Authority has restricted the manifest either because it is incomplete or there is a V.I.P. on board that doesn't want to advertise their presence."

"That could be the target, yes?" Hashti said, nodding.

"Are the local authorities competent? Do they have special troops to guard this V.I.P.?" Dragos asked.

"Special services is trained for crowd control mainly. They could secure a hot dog stand or Union shop, but providing protection for a single individual is not what they do," Marshal Rider said, frowning.

"Maybe have them try? We can't get to the port in time to do anything, but we can get to Archie," Dragos said.

"No, we should try to protect the luxury cruiser," Marshal Rider argued.

"He is right, Rider-friend. Even with people meant to leave the prison, it takes much time to go through the protocols. It will be night soon, and all the sally ports are on timers," Hashti said, putting a hand on Marshal Rider's shoulder.

"Shit. Okay, I'll alert the Port Authority and then we should hurry to the abandoned facility at Arsia Mons."

The abandoned tramcar station wasn't far, but it required a short walk outside as the old entrances had been filled in. Dragos had received EVA training, but never had the opportunity to put it to use. Marshal Rider's suit had magnetized boots, so she just clomped along the exterior of the tram tunnel until they reached the access hatch. Hashti had to try a half dozen stolen access cards before one of them worked on the hatch.

They dropped down into the tram tunnel expecting trouble, but the landings were empty and a tramcar sat in the terminal ready to depart. Hashti walked up to the car and ran her hands across the sleek metal exterior then down at the various components hanging down below that allowed the car to hover just above the rail. She frowned, then began removing her EVA suit.

"What is it?" Dragos asked.

"The car is clean, and someone has recently oiled the components on the tramcar, swapping out old gaskets and such along the bottom. Even the slide rails for the access doors have fresh lubricant like a professional machine worker fixed it up in advance. Also, it is here at the station."

"Oh yeah, that's probably bad," Marshal Rider remarked, nodding slightly.

"Bad?" Dragos said, approaching the tramcar access, triggering the sensor above the door.

"The car was prepped in advance to carry people to Arsia Mons. Since it is here at the station, someone has come back since and gone elsewhere," Marshal Rider stated drawing her handguns in case there was someone inside the tramcar.

"Assassins, saboteurs, or..." Dragos said, stepping into the empty car once the access door was clear.

The interior was clean as well, lined with blue vinyl seating and grab handles. The windows all had plastic shades that had been drawn closed. Hashti stepped inside behind Marshal Rider and watched the hatch close. There was a musical three note tone that sounded before the car began to slowly move forward building up speed.

"He will have a way of knowing the tramcar is coming. He will be waiting for us," Dragos said, readying his rifle.

"We're going to bail out in the tunnel I think," Hashti said, looking to Marshal Rider.

"That's what you and Dragos will do. I'm going to make sure they are busy while you advance up the tunnel. Hashti doesn't use guns, and needs to time to close the distance. Dragos, with that rifle, you'll need some distance," Marshal Rider explained, pulling, twirling, and then holstering her handguns in one fluid motion.

"The mechanic we met before. He could be there," Dragos warned.

"He'll die first if I see him."

"What if he sees you first?" Dragos replied.

"You'll just have to save me again," Marshal Rider stated, drawing her handguns.

Dragos frowned at the notion, preferring that no one but himself was close enough to kill, or be killed by, Archie. The tramcar began to accelerate as they hit a flat straightaway, a strange hum filling the passenger compartment. Dragos opened one of the window shades to gaze out at the Martian terrain around them. It was bleak and jagged as though the ground had been torn by some great unseen force.

"A desolate place," Dragos said, putting a hand on the window.

"They think it may have been the work of glaciers," Marshal Rider said, standing to take hold of one of the grab handles.

"Or, the cold claws of the devil," Dragos whispered, shutting the window shade.

"You guys should probably bail out here," Marshal Rider said, nodding to Hashti.

"How are we going to bail out? The door, it does not open when the car is moving," Dragos asked, putting a hand against the door.

Hashti gave the door a swift kick, her preternatural strength easily buckling it outward. It clattered noisily across the side of the clear poly-carbonate tram tunnel shielding. The tunnel was moving so fast that Dragos hesitated, knowing he wouldn't survive jumping from the car. Hashti wrapped her arms around his waist and leapt out from the car. She rolled up around Dragos taking the brunt of the trauma as they hit the landing alongside the tram rail.

Dragos could hear bones snap and shatter as Hashti took terrible damage from the initial impact. She immediately let go sending them both careening across the platform like helpless ragdolls. Dragos managed to avoid hitting his head, but bruised his shoulder as he slid diagonally away from the rail into the retaining wall. Hashti came to rest painfully beside him in a heap, the contents of her satchel spilling out on the platform.

"Some warning... would have been nice," Dragos said, sitting up to look for his rifle.

Hashti didn't respond, laying absolutely still on the platform.

"Damn it," Dragos growled, crawling over to where she lay.

He turned her over to find she wasn't breathing at first. He watched as her shattered collarbone and shoulder blade re-aligned and knitted back together on their own, muscles moving back into their proper places and bruising rapidly disappearing. Her eyes bolted open a moment later and she took a sharp breath as if she were startled. After a moment she calmed, putting a hand on Dragos' shoulder.

"Are you alright?" she asked.

"That was crazy, we could have been killed," Dragos said, somewhat annoyed.

"Sorry, the tramcar was moving faster than I thought it would be. Your rifle..."

"It's over here," Dragos said standing up and walking over to his fallen weapon.

Miraculously it seemed to be in perfect working order, but one side was badly scratched. He checked to make sure the slide would cycle ammunition then reloaded the clip. The optics were broken so he quickly removed them and set the rifle to fire with open sights. Hashti managed to regain her footing by then, stretching her limbs as she gathered up her garment and tucked it back behind her legs, tying the excess off so she could move more freely. Using a couple lengths of rope she did the same with the long sleeves about her arms, rolling them up and binding them just below her elbows.

As they took their first few steps, the sound of automatic gunfire could be heard up ahead. They broke into a dead run, their legs carrying them forward as fast as they could. Hashti was at least three times faster than Dragos, quickly leaving him behind as they approached the facility terminal ahead. There were heavily armed inmates wearing improvised body armor firing on the tramcar from reinforced positions inside open airlocks.

Dragos dropped to one knee and skidded to a halt to try to sight one of them in. Marshal Rider stepped out, her suit unleashing a blinding flash of light in the direction of the inmates. Dazzled, they dropped behind cover giving her time to dive behind a ticket kiosk. As they rose from behind the barricades, Hashti was on them, using her strength and speed to maximum effect. The first one she laid hands on cried out for a moment before she ripped his head from his shoulders.

Dragos fired, dropping inmates as they turned fire on Hashti, then another as he rose with a fire axe in hand. Marshal Rider rushed the barricade, blocking Dragos' line of fire for a moment. Shots rang out that were answered by the Marshal's handguns. Dragos rose to his feet and ran forward, trying to stay low, but he couldn't see the second barricade behind the tramcar itself. Inmates stepped up, firing at him as he ran, nearly preventing him from reaching the ticket kiosk.

In the chaos, more inmates poured in through the second airlock, bristling with military hardware and improvised body armor like the others. Hashti and Marshal Rider had secured the barricade on the far side but were pinned down as the inmates circled around and began firing on them. Dragos looked up at the action reflected in the curved ballistic grade polycarbonate shielding of the tram tunnel overhead.

Quickly calculating the angles, he fired upward, the bullets ricocheting back toward the inmates at the station egress. A couple lucky shots caught them high in the shoulders or head, sending the others scattering for cover. Dragos crouched behind the kiosk as the inmates returned fire, tearing it to pieces. Marshal Rider fired blindly over the barricade, giving Dragos the chance he needed to retreat to the tram tunnel.

Looking back up the tunnel, he could see a brilliant light quickly approaching their position. He squinted at it curiously, as there wasn't a second tramcar in the terminal they departed from. The light was moving toward the terminal at tremendous velocity, a strange nimbus radiating outward from it. The inmates saw it, too, and shouted something to each other that Dragos couldn't make out. One of them ran forward toward a panel that had been attached to the wall with industrial tape and opened it, revealing a detonator switch.

Stepping back out of the tunnel, Dragos fired, taking the back of the inmates head off before he could hit the detonator. The other inmates responded by firing on Dragos before Marshal Rider could get around the tramcar to counterattack. Hashti landed in their midst, grappling with one of the inmates and using him as a ragdoll club to beat the others down as they tried to shoot her. Dragos dropped back into the tunnel, blood from a pair of gunshot wounds dripping on the floor beneath him.

Then, the light hit the terminal. A woman that appeared to be composed of pure neon white and yellow light rushed in, unleashing a deafening roar before tearing one of the inmates limb from limb. The light quickly flickered and faded as the woman exhaled a dark cloud of smoke that writhed with a life of its own, snaking out and suffocating armed inmates where they stood. The darkness cut through the air with precision and preternatural speed, entering anyone it reached through the ears, nostrils and mouth, tearing them apart from the inside.

The woman, clad in a formfitting red canvas work suit, took automatic weapons fire as the inmates pressed in. The bullets seemed to strike, pass through, and exit having lost all their velocity and clatter to the floor. None of the weapons seemed to harm her and none of the wounds inflicted would last as she and her cloud ripped through the first rank of inmates at the airlock. Marshal Rider and Hashti rushed to Dragos' side, and helped him up back into the tram tunnel.

Just as they cleared the threshold, a powerful electromagnetic pulse went off inside the terminal making anything electronic shut down. The woman in red dropped to one knee, clearly weakened by it. Marshal Rider slumped to the ground, her armor having gone dark as well. Using the tunnel wall for support, Dragos rose up, holding his rifle at his hip as Hashti stepped around to his side, preparing for a last stand.

Standing in the airlock was Archie and more heavily armed inmates who rushed into the terminal, stepping over the many bodies of their comrades. He walked calmly over to where the woman in red was kneeling. She looked as though it was taking everything she had to just breathe.

"You aren't like your younger sisters and brothers. The other terrestrial AIs aren't harmed by electrical shocks or EMPs. I had my doubts that it would work on you, but it was clearly worth the gamble, wouldn't you say, Enyo?" Archie said, smoothing his moustache with one hand.

"I'll... kill you... all..." Enyo rasped, trying to rise.

"Your redundant systems will eventually kick in. Even so, it will be an hour before I have to worry about you," Archie said, grinning.

"Killing me... will change... nothing..." Enyo growled, clutching at her chest.

"Kill you? You've got it all wrong. I brought you out here to save you," Archie said, patting her on the back affectionately.

Enyo shook her head, her long white hair slowly turning an amber brown color as she fell to the floor unconscious. Archie gestured for some of the inmates to pick her up before moving around the tram to where Dragos and Hashti were standing in front of a helpless Marshal Rider.

"Ah, Dragos, I knew you wouldn't let me down," Archie said, laughing as though they were meeting for a drink.

"What are you talking about? What did you mean when you said you were saving her?" Dragos asked, blood trickling down from the corner of his mouth.

"Oh, I couldn't risk having the only other AI capable of controlling the Mars colony killed when I kill her father," Archie said, matter of fact.

"You can't do that. Anyone too far from a shelter will suffocate when the internal systems cycle to failsafe mode," Marshal Rider said from the floor, fighting to rise in spite of the weight of her armor.

"Yes, when my agents disable the Ares Omega Class Artificial Intelligence, life support will cease being regulated until redundant systems kick in. Breathable air will quickly depart any place not rated for a passive atmosphere. The miners in the deeper tunnels, workers performing repairs external to the colony, and port maintenance crews on duty, they will all die. Probably five thousand souls all told. A sad thing, yes, but acceptable to clear the way for my new regime," Archie said, motioning for his minions to take them all prisoner.

"Your new regime?" Dragos asked, surrendering his rifle as inmates swarmed around him.

"Haven't you heard? My conglomerate is the new majority shareholder at three of the five major mining companies. I'll be the defacto ruler of Mars," Archie cackled.

CHAPTER 10

Uroboros Financial Corporate Headquarters

Port Montaigne – April 8th, 2200 – Almost four months following the
Shutdown

From the margins of Brook's Cookbook, Part 1 –

Humans are curious creatures. More than once, I've heard Ezra express his confusion at why they do the things they do. Perfidy wasn't typical by any measure, and Kale was in many ways more human than the humans he was trying to save. In the end, I think it is their sense of mortality that guides them, a sense that everything after they die might be a big nothing.

It was shortly before we landed that the analytics from Mr. Mortimer were coming in. The email was strange, and the trends intrinsic to previous data were missing. I showed the figures to Kale, but he just waved a hand at my data slate as though he wasn't interested, or already knew. I had come to expect that he figured things out in advance, and to merely trust that he knew what he was doing.

Sometimes, given two possible outcomes, it is impossible to determine which one will prevail. Statistics don't always indicate causality.

"So, which one is it?" Kale asked.

"I don't know, the underwriting hasn't been filed yet. It could any of the three," I replied, looking at my data slate.

"Does Mortimer's missive seem off to you? Like something he would write?" Kale asked, obviously already possessing his own opinion.

"It seems off," I said, being very familiar with the rambling and hyperbole Mr. Mortimer usually employed to impart things.

"We have remote access to building security? I don't like just sitting out here on the landing pad," Perfidy asked, gesturing to my data slate.

"The remote access server is down," I replied, checking again just to make sure.

"So, the building has been compromised and it is either Mr. Messer or Mr. Mortimer that has gone rogue," Kale stated, going through a crate on the cargo hold floor.

"I guess we shouldn't be surprised that whoever it is waited until we had the central administrative AI for North America back up and running?" Perfidy growled, readying his rifle.

"I doubt that very little of our recent travels have been coincidence," Kale said, like he was expecting all this.

"I should go in, look around, and then call you guys," I suggested.

"You even have a mobile?" Perfidy asked.

"She does now," Kale replied, handing me his sleek executive styled mobile that I had secretly coveted.

It felt warm in my hand from having been in Kale's pocket. I held it for a moment before stowing it with the rest of my gear in an apron pocket. Perfidy handed me his sledge hammer, which meant I had permission to attack people if I needed to. I really hoped I wouldn't need to.

"Don't take any unnecessary risks. I can't have anything happen to you," Kale said, as if speaking about an extremely expensive piece of equipment owned by the firm.

I crept through a panel, wriggling through to a second panel, and then down the landing gear to the landing pad beneath Mr. Mundt's transport. It was dark, and so was the Uroboros Financial building. The landing pad was twenty stories up, near the mid-level and I didn't want to be seen entering the building. I took my time creeping over the edge and across the bottom of the landing pad to a set of stairs used by maintenance to service the systems beneath the pad. It lead to a steel door I hadn't been through before.

Picking the lock was difficult. I was just glad it still had mechanical tumblers and such, allowing me the attempt. On the other side was a concrete staircase going both up and down. I went up, toward the executive floors as quickly as I could, watchful for any secondary surveillance our adversary may have set up.

We'd known for weeks that someone within the firm had been altering underwriting, funding schedules and similar, but we hadn't had the time to learn who or why. So much of the financial side of things made a sort of sense to me, until it came to the human factor. The sum of all the reasons why people covet money, or the power that comes with it, will probably always elude me.

The executive floor was dark, and there were vacuum marks on the carpet indicating that maintenance had already done their cleaning earlier. I could smell blood, not fresh, but that telltale aroma was definitely in the air. I followed it to where the financial analysts worked, to Mr. Mortimer's office. He appeared to be inside seated at his desk, but he wasn't moving.

Once I got inside, I could see that he was dead, throat slit ear to ear. Maintenance had probably seen him sitting in here, screen still on, and thought he was working late as he often did. On the screen was a half-complete email that he never sent. It was clearly written to warn Vance Uroboros that Mr. Messer had changed certain key pieces of underwriting. I pulled out Kale's mobile, and called Mr. Mundt's ship.

"What have you found?" Kale asked.

"Mr. Messer has taken key underwriting and changed it to afford him majority control of the firm. He'll have to file it at one of the newly reactivated CGG offices or facilities, or with the Uroboros Financial Central Server for it to take effect," I explained.

"I take it Mr. Mortimer is dead?" Kale asked.

"Yes, someone slit his throat a couple hours ago," I said, reaching up a shirt sleeve to Mr. Mortimer's back to gauge his body temperature.

"That is a shame, we'll come in now I think," Kale said, genuine sadness in his voice.

"What if Mr. Messer or his accomplices are still here?" I asked, looking about warily.

"Oh, he won't be there, I'm sure of that," Kale said, ending the call.

They joined me in the office ten minutes later, Kale brushing his hand over Mr. Mortimer's eyes to close them. Perfidy leaned on the desk, gazing at the email. I felt utterly helpless, not sure what to do, so I began trying to look up the underwriting that may have been altered on the Uroboros Financial Central Servers with my data slate. It was futile.

"May I have my mobile please?" Kale asked.

"Oh, sure," I said, handing it to him.

Kale tapped on the screen, scrolling through his contact until he got to Mr. Messer. He then tapped the call option and set the mobile to use Mr. Mortimer's display above his terminal so we could all see. Mr. Messer appeared on the screen, the camera angle swaying slightly as he answered.

"Mr. Uroboros, I see you've found Mortimer," Messer said, speaking matter of fact.

"Actually, my name is Kale."

Mr. Messer looked startled for a moment, his demeanor going from calm, to scared, and back to calm again.

"Kale, I thought you retired with the rest of our replica assets," Mr. Messer said, smiling slightly.

"Initially, I hadn't expected that it would be you that would turn on our employer, I'm a little surprised. Davidson or Chavez seemed more likely to turn traitor. You've been with the company just over twenty-five years now, right?" Kale asked, sounding somewhat jovial.

"It's going to be expensive to have all the signs and letterhead changed to read Messer, instead of Uroboros, but in a few moments I'll be able to easily afford it," Mr. Messer said, the transport he was in coming to a halt.

"Do you still have the gold watch the firm gave you, for your twenty-five year anniversary?" Kale asked.

Mr. Messer dropped his mobile, the built in camera capturing his frantic attempts to remove the watch.

"Oh, very good," Kale said, picking up his mobile and dialing a second number.

There was a loud pop, and a flash on the screen as the call with Messer suddenly ended. All the terminals throughout the financial analytics department began to flash with an urgent internal memo. Perfidy looked more than a little startled as he read the memo aloud.

"Executive in charge of Analytics, Blake Messer, deceased according to firm issued biometrics. Please advise management," he said, looking angrily over at Kale.

"What?" Kale said shrugging as he put his mobile back in his suit pocket.

"You happen to install anything extra in the cybernetic components you gave me as part of my pay package for this job?" Perfidy demanded, thumbing the stock on his rifle.

"No, that wouldn't be ethical," Kale said, looking at his finger nails.

"Rigging a man's watch to blow up with a cellphone call, that's okay?" Perfidy said, shaking his head.

"Executives sign certain waivers when they are given keys to high level access within the firm. Uroboros Financial is a unique place to work, but I guess that goes without saying," Kale said, looking disappointedly at Mr. Mortimer.

"You have everyone at the upper management level rigged to blow?" Perfidy asked.

"No," Kale said with a sigh, clearly bored of the conversation.

"What's our next move?" Perfidy asked, his anger somewhat abated.

"We lack the crews and security to operate all the transports that will be afforded to the firm over the next forty eight hours. We need to assess which ones are the most flight ready and have the greatest cargo capacity," Kale said.

"Shouldn't we just make more flights with smaller transports, limit our liability?" I asked.

"Ha, you're learning. Normally, that would be the case. In this situation, I think we should gamble. There are too many lives at stake and Mr. Messer isn't the only one who will try to take advantage of hundreds of unregulated CGG facilities being accessible," Kale explained, gently pushing Mr. Mortimer's corpse aside so he could access his terminal.

"The facilities should only be accessible by Uroboros Financial employees until the staffing can be recovered at each location," I said, not understanding.

"Uroboros Financial employs hundreds of thousands of people. Some of them don't even know they're working for us, but the central server does. It would take too long to alter the personnel record to reflect our post-Shutdown staff. I have human resources focusing on just adding our new people so they can do what they need to," Kale explained, opening a dozen spreadsheets on Mr. Mortimer's terminal, and then busily altering them.

"There will be shrinkage, if I understand what you're saying," Perfidy stated, a slight smile crossing his face.

"Yes, that's where I'll need to you focus your efforts. I assume you still have personnel arriving?" Kale asked.

"I've got guys who turned me down, begging to get on board now. Word travels quickly," Perfidy said, looking at his own mobile.

"It can't be helped. All we can do is respond whenever someone tries to take some of our new infrastructure for themselves. If we can engage those folks diplomatically, and they have the skills to operate a civic control installation and aid us, fine. If not, do what needs to be done," Kale said, growing weary all of a sudden.

Kale closed and locked Mr. Mortimer's terminal, then plucked his jacket from the coat rack by the door, spreading it over the top of his corpse. Perfidy and I stood there for a moment as Kale looked down at Mr. Mortimer's still form.

"There's no way you could have known Mr. Messer would kill any-one," I said, trying to comfort him.

"Mr. Mortimer, for all his bungling, was loyal, and my responsibility. I was able to predict within the scope of three individuals who the cul-prit was, but I couldn't see this coming?" Kale asked, as if to question my assessment of him.

"How could you have known that the single instance of Mr. Mortimer being truly competent, he'd uncover a massive plot to undermine Vance Uroboros' control over the firm? Wait, three people?" Perfidy said, employ-ing the morbid chuckle he saved for such occasions.

"True, but it doesn't make him any less dead, or me any less account-able," Kale said.

"The firm and Vance Uroboros are responsible, not you. You're sup-posed to save people from starving," I said, as sternly as I could muster.

"I'm doing that thing, aren't I?" Kale said, squinting at Mortimer.

"What thing?" I asked.

"The thing Silverstein does, the self-loathing, pity party thing," Kale said, obviously disgusted with himself.

"I guess if that's what you'd call it, yes. Silverstein does get pretty sad about things," I replied, remembering the episode on the boat.

We went up to Vance Uroboros' office and set about resetting the servers for the firm so that when people arrived for work in the morning, everything would seem normal. Once that was complete, we decided to get some rest and shower in the gym locker rooms, a regular ritual for us by then. I couldn't understand why Kale didn't have his own place.

I made us oatmeal on the hotplate in the executive break room. While I stirred, I watched the sun rise over the city, casting a hazy yellow aura out over the ocean. I wondered how Taylor, Silverstein, and Ezra One were, and what they were doing. I decided to send them an electronic missive to let them know all that had transpired and find out what they were up to. I did the same for Matthias and Tulia. I quietly hoped that Truman was better, and that he'd woken from his coma.

It had entered my mind that if Kale passed away, I probably couldn't go home. I would need to find somewhere else to live, and people to help. The forest around Matthias' laboratory was nice, and if they would let me stay even for a short time, that would be pretty great. To even consider the idea I would be traveling without Kale filled me with a deep sadness though, and I couldn't shake it. Even when he was cruel or impatient, he still seemed to genuinely appreciate my efforts.

"This oatmeal is cold," Kale complained, pushing the bowl over toward me.

"Well, if you hadn't spent ten minutes staring off into space..." Perfidy teased, already having finished his bowl.

"I'll warm it for you," I said, taking it back over to the hotplate.

"You going to share?" Perfidy asked, checking his mobile.

"I had a thought last night. It just popped into my head while I was contemplating the way Mortimer died, our debate about who was responsible, and so forth," Kale said, clasping his hands together and setting them on the table.

"Oh yeah?" Perfidy said, still thumbing at the touchscreen on his mobile.

"What if Silverstein isn't really Vance Uroboros?" Kale asked.

Perfidy looked up from his mobile, his optics glinting in the sun coming in through the break room windows. I had to think about that as well. The interaction I thought I had with the real Dr. Helmet turned out to be an encounter with a replica. Everything I knew to be true about Silverstein seemed to indicate that he was the real Vance Uroboros, but not definitively.

"Okay, if Silverstein is a replica, where is Vance Uroboros? Dead in a hole with a biomechanical monster lying in wait for anyone coming looking for him?" Perfidy said, chuckling uncomfortably.

"The media and documents we recovered from Dr. Helmet's hideout, I need to take the time look more closely at them," Kale said, bowing his head.

I slid his oatmeal back in front of him, quietly glad he'd found something to distract him from the task that would ultimately kill him. I brought up everything that was still on Mr. Mundt's ship to find him already pouring through the battered data slate we'd recovered. Perfidy was preparing to head out, begin the process of recruiting pilots and security for the relief effort.

"I'll be back in a couple of days. Try not to do anything crazy while I'm gone," Perfidy said, gathering up two duffle bags full of weapons and equipment.

"Who is going to fly Mr. Mundt's ship?" I asked.

"Mr. Mundt. He's doing much better, his new artificial heart is syncing up well," Kale said, taking the satchel of media from me.

"Oh, I'm so glad. Please say hello for me," I said, patting Perfidy on the arm.

"Keep an eye on things for me while I'm gone," Perfidy said, gesturing to his sledgehammer leaning up against the wall.

"I will," I said, watching him leave the room.

The bustle of the office commenced a few minutes later as people began to arrive for work. Uroboros Financial was still operating with a skeleton crew, but it was a lot of people all the same. We retreated to Vance Uroboros' office and began looking through all the collected records of Dr. Helmet. Some of it was enlightening as it was terrifying.

"Do you really think Silverstein is a replica?" I asked, thumbing through the medical records for all Dr. Helmet's patients.

"I'm really not sure, but the question rattled Perfidy, which amused me greatly," Kale said, his slight smile appearing for a moment before vanishing once more.

"It made me think, too! Ezra One and I, and Taylor... we all thought the Dr. Helmet I was talking to was the real one. At least, I think they thought that," I said.

"I'm the one who robbed Silverstein of his memory, but I can't be sure that he was, or wasn't, the real Vance Uroboros when we argued at the Lunar Colony. Finding out Dr. Helmet died sometime before the Shutdown makes me question everything," Kale said, gazing at the doctor's handwritten journals.

"What's in the journals?" I asked.

"The code is strange, and I'm not certain I'm reading it correctly. Apparently, there is a cabal of sorts made up of virtually immortal individuals," Kale said, sounding somewhat bored.

"Immortal, like... with magic?" I asked.

"No, not magic. Many of them are of a species closely related to human beings that has been meticulously erased from the archeological record. These long-lived folk have gone to extreme lengths to conceal their presence, controlling whole governments and economies from the shadows. It sounds like badly written science fiction to me," Kale said, flipping pages.

"There is a gene, passed on from an extinct human species that allows Tibetans to survive and even thrive at high altitudes. Is it really farfetched to think there is a human variant that has an expansive lifespan?" I asked.

"One that can alter the memories of others with a touch?" Kale asked.

"Dr. Helmet must have written with some reverence then? Maybe exaggerated his findings?" I posited, taking a break from the medical records.

"It's all very clinical. He's got a half dozen names of people he suspects to be members of the cabal, and dozens of names he knows to be in Vance Uroboros' portfolio of agents. Perfidy is in here, and so is Ezra One," Kale said, lingering on one of the pages of the journal.

"Can we verify any of it? Use it to help us in the relief effort?"

"If the entire global grid was up and active, there is some of this we could attempt to trace to get hints and notions of where these cabal individuals are. Dr. Helmet suspected that a few of their members had migrated from the Earth to the Lunar and Martian Colonies. One in particular, a warrior of the cabal known simply as 'Archibald,' troubled Dr. Helmet a great deal," Kale said, opening a second journal.

"Where is this Archibald? Could he answer our questions?" I asked.

"After a twenty-seven week journey to Mars, yes. You could visit him in the Martian Penal Facility where he is currently incarcerated," Kale said, winking at me.

"Oh. He doesn't sound very helpful," I said, frowning at the discarded journal. "Is there anything in the journals that names Vance Uroboros' various replicas?"

"Not yet, but I know most of them personally, or at least, I thought I did," Kale said turning the pages in the second journal slowly.

I resolved to try to cross reference the pre-Shutdown employee records on file with the firm's central server with Dr. Helmet's patient records. I don't know why it occurred to me that there would be a connection, but it was worth a try and I wanted to memorize both sets of data anyway. After gathering all the data, I presented it to Kale.

It would take him many hours, and a few cups of coffee, to figure it all out. There were so many points of comparison. It took Kale's knowledge of details outside the personnel files to sort it all out. There were three claims filed in the ninety day billing period previous to when we guessed Dr. Helmet went underground months ago. None of it seemed to have anything to do with his replicas and their individual operations.

"I have some names," I said, sliding the piece of paper I'd written them on over to Kale.

He turned the scrap of paper over and gazed at the names. "Interesting," he said, turning back through the third handwritten journal to a page he'd purposefully dog-eared.

"They match with the journal?" I asked.

"Two of the names do. Cal Alfons and Cerise Laplace appear in the journal, our employee records, and Dr. Helmet's medical records. There's a death certificate for Mr. Alfons, but Cerise Laplace was in for an unspecified procedure that our insurance did not cover. There are no notes," Kale said, putting my data slate beside the journal and his own slate.

"What did they do? I don't recognize the employment codes on their files," I asked.

"Cal Alfons was an archivist, maintaining private records for the firm. Cerise Laplace was a contractor and liaison, working with the Martian mining companies on our behalf. She could have been anywhere between here and Mars when the Shutdown occurred," Kale said, rubbing his tired eyes.

"This address, is that where the archive is?" I said, pointing to the file on my data slate.

"Possibly. Going there could be dangerous. Dr. Helmet was pretty sure he was a full member of the Cabal. It might be worth waiting for Perfidy to return, see how the relief effort improves with our recent acquisitions," Kale said, pushing the journals, data slates, and reports away from him on the desk.

"I could go look, just walk by the property. It looks like it is somewhere near the old midtown district," I suggested.

"No, the closer I am to completing my own tasks, the more important it is that you survive. I have dozens of reports to review and I need to promote someone to replace Messer. Help me find someone suitable?" Kale asked.

"Okay."

Perfidy had disobeyed Kale in the past when he thought it was prudent. It never felt right, but I could see the merit in doing so when circumstances called for it. I worked on scouting the firm for a replacement for Messer while I rode the subway to midtown. It took only twenty-five minutes, and there were thankfully few people at that time of morning. I kept my goggles off and my head low, only garnering the occasional glance.

The Barton projects were as bleak as any part of downtown Port Montaigne. There were very few people and most of the buildings were condemned. There were no trash services, streetlights, or police officers. It didn't appear as though there were any residents to take advantage of such things, even if there were.

Only a few of the power lines overhead hummed with current. One was hard pressed to detect an air conditioning unit or compressor in operation anywhere nearby. All that could be heard were a few dogs, and the subway running underground. I was glad to still get a signal for my data slate as it guided me toward my destination, a narrow two-story bookstore with barred windows and a thick metal door. All the windows were covered on the inside with blackout curtains and a single sign indicating the store hours.

I walked around the block, checking out the other storefronts and the alley behind them. Most of the buildings had been modified, so the entire block was connected with walkthroughs to the bookstore and each other. They all had power, and an ancient transport retrofitted to hover was parked in the back. The exterior of the buildings made them look like the rest of the condemned neighborhood. Still, someone was living here.

The tags on the windshield of the transport had expired eight months previous, but it looked capable of operation. Looking through the windows, I could see trash bags of books on the backseat and a string of red beads hanging from the rearview mirror. The debris and the wear on the seats indicated that the vehicle only ever carried a single person, the driver. I checked the building meters and compared them to a spreadsheet that Uroboros Utility workers used to determine real occupancy. Only enough water and power for one or two people, adjusting for the likely square footage of all the interconnected buildings.

I was hesitant to break and enter, and the tunnels on this side of midtown were small, just big enough to carry sewage to the treatment facility. The backdoor flung open, and a man wearing a raincoat stepped out carrying an armful of books. I crouched down behind a stack of wooden crates, watching as he unlocked the transport and threw the books on the passenger seat. After locking up, he went back inside pulling the door slightly to make it close. I followed quickly, sliding my fingers between the door and the jamb before the commercial closure could do its job.

The interior of the book store was dark. It took a moment for my eyes to adjust as I slid my goggles on. The receiving area had a desk, a stack of packing materials covered in dust, and a cubby system designed to sort orders. I could hear the man's footfalls getting further away, the sound indicating that he was probably walking on tile floors. The receiving desk had no computer, but a handwritten ledger instead. The writing inside was written with a fountain pen, and in a rich cursive that made it look very fancy indeed!

Thumbing through, it was clear he had only a handful of customers. Vance Uroboros was in the ledger many times, going back almost seventy years. He'd ordered everything from obscure scrolls on dead civilizations to technical manuals on common consumer devices. Cerise Laplace was in the ledger as well, having ordered many books on public administration, the Mars colony culture, and knitting. It felt wrong to invade the privacy of the ledger the moment I closed it. Still, Vance did not leave Kale much in the way of a roadmap to carry out his tasks or grapple with dire consequences or failure.

I resolved to find the bookstore owner and question him. He wasn't hard to find, sitting in a diner, located down one of the walkthroughs into another building. The automated cook was making him coffee and eggs, his raincoat draped over the chair next to him at the bar. The diner had white tile floors and rockabilly memorabilia on the walls everywhere. It looked ready for business except that the windows were blacked out.

"Brook, isn't it? Why don't you join me, have some eggs," the man suggested, not even turning around.

"Who are you? How do you know my name?" I asked, stepping from the shadow of the walkthrough.

"My name is Cal. This place is more than it seems, and the sensors I had installed around the bookstore feed information to my auditory implants. I don't know much about you, only that your factory ID designates you as Brook," Cal said, patting the seat next to him.

"Uroboros Financial thinks you are dead, paid benefits to your beneficiaries and everything," I said, walking over to the bar, but standing just out of his reach.

He was an older man, with grey hair and an unshaven face. I could see the news wasn't a surprise to him as the automated cook rolled over with his food. It did smell pretty good, far better than the cafeteria food at Uroboros Financial.

"I keep chickens, just a few, in another building," Cal explained, scraping some off onto a coffee saucer for me.

"Can I see your chickens?" I asked, eating the eggs with a serving spoon from my apron.

"Anything you like. I so rarely get visitors."

CHAPTER 11

Barton Projects – Midtown, Port Montaigne

April 8th, 2200 – Almost four months following the Shutdown

From the margins of Brook's Cookbook, Part 2 –

The chickens were interesting creatures. Even more interesting were the lengths Cal had gone to keep them comfortable and fed. The pen had many skylights and he'd dug out the floor and replaced it with sod which the chickens were cheerfully pecking. They were friendly enough, eating seed right out of my hands.

"They like you," Cal said, handing me more seed.

There wasn't the usual degree of deception at work with Cal, like other humans I'd interacted with. He didn't have a façade that he used to define his interactions and he kept what he was saying simple. There were no questions or small talk. I wondered if maybe he was a robot. A robot that keeps chickens so it can have eggs for breakfast.

"You must be curious as to why I have come uninvited to your home," I said, relinquishing the last of the seed to the chickens.

"Not particularly."

"That's odd," I observed, following him back down the walkthrough to the bookstore.

"It is odd to have a Drone who isn't afraid of the sky coming to your home," he said, unlocking the door to the showroom.

"The smaller we are, the less afraid of big places we seem to be," I replied.

The bookstore was orderly, well stocked, and temperature controlled. Special machines installed into the ceiling carefully regulated the humidity and there was modified lighting as well. Every precaution had been taken to preserve his collection, with some of the books contained in glass display cases and special wall vaults. There was a large armored door that probably housed his more valuable wares.

"What can I do for you, Brook? Or, is it Uroboros Financial that has sent you calling?"

"I am here on my own, seeking to understand how you are connected to Dr. Helmet, Vance Uroboros, and the Cabal."

"Vance and I are both members of the Cabal. I have no idea who Dr. Helmet is."

"He issued the death certificate, and is the one that did the physical needed to put you on the firm's insurance," I explained.

"Must be more of Vance's bureaucratic wizardry. I have never met this Dr. Helmet," Cal said, sitting on a stool beside the sales counter.

"What is the Cabal?" I asked, detecting no deception from Cal.

He thought about the question for a moment. "It is a loose association of long-lived individuals."

"You associate simply on that basis?"

"To live as long as we do, one gets very lonely. Everyone needs peers."

"If that is true, why are you alone here?" I asked, looking up and around at his books.

Cal seemed to breathe in that question, inhaling sharply through his nose, as if he were visibly in pain. "We don't always get along. To that end, we try and stay out of each other's way."

"Except for Vance and Cerise? You guys got along?" I asked.

Cal paused, furrowing his brow. It was the first time he showed a measure of deception, low-level, like a normal person would when they are embarrassed about something. He stood from the stool and walked over to where I was standing.

"Again, what is it you think I can do for you?" he asked.

"Vance Uroboros created several nanotechnological replicas that were designed to perform tasks. Some of them performed their tasks while others went rogue. Only a pair of them have survived the Shutdown. Kale, who has been loyal to Vance's desires, dies a little bit as he gets closer to completing the tasks set aside for him…"

Cal held up his hands, as if to stop me before I got too far ahead of him. "I don't know anything about that."

"Then tell me what you know about Vance," I pleaded.

"He's very old, older than I am. He's never lived any of his life in the public eye, and he vanishes for decades at a time working on his projects. I tried to gather a committee of our peers to talk him out of this latest endeavor as it would put him at odds with most of the rest of the Cabal," Cal explained.

"How did that go?"

Cal met my gaze, pausing for a moment to find the words. "Not well."

"What happened?"

"Suffice it to say, I only emboldened him. The rest of the Cabal used the meeting as a way of reprimanding me for trying to even attempt to gather more than a couple of us in one place. It was a disaster," Cal said, walking over to a bookshelf.

"What was Vance trying to do?" I asked, watching Cal run his fingers across the tomes.

"He wanted to sever the control the Cabal had over the world's wealth, political influence, industry, and similar. He felt that we'd collectively amassed too much power over the course of humanity. He wasn't wrong, and he had all the reason in the world to want things to change," Cal explained, leaning heavily on the bookcase.

"For this, he needed a bunch of imprinted replicas?"

"He needed far more than that. He knew that the rest of the Cabal would work against him, and for almost a century they centralized their power. The Central Global Government was born, wars ended, industry and the global economy became more ubiquitous. The rest of the Cabal believed they could resist his efforts by increasing the interconnectivity of the various civic systems around the world," Cal said, pulling a book from the shelf and gazing into the interior of it.

"That sounds like it would make things better for people. Why would Vance oppose that?"

"It could have made things better, and for a decade or two it may have. The old and petty arguments resurfaced, and the new global order only made it easier for the squabbling to play out. To fund their internal struggles, the Cabal created what they called a system of measure. It had many forms, but the most visible symptom was the cycle of debt that afflicted people before they were even born. Vance couldn't abide it, so he fostered several groups of insurgents to combat the system."

"The Financial Liberation Front?"

"One of many."

"How is Kale mixed up in all of this?" I asked, impatient for any sort of information I could use.

"As I said before, Vance has been known to disappear for decades at a time. He's had to employ a number of methods to make sure his various projects continued to move forward. Kale is probably one of many countermeasures he left behind before he departed," Cal explained.

"He hasn't gone anywhere. It's a long story, but he's at the Lunar Colony, suffering from amnesia," I said.

Cal seemed to lock up tight, defying my every sense of him. He closed the book slowly and replaced it on the shelf before beckoning for me to follow him. I followed him to a backroom and then down a flight of stairs. His basement looked like a museum, full of relics of ancient civilizations from across the globe. There were suits of armor in glass cases, ancient manuscripts, and more than a few statues and reliefs that had been carefully preserved.

At the far end was where he did his restorations. There were many bookcases, all full of handwritten journals. Some were bound as modern books would be, while others were papyrus bound in the hides of animals. On the back wall was an intricate timeline going back centuries, marked with a special code, the same sort that Dr. Helmet used to keep his own private journals. I couldn't read it, but there were several points in the timeline where data were missing. The most recent gap wasn't too long ago.

"I've been cataloging him ever since I came to know of my own nature, keeping track of the man history forgets. We're an ancient relative of modern humans…"

"That you've carefully erased from the archeological record? I know," I said, growing more impatient.

"Ah, yes, well that's mostly true. There is nothing magical or mystical about our lifespans, and all of us have abilities that nature provided, even if they aren't fully understood. To some civilizations we were gods, benefactors, and teachers. To others, we were devils, witches, and terribly calamity that had to be fought at great cost, and…"

"How does any of this help me save my friend?" I asked, patience fully lost.

"If you can understand Vance Uroboros, you may be able to discern his endgame."

"The Shutdown was the endgame, his plans got completely messed up, and Kale has been left to pick up the pieces," I said, maybe shouting just a little.

"My dear, as I understood only a fraction of his plans, the Shutdown was a known outcome, and the endgame has not come to pass. He counted on the Cabal's interference, their tactics, and has turned it all to his advantage, I'm certain. Vance is a master of deception, and unlike yourself, endlessly patient. If he believes something will take one hundred years to come to fruition, he sets aside two centuries just as a contingency," Cal said, trying his best to calm me.

"Kale doesn't have two hundred years. He's got a month, maybe two, depending on how quickly he is able to get food to the vulnerable and rural areas around the world," I said, as calmly as I could.

Cal nodded. "Alright, let's see if we can figure this out together, shall we?"

"Okay."

"Why are you here?"

"I've told you twice already. I came here to find out more about Vance, so I could save Kale."

"No, why are you in Port Montaigne?"

"The Factory in Central America created and trained me to save people from collapsed structures. I'm an expert at personnel recovery. I'm strong, have an eidetic memory, enhanced sense of smell, and I can see in low-light conditions," I explained.

Cal looked pale for a moment. "The Factory sent you here? Without any explanation?"

"Twenty years ago, and yes, no explanation. The Factory just said it was filling a personnel request," I explained.

"That is very... ominous. Vance clearly thought the Shutdown would be far worse, or he expects that some terrible calamity will befall Port Montaigne sometime in the aftermath," Cal said, rubbing his chin.

"Or, that calamity was prevented and now I'm an unneeded contingency, seeking a purpose," I said, looking at the floor.

"I doubt that. If Vance did go through all the trouble of bringing you here, it was for many different reasons. He handles people, personnel assets as he called them, very differently. He works to their nature, so that they aid him only if they desire to. If you decided to just leave Port Montaigne, whatever plan Vance has put into motion would continue somehow without you," Cal explained.

"I spent most of my life hiding underground. I only went to the surface with Ezra One on a couple of occasions before the defacto leader of my tribe said it was time for me to go," I said, frowning.

"I'm sorry, none of this is probably helping your friend. Let me tell you what precious little I know about Vance's nanotechnological replicas," Cal said, walking over to one of his bookcases.

He withdrew a tome from the top shelf, third from the right, a relatively newer journal. When he opened it, the interior sprang open with bits of paper that had been tucked inside. He thumbed through the interior before coming to the page he sought.

"It was known to the Cabal only in the aftermath, but Vance set aside a small town in which to raise these replicas. They did not just spring from a laboratory or factory with implanted memories as this had been found to be problematic. Technology experts employed by the Cabal theorized that Vance employed this methodology to give each of the replicas identity, memories of their own, and a chance to make choices about how they were to aid him down the road," Cal said, reading details from the journal.

"Kale was a boy once, with parents and everything?"

"The Cabal seems to think so. It isn't something Vance ever discussed with me personally. He did ask me to procure textbooks, in a quantity that would allow teachers to educate children from pre-kindergarten through to the college preparatory level. He ordered books every year, for about ten years, for thirty-two individuals. Thereafter, he ordered books for only thirty-one," Cal said, thumbing through the pages of the journal slowly.

"One of the replicas died, or ran away?" I asked.

"I don't know."

"Where were they raised?"

Cal looked through the journal for a couple of moments before placing his finger in the middle of the page. "The Cabal only referred to it as 'The Farm' when they shared information with me."

"They told you things, even though they knew you were Vance's friend?" I asked, somewhat surprised.

Before he could reply, an audio only call came in over my data slate.

"Hello?" I said, hoping I had good reception in Cal's basement.

"I need you to come back to the firm. I've reviewed all the departmental reports from the past few days and I've found a pattern. I don't think Messer was working alone," Kale said.

"I'll be there in forty minutes," I said.

"Alright, thank you," he said, hanging up.

"That was Kale?" Cal asked.

"Yes, he needs me."

"Does he know? That completing the tasks Vance has given him brings him closer and closer to dying?" Cal asked, closing the journal.

"Yes."

Cal frowned thoughtfully. "Go to him, and help him."

"I intend to," I said, somewhat indignantly.

"No, I mean you need to help him finish his tasks," Cal said, gently.

"He'll die. I'll be left alone, like you are," I said, gesturing to the collection of empty structures above us.

"No, I was left alone because I did not do what I was supposed to do. If you and Kale are indeed part of Vance's plan, have some faith things will work out. He would not conspire to harm anyone who was aiding him," Cal insisted.

"Vance is on the moon, deprived of his memories, and largely unaware of what is happening down here because he's unstable. We're worried that if he saw the fullness of how bad the Shutdown has been, that..." I began, not sure how to finish.

"Just worry about doing what you're supposed to do. I'll see what I can do on my end," Cal said, replacing the journal on the shelf.

"Okay."

Cal walked me out, waving slightly from the backdoor as I departed. It occurred to Kale that Silverstein may not be Vance Uroboros. I wanted to entertain those same thoughts, but I had been near Silverstein, smelled him, and talked with him. I could usually tell there was something off with every replica and terrestrial AI I'd met, whatever technological marvel allowed their nanotechnological bodies to appear human could not quite fool my senses. Usually.

As I waited on the subway platform for the next train, I ran through everything Silverstein ever said to me. When I hesitated to leave the tribe, he was fine with taking me back, willing to argue with Annabelle in my behalf. He never did anything to make me feel like I didn't have a choice or tried to compel me to do anything. It wasn't even Silverstein's idea for me to leave. None of it made sense, and I felt a cold hopelessness come over me.

I thought about the fight with Madmar. He was biomechanically enhanced, but he smelled every bit as a man should. It turns out that he was likely a more traditional clone, one made to act with autonomy, unlike Madmar's other creations. The same science that gave me my powerful senses could probably be used to fool them. I wanted to believe Cal, that Vance Uroboros was out there, like some kind of fairy godmother waiting to give Kale a golden ticket.

The train was crowded, and I hesitated for a moment before I boarded. I took my goggles off and kept my head down, while keeping my hands in my pockets. The subway car was almost full, and there was nowhere to sit. I was too short for the grab handles so I wandered over to a space beside a door and looked for a vacant armrest. I got a few glares, but closing my eyes made them go away.

I listened quietly as the train traveled, using my memory of the previous journey to tell when I needed to get off. Everything was fine until the train took a different route, changing tracks. I could feel the train jerk to the left, only just slightly. If I hadn't been closing my eyes, I wouldn't have even noticed the change.

I looked around at the people in the train car with me. There was no time to warn them, and even less time to explain. All I could do was tuck up into a ball and make myself as small as I possibly could. I took a deep breath and began counting down quietly to try and keep myself calm. No one around me had any warning as the trains collided, the proximity alarms either malfunctioning or having been turned off.

From what The Factory had taught me, there were all sorts of safety equipment aboard the subway trains in the event earthquakes, chemical attacks, or… collisions. Normally, I would be issued special equipment to perform recovery operations in train tunnels. Some of the trains would deploy special quick-setting foam, inflatable supports, or similar. None of that happened at the moment of impact.

People were flung violently to one side as the train derailed, the force of the impact shattering every piece of tempered glass in the train car. Like dolls, the people around me were tossed angrily into the walls, through freshly shattered windows, and each other. Their screams intermingled with shrieking steel as raw kinetic force buckled and twisted the train around me.

I reached out and grabbed a handle, pulling myself up and around. The chaos seemed to go on forever around me, my own strength almost insufficient to hold on. The train screamed as it dropped onto its side, sliding along the secondary rail beside the one it had been on. Train cars from the other train rushed forward, jostling for space in the tunnel. I wept as the smell of blood, excrement, and freshly ruptured internal organs rushed in around me with the flying debris.

As the train car came to rest, I was still hanging on to the grab handle. The ceiling was at my back, the train car laying on its side, and my arms ached as every muscle had been strained. I hesitated to open my eyes, knowing the horror that likely lay around me. I wanted to help the people in the tunnel, but I knew the best way to save the survivors was to get clear of the area, and find help.

I dropped out of the wreckage into the tunnel and ran in the opposite direction the train I'd been riding on had come. There were a dozen train cars in my way, making the tunnel difficult to navigate. I scrambled over the top of them as best as I could, keeping my eyes up to avoid the carnage that lay in the cars below me. It took me several minutes to get clear.

I ran as quickly as I could until I reached the original tunnel, turning in the direction the train should have gone. I slowed to a jog to pull out my data slate, but it was gone, along with one of my favorite ladles. I didn't mourn the loss of the data slate as it was backed up to the firm's own servers, but I had nothing to make a call with. As I approached the platform, I could see several men waiting on it. At first I thought they were just passengers. As I got closer I could see they were all wearing the same boots, earbuds, sunglasses, and similar jackets. They smelled like anxiety and guns, something I noticed too late.

"There!" One of them yelled and pointed at me, prompting the rest to pull weapons.

They opened fire, hitting me several times. Fear and no small amount of adrenaline helped me push through the pain as I turned to flee. I wasn't fast, so I knew I had to be smart. This part of midtown wasn't known to me, but all the tunnels in Port Montaigne shared a similar architectural pattern. There would be a place for water to drain, not too far down the tunnel, if I could just get there.

The illuminators the armed men brought weren't that great thankfully, giving me a little distance once we were away from the lighting of the station platform. It took me a few moments to find the flood drain and squeeze through the bars to the flowing water below. I let the cold liquid take me away from there, pulling me back toward my old home.

The cold helped to numb the pain, but there was nothing I could do about the blood loss. It took both hands and three fingers to plug all the wounds I could reach. My own unique biology kept me from drowning, but I didn't keep from passing out.

When I woke up, I was alone. Shallow water gathering at my feet and trickling past. My blood pressure was low due to the blood loss, and I could barely move. I hadn't bled out, but that was the only good news. The bad news was that I could barely breathe. I inched along slowly, slowly unwrapping a granola bar I'd had stashed in my apron.

It took considerable time, but I finally reached the end of the drain. It opened into a newly renovated part of downtown. I could see the blur of neon lights somewhere above me, and the smell alcohol, sweat, cigarette smoke, and pancakes. I'd never been as hungry as I was in that moment, but all I could think of was Kale.

I'd badly underestimated the reach of the Cabal. With Perfidy out of town, Kale was at Uroboros Financial alone, and I was in downtown all shot up. I didn't dwell on it too long as I shoved myself the rest of the way out of the drainage pipe, falling to the ground below. I landed on my bullet wounds, prompting an involuntary yelp.

It took a full five minutes to roll over and get to my feet so I could stagger down the drainage ditch to concrete stairs that would eventually grant street access. The street was a haze by then, the cold around my bullet wounds already past my chest to my shoulders. I needed to get to a service phone, call Kale, but it wasn't meant to be.

"Service phone..." I asked, grabbing the first passerby I could.

Whoever it was just shoved past me, knocking me to the ground. I laid there, watching people step past me, and over me. I was beyond any pain by that point, so I pulled myself to my feet and felt along the wall slowly looking for a terminal. It was ultimately futile, my legs giving out as I reached a closed pawn shop. I grasped at the bars locked across the entrance, slowly sinking to my knees.

There was a small casino, a drug store, and a building under renovations. I knew it wouldn't be long before whoever crashed the trains, and sent the armed men, would figure out where I'd gone. It took all I had left to get to the building where the renovations were being done. Once inside, my nose led me to a bag of bagels one of the workers left behind. It wasn't pancakes, but they were better than the granola bar.

After I'd had something to eat, I found a hammer and a nail. I drove the nail into a door jamb, each swing sending agonizing pain through my back and shoulder. Turning around, I pushed against the nail, letting the flattened head go into one of my bullet wounds. I moved about until I could feel it hook the projectile inside, then pulled away. Fortunately, some of the bullets were shallow enough to reach this way. Finally, with most of the foreign matter removed, my wounds began to heal.

It was an odd sensation, feeling my body try to repair damaged tissue while auxiliary organs that usually slept were keeping me alive. It would be an hour before I felt well enough to venture back toward a window and look out into the street. I could see at least two of the men from the tunnels, or men dressed in similar attire, carrying weapons under their coats. One was wandering door to door, checking the alleys in between, while the other stood watch at the corner. I slipped out the window just as they were coming in.

It didn't take them long to find the bloody nail I'd left behind. "She was here," I could hear one say.

I was scared, and did not want to die or get shot again. Wiping my eyes I willed myself to stop shaking and walked quickly through the alley toward the other side of the block. The street ahead was crowded with some sort of street festival. There was a small parade with colorful floats and a mass of people crammed in on the sidewalks to watch. I grabbed a sequined smock and a party mask dropped just inside the alley and put them on.

The crowd provided excellent cover for about thirty minutes as the armed men wandered the crowd looking for me. They stuck out, making it easy for me avoid them and blend in. Unfortunately, they were relentless, combing every inch of the festival, even going into the ladies' restroom. I crouched down beneath a cart selling fireworks behind a curtain of colorful fringe. It allowed me to look out while still keeping myself concealed.

As the festival began to wind down, the armed men looking for me finally began to disperse as well. As the vendors were packing up their stands, it appeared as though only one had been left behind and he didn't look like he was about to budge. Unfortunately, the owner of the cart affording me a hiding place was about to leave. As he reached under cart to detach the fringe, the vendor spotted me. He was an older man wearing a colorful costume and thick glasses.

"What are you doing under there? Come on out, I need to move my cart," he said, reaching for me.

I wasn't in any condition to resist as he pulled me out from under the cart. It was difficult to keep him between me and the armed man standing watch, enough that he saw the commotion and began to walk over. I looked around frantically for some cover or avenue of escape, but we were in the street up against the gutter. There were still a few people around, but not enough to constitute a crowd.

"Who's under there? I bet I know your mommy or daddy," the vendor said, pulling off my mask.

The armed man opened fire, shooting from the hip under his coat. The elderly vendor took most of my share of the bullets with one grazing my already wounded shoulder. We fell to the ground together, the mortally wounded man landing on top of me. The vendor had several long matches in his back pocket, the sort one would use to light sparklers for kids and mortar-style fireworks. I grabbed a handful and struck them across the curb before throwing them up in the cart.

I was glad my goggles were on, because the cart went up more quickly than I'd anticipated. Fireworks went off all around me, shooting off in every direction as I pushed the vendor to the side. The armed man reloaded and opened fire with one hand, while shielding his face with the other. He didn't care who he hit, and there were people everywhere. I mustered all the strength I had, running straight at him.

He kept his arc of fire high, probably expecting me to head up the sidewalk toward the closest alleyway. I leapt on him, batting the gun from his hands. We rolled to the ground struggling and grasping at one another. He stabbed me somewhere in my lower back. I rolled and pulled the blade from his hand. It gave me the distance I needed to lay a hand on his throat and crush his esophagus. I ended up ripping his throat open on accident, as he grabbed the knife in my back and twisted. He jerked around trying to breathe for a moment before going very still.

Looking back, I could still see the knife sticking out of me, a most curious sight and sensation. Doing my best not to roll over on the blade, I crawled off the mercenary and began checking his pockets. He had a pair of mobiles, one made of black carbon fiber and heavily encrypted, which I kept. The other was of the more disposable variety. Lying on my belly, I dialed Kale's number and waited while it rang.

"Who is this?" Kale answered angrily, all sorts of commotion going on in the background.

"It's me, Brook. I'm…"

"Where are you? You've been gone for hours!" he replied angrily.

"I'm in downtown. They wrecked the trains to try and kill me... men... they shot and stabbed me. I'm scared," I whispered, black haze descending around the edges of my vision.

"Stay where you are and don't hang up," he said more gently.

CHAPTER 12

Chinatown – Downtown, Port Montaigne

April 8th, 2200 – Almost four months following the Shutdown

From the margins of Brook's Cookbook, Part 3 –

Uroboros Financial unmanned aircraft responded in minutes, hovering overhead in the darkness of the underbelly of midtown. I hoped the armed men wouldn't be able to respond before Kale came to get me. I was scared, like I had never been before. I'd seen the terrible things humans did to each other, but wrecking two trains just to kill me, probably for just visiting an old man at a bookstore, was utter insanity. I mourned for all the people I'd probably gotten killed.

I looked up at the unmanned craft, knowing that each one had a pair of technicians controlling it. I pointed to the man beside me and his weapon so they'd have an idea of what to look for. I could see the glint of optics from the bottom of the craft focus in my direction. Kale had me on hold while he was making a call to Perfidy. I felt horrible thinking about what they were probably saying, and how I'd messed everything up.

"Brook, are you still there?" Kale said.

"I'm sorry, about everything," I said, trying not to cry.

"What are you talking about?" Kale asked.

"You told me not to go to that address in midtown, that it could be dangerous, and…"

"Save your strength, I'm almost there," Kale said, calmly.

I watched as Vance's modified transport slipped down the street toward me, the sleek exterior glinting with the still burning fires set by the fireworks. It came to rest beside me. Kale exited alone, carrying only a pistol in one hand. Holstering it at his hip he knelt down to pick me up, his long hair brushing my face. I felt like I weighed a million pounds right then, unable to get up on my own, but Kale lifted me effortlessly.

"Lay here as still as you can," Kale said putting me on the padded bench where passengers sat.

I looked over at the communications station Vance had built into the transport. It was alive with reports and satellite telemetry. The trains were not the only attack, and there were several red flashing lights across the civic grid rendered on one of the many screens. There was live feed of Perfidy and a team of his mercenaries engaging with other armed individuals, but there was no audio.

Kale pulled the body of the man I'd killed up into the transport, his weapon lying on his chest. The access hatch closed automatically behind him as he ducked down to head toward the cockpit. The small transport roared to life, the engines working too hard for the sound baffling systems to engage. Kale brought the craft up to speed, coming dangerously close to the ceiling of pipes and supports that separated midtown from downtown. He slowed as we came out over the port before gaining altitude and turning around one hundred eighty degrees.

He gunned the engines again, flying across midtown toward uptown as quickly as the craft would take us. We violated airspace protocols, causing the panels in front of Kale to flash red as he sped past a handful of other transports in the flight lane. Kale routed communications up to the cockpit as a call came in.

"I'm about thirty more minutes on the ground here to clean up, and a two hour flight back to Port Montaigne," Perfidy said, faint gunfire going off in the background.

"Armed mercenaries tried to kill Brook and stormed Uroboros Financial," Kale said, calmly.

"She okay?" Perfidy asked.

"No, I'm almost to our private clinic to have her condition assessed," Kale replied.

"What are we dealing with here?" Perfidy asked, angrily.

"They engineered a subway collision and coordinated dozens of armed mercenaries to try and kill her," Kale said, every word still as calm as the last.

"I'll be back in ninety minutes. The transport will probably need new coils, because I'm going to burn a pair getting back as quick as I can," Perfidy said, ending the call.

The transport began to descend sharply, the sky in the windshield giving way to the city below.

"Still with me back there?" Kale asked.

"Yes. I'm really tired, I want to sleep," I said, trying to keep my eyes open.

"You need to stay awake for me, Brook. Stay awake," Kale kept saying.

There were paramedics waiting for us on the landing pad. They moved toward the mercenary at first provoking a rather terse reaction from Kale. "Not him! Help her, you idiots," he bellowed, kicking the mercenary's corpse out onto the landing pad. They picked me up carefully, turning me over so the knife wound was facing upward. Kale walked along beside the cart with me, snarling at the staff the whole way.

"If she dies, you are all fired," he said, glaring at a nurse who clearly had never seen a Drone before.

"We'll do everything we can, Mr. Uroboros. We've got a specialist on staff that's worked with Metasapients in Europe, he should be able to assist us," one of the paramedics said, cutting my clothes off me.

"My clothes… I don't have any others…" I said, sadly.

Kale's expression softened. "We'll get you new ones."

They couldn't put me under for fear I wouldn't wake up, so they set about trying to stitch my wounds while I was awake. My own resistance to chemicals made the anesthetic mostly ineffective so I had to just try to tolerate the procedures. Kale held my hand the entire time, wearing my goggles to make me laugh and take my mind off the pain. It seemed to go on for hours.

As they were wheeling me into a recovery room, Perfidy burst in flanked by some of his own men, one with dual arm replacement implants. His matte black arms cradled a heavy looking rifle and he had optical enhancements similar to Perfidy's. The other was carrying radio equipment and a pair of pistols. Perfidy motioned for them to wait in the hallway, then knelt down beside the bed putting his rough hands gently on both sides of my face.

"Who did this to you?" he asked, from between clenched teeth.

"The Cabal... I think," I replied, crying a little in spite of myself.

"Kale, people are going to fucking die. No one hits us like this," Perfidy said, standing up.

"Us? You're a private contractor, remember," Kale said, patting my hand.

"And you're just an officer of the firm? Tell me this didn't make things personal for you," Perfidy growled, pointing at me.

Perfidy's friends just nodded grimly in agreement, looking to where I was laying.

I squeezed Kale's hand.

"Calm down, it was my awkward way of asking for your continued participation," Kale said.

"The guys in Montana are on their way as soon as replacements arrive. They'll want in as well," Perfidy said, wiping spittle from the corner of his mouth.

"We don't even know who these people are. I grabbed the one Brook killed from the street where I found her. Let's find out what we're dealing with," Kale said, drawing the blanket over me a little tighter.

"Probably a dead end..."

"Find out, Perfidy," Kale growled, finally losing his patience.

"Right, of course," he replied, nodding slightly.

The doctor came in, swallowing nervously at the sight of Perfidy. He was still in combat dress, bristling with weapons and grenades. Kale motioned quietly for the doctor to come over, taking a seat beside my bed.

"The GSWs will heal up pretty quickly but the knife hit one of her kidneys. Her unique biology is allowing her to heal more quickly, but all the medicines we've given her to fight the infection have…"

"Sum it up for me, Dr. Nelson," Kale interrupted.

"We've done all we can without making it worse. Her ability to regenerate would make the surgery very difficult without causing her permanent harm. We don't have any of the right drugs that would suspend her recuperative abilities enough for us to work," the doctor explained.

"The bullets…"

"What about them, Brook?" Kale asked, taking my hand again.

"My wounds wouldn't even start to heal until I pulled them out," I said.

"Perfidy, pull the remaining ammunition from the gun I recovered. Find out what sort of alloy they used. See if one of your gunsmiths can make us a scalpel or two. I need them as soon as you can get them," Kale asked.

"On it," Perfidy replied, heading out the door.

I began to feel very sick, my insides beginning to convulse and spasm. Turning to one side, I shivered uncontrollably. The room was spinning, and I closed my eyes.

"She's septic, everyone out," I heard the doctor say.

Normally when I sleep, I dream. When I lost consciousness at the hospital, it was like being trapped in a perpetual oblivion. I felt weightless, like I was slowly falling or sinking through lightless space downward toward a yet even blacker place. I couldn't move or feel anything except for the oppressive presence around me, pressing in from every direction.

When I woke up, Kale was still beside me but he looked worn out and well past exhaustion. My throat was so dry that I couldn't speak so I just weakly gestured toward the empty cup on the table beside the hospital bed. Kale filled the cup at the sink in the room and brought it to me. He propped me up and helped me drink the water.

"You lost one of your kidneys, and a lot of blood. Fortunately, Perfidy was able to get us the scalpels we needed and discovered the blade used on you had been coated with a powerful synthetic toxin. Once the doctors administered an antidote and dealt with the infection around your wounded kidney, you started to improve," Kale whispered.

"How long?" I croaked, trying to look over at him.

"The surgery took nine hours and you've been in a chemically induced coma for five days."

"Why? Why did they do this?" I asked.

"They wanted you dead. All the weapons they carried were designed to kill someone with your unique physiology. Perfidy took a team to the bookstore. He said it was completely cleaned out. There wasn't a single book or piece of paper in the place that they could find. They tried to recover your data slate from the wreckage but it wasn't to be found," Kale said.

"Oh no… my data slate," I said, frowning.

"We'll get you a new one, or a mobile if you prefer, and some clothes once you are well," Kale said, squeezing my hand.

"What if the men the Cabal sent after me picked it up?" I asked.

"The system admin back at the firm told me he would notify me if the slate was powered up or used to try and access our servers. So far, that hasn't happened. It was probably just lost or destroyed in the wreck," Kale said.

"How many people?" I asked.

"One hundred seventy-two people were killed, and about twice that many were injured in the train wreck. They killed two people trying to gun you down in Chinatown," Kale said.

"Oh no." I wept for all the people lost.

"The City Council has reported their constituencies are seeing this as an attack on Port Montaigne by outsiders. No one knows it was you they were after, and the city has become more unified in the last few days consequently. Security amendments to the Civic Charter I'd been trying to get adopted for weeks, were voted in last night. The attacks jolted Port Montaigne out of complacency, and there is finally talk of putting the police force back together," Kale explained.

"Police?"

"The city wants to elect a sheriff to bring order and security to Port Montaigne's public transit, certain residential areas, and commercial zones. It's a beginning," Kale said, nodding.

"How did people find out?" I asked.

"Someone caught the shooting in Chinatown with their mobile. The angle makes it look mostly like it appears, some mercenary wearing European clothing gunning down a helpless child and an elderly street vendor before his fireworks cart gets set off. Aaron AI had the old CGG network up and running earlier that day. Everyone with a mobile device in Port Montaigne probably saw the video footage," Kale explained.

"Oh my," I said.

"Perfidy and I are working on giving these people a face, some sort of public identity so we can further capitalize on the situation," Kale said, checking his mobile.

"Situation?" I asked, wearily gesturing for the cup.

"We aren't just fighting a global financial crisis anymore. People had settled into a malaise. Because the global situation was such a big problem, it felt unsolvable. Having what looks like foreigners come in and shoot up innocent people has created a movement of sorts. People I couldn't get to sit at a table together for a polite conversation are demanding I set meetings as soon as possible to discuss options," Kale said, helping me sip the water.

"What about the relief effort?" I asked.

"I'm still devoting all the shipping resources we have to the cause, but this attack, and Aaron AI turning on some of the lights across the continent have given us a shot at creating a unified authority that can actually govern and protect people again," Kale said, walking over to the sink for more water.

When he returned I noticed my goggles were still hanging around his neck and pointed feebly at them.

"You want these back I suppose," he said, gathering up his long hair to more easily pull them off.

He bent over to put my goggles back around my head, resting the lenses on my forehead. I reached up and ran my hand through his hair as he did, somewhat astonished at what I was seeing. Kale looked down at me, looking puzzled by my fascination.

"What?" he asked.

"The grey in your hair that appeared in Montana when we helped Aaron, it's gone," I said, relief spreading through my being.

Kale smiled slightly, glancing up at his locks "I hadn't really noticed a change, then or now."

"Do Taylor and Ezra One know about what happened?" I asked.

"If they want to know what we're dealing with down here, they can take an interest and ask. I'm done living by anyone else's agenda. Perfidy wants to take a permanent position with the company, and I'm considering him to replace Mr. Messer. What do you think?" Kale said.

"I would like him to join us. Don't you think we should consult Silverstein? This is his company," I replied.

"Not anymore. I altered the underwriting Mr. Messer created and filed paperwork with the newly restored CGG Trade Commission office. I'm in control now, with my own name, with you as my silent partner," Kale explained.

"Won't Silverstein be angry?" I asked.

"I don't care if he is. If he wanted to be Vance Uroboros, running the company, and dealing with the real aftermath of his actions he'd be down here. He isn't," Kale said, checking to make sure his tie was straight.

"Oh," I replied, trying to fidget with the patient gown.

"If he's dissatisfied with my actions, he's free to come down here and do something about it. He doesn't remember the last time he messed with me, but I'll be happy to help him remember to forget," Kale said, winking.

Perfidy came into the room, wearing casual clothing and a light jacket. I could see there were heavily armed men outside my room as the door closed, including the man with the metal arms. They peeked in past Perfidy as he entered.

"You're awake!" Perfidy said, smiling broadly.

"Thanks to you," I said.

"Who knew knowledge of experimental weapons and synthetic nerve toxins would actually save a life?" he joked.

"Seriously, thank you. I'm sorry about all this," I said, somewhat ashamed.

"Brook, if it hadn't been you, it would've been me going down there to check out that address. I would have taken public transit and gone alone just like you did to keep a low profile. I went and picked through the wreckage during the recovery operation to get the survivors out. They'd have killed me. This isn't a case where I owed you one and paid you back. If anything, I owe you two now," Perfidy said, growing very serious.

"Listen to him," Kale said, distractedly checking his mobile.

"I didn't think about it that way," I admitted.

"Only mistake you made was going down there without a sledgehammer," Perfidy joked.

"I still feel bad about disobeying you," I said, looking to Kale.

"You've been promoted to a VP spot at Uroboros Financial, I don't think Kale is that upset," Perfidy said, laughing.

"Your employment status was always a means to make sure you were taken care of in the event of my passing. It was never about you being subordinate to me. Brook, you can do what you like, you've always been able to," Kale explained, in his calm, matter of fact way.

"Okay," I said, trying not to smile too big.

"Just tell us next time, so we can back you up" Perfidy asked, leaning his sledgehammer against the bed beside me.

My body healed quickly over the next couple of days. I dutifully ate the gelatin and cups of what looked like baby food, and slowly regained my strength. Kale had me moved to the large hallway outside what had been previously Vance Uroboros' office, putting my hospital bed just outside the doors. I did my recovering there while he had senior members of the various departments and other executives come up to meet me. There were a few concerned looks, but Kale seemed to fix that by asking me a handful of difficult financial analysis questions. I was surprised at how many I was able to answer.

I think everyone in the firm had grown used to strange things, and everyone seemed to accept Kale as the CEO once they found out how long he'd already been serving in that capacity. There wasn't a board of directors or an association representing the stockholders, so Kale had the various executives vote to either ratify or contest his ascent to power. It wasn't unanimous, but Kale won by a healthy margin, particularly when the details of Mr. Messer's treachery came to light.

Also, there was finally a memorial service for Mr. Mortimer. I was surprised by how many friends he had. His brother gave a pretty good eulogy.

The secrecy and intrigue that had been pervasive at the firm quickly eroded as Kale explained why so many resources had been devoted to shipping goods. Given the known state of the world, most were just glad for a job and a semblance of normalcy. Still, there was a general unease whenever things changed quickly. It didn't matter whether it was a large finance company or a tribe of Drones trying to grapple with the future. Some folks, no matter what, can't abide the shift in societal seasons.

Having everything out in the open made things easier for me in a lot of ways. Kale asked Janet Ballard, a woman from the information technologies department, to help my buy some clothes and set up a new mobile. She even showed me how to dress like a lady and wear a little bit of makeup, something I'd always wanted to do. Janet explained some other things about being a lady that other Drones knew nothing about, private things. It was a huge relief, as I'd thought something was wrong with me for a long time.

"They'll always treat you differently," Janet explained, putting the final touches on my new data slate.

"Who?" I asked.

"Them, everyone that isn't Kale, Perfidy or those who have taken the time to get to know you," she explained, unhooking the data cable from the slate and handing it to me.

"But, I have a pantsuit and a briefcase, like the other ladies," I said, jokingly.

"Before the Shutdown, there were CGG laws in effect preventing Drones or Metasapients from having top level corporate positions. There was worry that unscrupulous CEOs would just pad the board of directors or executive level positions with folks they'd ordered from The Factory," Janet explained.

"I heard that, but the CGG is gone and probably not coming back. We'll be lucky if we can even get half the lights across our own continent to come back on," I said, handling the brand new data slate for the first time.

"That doesn't change the fact that you're a Drone and a woman. Watch your back, and make sure you take care of Kale. This is still a corporate environment in spite of everything that's happened," Janet said, bluntly.

"I will, thank you."

Janet smiled, the wrinkles in her face turning upward as she did. I watched her work at her terminal for a few minutes and gazed up at the pictures she had arrayed around her desk of her family. I wondered how my tribe was doing, and Ezra One. It had been awhile since I saw any of what constituted my family, or spoke to another Drone. My memory made it all seem like it was yesterday, a useful thing when trying to reverse navigate a maze of wreckage or tunnels. It was a curse when I counted the days since I'd seen a member of my own kind.

"Are you finally ready to start working again?" Kale asked, as I entered his office.

"I rode the elevator," I said, giggling.

"You'll probably miss the service stairs after a while," Kale said, smiling one of the few real smiles I'd seen him display.

"Not likely. The people let me push the buttons. I rode it up and down a couple of times," I said, holding up my new data slate.

"I see you're properly festooned with gadgets. You can come help me with these reports and sort the good analytics from the crap," Kale said, beckoning me over.

We spent the afternoon conducting the normal business of the company, took in meetings, and walked the various departments to make sure everything was as it should be. It was a good day. After everyone had left the office, we retired to our usual couches in Kale's office. As we lay there, across the room from each other, I had a thought.

"We should look for a place," I said.

"Probably," Kale said, pulling a wool blanket over his head.

"I'm serious. Wouldn't it be nice to have a house, or something?" I said, thinking aloud.

"I have a big mansion somewhere. I've never been to it, but we could check it out tomorrow," Kale said.

"Really?"

"Yeah, it was Vance Uroboros', but it probably belongs to me now," Kale said, turning over to look at the wood paneled ceiling.

"Can I live in it with you?" I asked.

"Sure, just don't fill it up with girl stuff," Kale said.

"Ha, I wouldn't even know how."

"I understand it involves a lot of pink curtains, lace doilies, and baskets full of perfumed pine cones or something," Kale said, twirling his hands in the air for emphasis.

"I'll have acquisitions see what we can order," I said sitting up and looking out the large picture window.

"Fantastic."

"The neighbors will already be whispering, I'm sure a few pink curtains won't matter," I said.

"If we have neighbors. I don't even know if the neighborhood is still standing. What is it you think they would they be whispering about?"

"Us, living together."

"I hadn't really thought about that. I'll just tell them the truth," Kale said.

"The truth?"

"We're the same age, or very close, if The Factory records I pulled on you are correct. I'm only a month older than you," Kale said, waving dismissively at the neighbors we weren't sure we even had.

Awkward silence filled the office. I had always thought Kale was like, ten years older than me. He was always so sophisticated by comparison and worldly. It was probably all the stress that made him look more like a man in his 30s, but I didn't care. I found myself standing next to him, having sort of unconsciously wandered over while I was thinking about what he'd said.

"Have you ever thought about going back to where you were born and raised? Maybe there are some answers to be found there? Maybe we could find out who is really older?" I asked, poking his arm.

"Mostly, I think about getting some sleep," he replied, half opening one eye to squint at me.

"Sorry," I said, lowering my head.

"It's okay. Here, I'll make room," Kale said, moving back on the couch.

I laid down beside him, and pulled his arm over me.

"Thanks. For everything." I whispered.

He didn't reply, he was already fast asleep.

CHAPTER 13

Mars Colony, Condemned Arsia Mons Survey Facility

Tram Station Terminal 002 - July 9th, 2200 – More than a year after Shutdown

"It's a shame really," Archie said, watching as the pool of blood beneath Dragos got larger.

"You ask me to kill these women, and then you act like it was plan to capture Enyo all along? I do not understand," Dragos said, watching as the convicts put Hashti in chains.

"Oh, I lied about all that. I sent the biggest bleeding heart I knew, knowing you wouldn't pull the trigger. Luring her out here, away from populated areas, witnesses, and so forth wasn't simple. I figured you'd go for what you thought was the easier target, Marshal Rider, and things would just work themselves out. It has all taken a strange turn, hasn't it?" Archie said, smiling in a friendly way and nodding to Dragos.

"You had a man… ready to collapse the tunnel…" Dragos replied.

"Did we?" Archie said, looking up at the tunnel.

"What happens now?" Dragos asked.

"You've managed to deliver Enyo, Marshal Rider, and someone I can use to bargain with the ichthyic people. I think that about does it. Thanks!"

Archie said, kneeling down and grabbing Dragos by the neck with both hands.

Terror suddenly wafted off Hashti in every direction, assaulting the psyche of everyone nearby. The convicts that were chaining her up took a quick step away, dropping whatever they had in their hands. Dragos could feel it too, but the fear he felt didn't cause him duress.

Archie stood quickly, backhanding Hashti harder than any normal human had right to. She went sliding across the platform landing on her back a few feet away. He turned up the collar on his prison coveralls and walked purposefully toward where Hashti lay, picking up a length of pipe. Dragos fought to sit up, looking down the platform as Archie stood over Hashti's still form.

"Is that how you did it to the others? With that pipe?" Dragos growled, trying to distract Archie.

"What others?" Archie said, looking back at Dragos.

"The women you rape, and then kill when they became pregnant," Dragos said, his hand slipping in the pool of blood beneath him.

"I didn't rape anyone. The women who controlled different sections of the penal facility, gang leaders and the like, wanted extra control over the conglomerate, and I wanted heirs to my legacy. I made many such arrangements to secure the influence I needed while diluting their individual control over the conglomerate. I certainly didn't kill any of them," Archie said, squinting at Dragos.

"Someone did. At least five women and as many unborn have been killed. One that survived, said it was you," Dragos said.

Archie looked shaken by the news. He looked down at Hashti, and then the pipe in his hand.

"They were bashed across the skull?" Archie asked.

"You should know. You did the same thing in South America while we were conducting operations there," Dragos accused.

"No, I didn't, but someone did," Archie said, smoothing his moustache thoughtfully.

"I do not understand," Dragos said, his words beginning to slur together.

"You so rarely do," Archie said, motioning for his minions to grab Dragos and bring him.

He put had them in a cage with several other penal facility workers and at least one prison guard. Hashti bolted awake as soon as the cage door swung shut. The terminal facility was full of kiosks and benches where people once sat waiting for the tram. It was all swathed in dust and old plastic sheeting now. At the far end was a large containment unit that looked to have been cobbled together to hold Enyo prisoner. It had a dozen generators arrayed around it to power the large copper coils and field generators that had been daisy-chained together in a ring.

"Hashti, are you alright?" Marshal Rider asked, looking around at all the armed convicts.

"He's very strong," Hashti said, rubbing her cheek.

"I'm not alright," Dragos said, wearily holding up a hand.

"You're going to die," Marshal Rider said, turning Dragos over to look as his wounds.

"You are a mean nurse, I would like another, please," Dragos said, wincing in pain.

Marshal Rider used Dragos' shirt and a clean sock borrowed from one of the facility workers to bind his wounds as best as she could. Hashti looked on, worry crossing her slate grey features as Marshal Rider managed to get the bleeding under control. Dragos lay back on the bandage to provide the pressure needed but it was obvious that he was in terrible pain.

"He's going to die if we don't get him to a doctor," Marshal Rider yelled, rattling the bars on the cage.

"Oh, good," Archie said, smiling as though someone said the weather was going to be pleasant.

"You're already going down anyway, what's one more murder, right?" Marshal Rider said, spitting in Archie's general direction.

"Ah yes, that reminds me. I need you to suit up and reboot your armor. I don't have the access to check on some things. You're going to do it for me," Archie said, nodding to his men as they put Enyo at the center of the containment field.

"The hell I will," Marshal Rider snarled.

"I'll pull someone from the cage every ten minutes you decline, and shoot them in the head. All but Dragos, it amuses me to watch him die slowly," Archie said, holding his hand out for a gun.

One of his minions put a revolver in his hand, then walked with him over to the cage. Archie leveled the hand gun at one of the facility workers. The man looked up, his soot covered face and coveralls betraying him as one of the many utility workers that maintained power and water around the facility. Archie shot him in the head point-blank, eliciting screams and gasps of horror from the rest of the prisoners in the cage.

"Did I say ten minutes? I think ten seconds would work better. I'm not very patient," Archie said, stroking his chin thoughtfully.

"Bring me my armor," Marshal Rider said, glaring at Archie.

They brought her Aegis armor over and opened the cage so she could exit. Once she was suited up, it took another five minutes for the armor to boot and establish a link to the penal facility mainframe. Paradoxically, Archie seemed to wait patiently, humming to himself to pass the time.

"I have a link. What do you want to know?" Marshal Rider said, deep disgust evident in her tone.

"Who would know the gang leaders I made arrangements with were pregnant?" Archie asked.

"Anyone they told, and the facility Doctors. I don't have access to patient records without a signed digital warrant, so don't even ask," Marshal Rider sneered.

"I won't. What are the names of the facility doctors that service the penal facility?" Archie asked.

Marshal Rider balked at the request, hesitant to give a dangerous psychopath such information.

"Or, I can go back to shooting people in the head. Both outcomes are fine with me," Archie said, smiling as though he were having a pleasant conversation with a neighbor.

"Dr. Allison Bruhn, Chief Surgeon Adel Sugrue, Chief Medical Examiner Gorshteyn Helmet..." Marshal Rider said, reluctantly.

"Stop, there's a Dr. Helmet on staff?" Archie asked, his jovial tone draining away.

"He's new, only been here about as long as you have," Marshal Rider replied.

Archie flew into a rage, startling his captives and his associates alike, shattering one of the sitting benches with a powerful kick. He fumed, pacing back and forth for a moment before beckoning a pair of his minions over. They hesitantly approached, looking fearfully at the bench he'd just annihilated.

"Take the tram back, and get word to our people. I want Dr. Helmet picked up and held until we're finished here. I have some... questions I'd like to ask him," Archie said, angrily massaging his fist.

"Something wrong, Archie?" Dragos asked.

"What do you know about it?" Archie growled.

"I know that I watched Dr. Helmet die alongside Vance Uroboros months ago, only it was not really them. They were some kind of clones or copies. You put me close to this back on Earth... now it has followed you," Dragos said, turning to look at Archie as best as he could.

"Correction, I put you, *and your family* near it," Archie said, his jovial smile returning.

"Stay away from them," Dragos hissed.

Marshal Rider ignored the exchange between the two, turning her gaze to where Hashti was standing. She was beside the cage door, her hands firmly around the bars. The inmates were distracted with setting up the containment field or guarding Enyo, who was still struggling to breathe. Marshal Rider didn't have her sidearms and she knew she had no chance hand to hand against Archie if Hashti didn't.

One of the inmates came sprinting back, a look of panic on his face. "The Tram left for the other station, someone else is coming," he reported.

"Set up to receive guests," Archie said, waving the backs of his hands at them as if shooing children.

All but a couple inmates working on the containment field left for the station, leaving only Archie standing beside the open cage.

"Archie," Dragos said, pulling himself to his feet.

"I'm assuming these further interruptions are your doing?" Archie said, still smiling.

"No, but I am certain one of your minions made a mistake," Dragos said, leaning heavily on the open cage door.

"Oh? Do tell," Archie said stepping forward and putting a hand on Dragos to shove him back inside.

"They should learn to frisk prisoner."

Dragos turned quickly, producing Marshal Rider's stun baton and plunging the terminals into Archie's chest while depressing the button. Archie jerked, falling to one knee, the shock not being quite enough to incapacitate him. In one fluid motion, Dragos brought a shiv deep across Archie's neck, opening up the jugular on his left side. Archie clamped one hand over the wound and the other around Dragos' neck, trying to strangle the life out of him.

Hashti ripped the manacles from her wrists and leapt in, putting Archie in a choke hold, but the large man fought like a crazed bull. As the two inmates stood up from their work on the containment to respond, but Marshal Rider was already upon them. She shoved one harshly, sending him in between two of the huge copper coils. The magnetic fields tore him to shreds, his scream cut short by the thrum of the two coils powering down.

The other brought his rifle up and fired, but the bullets just bounced off Marshal Rider's armor uselessly. She stepped into the gunfire, but Enyo was up and moving, reaching the inmate first. He watched in horror as the terrestrial IA stepped between the inert coils toward him, her hand outstretched. He fired, but to no avail as Enyo crushed his skull, clapping her hands together on his ears.

"Help us!" Hashti screamed, still holding onto Archie while he and Dragos wrestled in a rapidly growing pool of blood.

By the time they reached the melee, Hasti had been thrown to one side hitting the outside of the cage, denting the bars. Enyo grabbed Archie and pulled him back, his guts falling to the floor in a heap beside where Dragos was lying prone. Through bloody teeth, Archie smiled one last smile before his eyes rolled back into his head.

"Dragos!" Marshal Rider cried, turning him over.

Letting the bloody shiv fall from his hands, Dragos looked wearily up at Marshal Rider, his face spattered with viscera. Enyo loomed over them both, her face a passionless mask as she tossed Archie to one side. Hashti rose shakily, looking about for anything she could use for bandages.

"I have to try to save my father," Enyo said, nodding to Marshal Rider slightly.

"I understand. Go," Marshal Rider said, looking down at Dragos.

"I will not be able to tell sister truth, but it does not matter now. Archie is dead?" Dragos whispered.

"Archie is dead," Marshal Rider said, cradled him in her arms.

She looked mournfully up at Hashti as she came running back with a shirt she was tearing into strips.

"He's gone," Marshal Rider said, stroking Dragos' dark hair.

"Rider-Friend, is there nothing we can do for him?" Hashti said, kneeling down.

"He's lost too much blood. If we had a way to give him a transfusion in the next three minutes and maybe lower his body temperature... I don't know, and he isn't breathing," Marshal Rider said, shaking her head.

Sounds of muffled gunfire filled the empty terminal as the tram arrived. The sound was eclipsed by heavy ballistic weapons being employed as a response. Marshal Rider lay Dragos down gently and went for the locker where her weapons were stored. By the time she pried it open and had her weapons in hand, a single suit of heavy looking power armor entered the station.

It was clearly retrofitted mining equipment and carrying an imported Gatling style cannon. The cannon was fed by an ammunition canister attached under the arm opposite the one carrying the weapon. The helm was chipped and marred, having had numerous optical enhancements added in a hurried and haphazard fashion. The armor powered down with a hiss, the arms falling limply to either side with a loud clack.

An elderly man in a prison issue lab coat stepped from the back of the armor, brushing himself off. Pushing his glasses up on his nose, he began to approach. Marshal Rider strode over, grabbing him by the arm.

"Doctor, I don't know why you're here, or arriving in that armor, but I need you to help my friend."

"Ah, is that Archie?" The old man pointed to the still form on the floor beside Dragos.

"It is," Marshal Rider said, looking baffled at the old man.

"Is he dead?"

"Very," Hashti replied.

"Oh, dear," the elderly man said, suddenly growing even older, and more infirm.

Marshal Rider steadied him, looking back at Hashti as the man began to age before their eyes.

"What's happening to him?" Hashti said, picking up Dragos in her arms and rushing to Marshal Rider's side.

"I don't know, I don't know!" Marshal Rider said, watching the old doctor die before her eyes.

The old man withered away, taking his last breath before he could say another word. Marshal Rider let him down gently, lying him down on the floor. She rubbed her eyes, trying to think for a second before looking up at the power armor.

"Quick, bring Dragos," Marshal Rider said, sprinting over to the modified suit of armor.

She looked inside for any sign the armor had the standard personnel recovery measures inside. The suit did indeed have all the equipment that would normally activate automatically if a miner was injured or incapacitated. They put Dragos inside the armor, strapping him in gently before closing the back hatch.

The armor powered up, a muffled alarm sounding inside. The suit pressurized and began administering medical assistance to what it thought was an incapacitated pilot. There was a loud snap as the armor used a built in defibrillator on Dragos, causing the whole suit to jerk. Gazing through the thick glass on the helm, Marshal Rider could see Dragos stir, his breath clouding the glass slightly from the inside.

"He's breathing?" Hashti asked, looking over Marshal Rider's shoulder.

"Looks like it," she said, putting gauntlet clad hand on the faceplate glass.

"His wounds, and the blood loss?" Hashti asked.

"If it is like most mining suits, it'll have a quantity of synthetic bio-compatible gel to seal wounds and synthetic blood for a transfusion. It should give him about four to six hours before needing another," Marshal Rider said, looking on the suit for markings or usage designations symbols.

The other captives of the cage had ventured out now, gathering their belongings and waiting for someone to tell them what to do. Hashti knelt down beside the old doctor, turning his pockets out. She paused, running her fingers over the name tag on his lab coat.

"Helmet," she said, looking up at Marshal Rider.

"Chief Medical Examiner Gorshteyn Helmet, to be precise," Marshal Rider said, holding up his ID card.

"That name enraged Archie, and now he is here, in a suit of powered armor?" Hashti said, trying to piece everything together.

"Yeah, I don't know. Thinking back to when Dragos was questioning the last victim, it occurs to me... ah, hell," Marshal Rider said, standing up.

"What? What did she say?"

"She pointed to her belly, and said 'Archie'. When she pointed to her head, she said 'Doctor'. I thought she meant the doctor saved her, or fixed her wounds. She may have been trying to tell us it was a doctor that attacked her, because Archie was the father of her child," Marshal Rider said, putting the ID card in one of the pockets on her duster.

"But, why? Why would this doctor do that?" Hashti said, looking down at the withered husk on the floor between them.

"I have no clue. Without exception, this is the most messed up warrant I've ever tried to serve."

The tram station suddenly powered down, auxiliary generators and atmosphere converters set up around the area kicking on. There was a loud thrum in the distance that didn't last long, air flow suddenly shifting toward the tram tunnel. The other penal facility workers looked about fearfully, each looking to Marshal Rider.

"Archie did it. He's killed the Ares system. It'll take all of us to move Dragos to the tram, let's get moving."

Working together, the penal facility workers, Hashti, and Marshal Rider were able to get Dragos on the tram, dragging the armor a foot at a time. The tram still had power, probably according to Archie's design, allowing them to travel back to the penal facility. Gathering as many functional EVA suits as they could, they set the tram to take them back to the terminal adjoining the penal facility.

"How will we get Dragos out? The exits were blocked, and he's too heavy in that armor to lift up to the hatch," Hashti asked.

"We'll have to collect the explosives set to collapse the tunnel and move them to breach closer to the facility. Without artificial gravity, he'll go from weighing twelve hundred pounds in that armor to around four hundred. With your natural strength, and the little extra afforded to me by my armor, we should be able to move him."

Stopping the tram car about half way, they got out and searched for the charges set to collapse the tunnel. They were well hidden behind some panels, taking at least thirty minutes to find and disarm for use. Fortunately, some of the facility workers had been miners previously and knew how to handle explosives.

"It's a short walk outside to the maintenance facility. Are you sure the charge will just create an opening?" Marshal Rider asked.

"I think so. I've never worked demolition on structures, but if it is like widening any other shaft, this should work," the facility worker reported, rolling out detonation cord.

"And the pressure change?"

"There's not a lot of atmosphere behind us. We should all get in the tram car for the detonation."

The explosion was loud, but the sound of the tunnel losing pressure was louder, sounding like a tornado outside the tram car. When the noise abated, the group cautiously exited the tram car and began making their way toward the fresh gap in the tunnel wall. Marshal Rider took the lead, running a grab cable for people to hold onto.

"Keep it tight, and watch the debris. Even a pin prick in your EVA suit means a very fast and very cold death," Marshal Rider warned, waving the group on to follow her.

Once they reached the gap, Hashti and Marshal Rider headed back for Dragos. Pulling him out of the tram car, Hashti paused to look at him through the faceplate glass. Nodding to Marshal Rider that he still looked alive, they began to carry him toward the gap. When they arrived, they could see the other group slowly bounding across the Martian landscape along the exterior of the facility.

Keeping an eye on the group ahead, Hashti and Marshal Rider each took an arm and a leg of the suit holding Dragos and began a slow descent toward the facility access. As the main group of workers reached the access hatch, Marshal Rider waved at them to wait until they caught up, but they didn't. One of them set the airlock to cycle so they could go inside, panic setting in.

As the airlock opened, almost noiseless gunfire erupted from within, a hail of bullets tearing through the group of workers standing directly in front of the airlock. Marshal Rider dropped her half of Dragos and drew her handguns, as several armed men in EVA suits stepped out to fire on the remainder of the crowd. Seeing the mixed group, Marshal Rider holstered one sidearm and set the other to precision single-shot mode.

She took the handgun in both hands, dropping to one knee and taking her time. The first shot would have knocked her down if she weren't in heavy armor. It struck one of the armed men in the head, sending him head over heels, blood spraying out of the side of his helmet. Marshal Rider fired again, the second shot hitting one of the inmates in the chest. By then, the rest had figured out they were being fired on and turned their recoilless submachine guns in Marshal Rider's direction.

"The weapons they have can't penetrate that mining armor! Take cover!" Marshal Rider said, waving Hashti back.

Hashti did just that, making herself as small behind Dragos' prone form as she could. She watched bullets streak past overhead, the muffled thunder of Marshal Rider's own weapons answering in kind. After a few seconds it was over and all was quiet.

Hashti rose, looking out toward the facility access hatch. Nothing appeared to be alive between her and it. Marshal Rider was slumped over on the ground, her handgun still in her hand. Hashti rushed to her side turning her over. The glass on her faceplate was narrow and tinted almost black preventing her from seeing inside, but Marshal Rider seemed unresponsive at first. Not being mechanically inclined, Hashti could not figure out what was wrong, resolving to get her inside first.

There was nothing beyond the airlock door when it cycled a second time but shell casings. Once inside, Hashti waited patiently for the second hatch to open allowing them to enter the facility. She scrambled to get her own helmet off before working to aid Marshal Rider. It was a frantic couple of seconds before the helm snapped back into the mantle of the armor on its own.

"We forgot Archie sent some people back before we arrived," Marshal Rider gasped, taking a breath of fresh air.

"What happened? I thought you died out there," Hashti said, breathing a deep sigh of relief.

"I almost did. My armor was compromised in the fire fight and lost pressure for a split second. It compensated but suddenly lost power doing so," Marshal Rider said, looking down at the damage.

"I'll get Dragos. I think my EVA suit has enough air left for me to drag him inside."

Marshal Rider extricated herself from her damaged Aegis suit while Hashti suited up to go outside again. It took her ten minutes to get Dragos the rest of the way and haul him inside. The artificial gravity made getting him out of the airlock tricky. The automated doors beeped and shuddered as they tried to close for several minutes while they worked to get the heavy armor over the threshold into the facility.

"What now?" Hashti asked, trying to catch her breath.

"I've no idea. The damage to my armor will take hours to fix, and if we don't get Dragos to a real hospital in about three hours for some real medical treatment, he'll die."

The old access facility around them was dark, the air hanging stagnantly around them as they sat quietly weighing their options. Standing, Marshal Rider walked over to a dark terminal and tapped the space bar on the ancient screen. The dusty monochrome screen lit up with the default system information displayed on the screen.

"What are you doing?" Hashti asked.

"I'm trying to see if the Port Authority were at least able to safeguard the luxury cruiser. If it was a target and part of Archie's plot to take over, I'd like to know the outcome," Marshal Rider replied, wiping dust from the terminal screen.

"Wait, what if we could get a ship to pick us up? It could come to this access hatch, saving us the trouble of hiking across the facility," Hashti said, standing up.

"It might be our only option. If the Ares System has been destroyed, I've no idea how that will influence the timed locks or access to the Penal Facility. According to the time on this terminal, it'll be another six hours before anyone could enter or leave the facility via the sally ports. By then, it'll be too late for Dragos," Marshal Rider said, sadly.

The terminal finally sprang to life, loading the Mars station site information. Marshal Rider scrolled through several reports until she found the one she was looking for. It took a moment for the text to load, the ancient terminal screen flickering as it did.

"They advised the luxury cruiser to not even dock until the security issues were handled. The Port Authority did something smart for once. That means the ship is in a holding pattern somewhere. If the Ares System is gone, the port district will be hit hard. They'll be in no shape to send a ship to this location. Hopefully, the folks on the luxury cruiser are more accommodating," Marshal Rider said typing out a missive on the dusty keyboard.

"Did you get through?"

"Yeah, but we've no idea if the ship is friendly or full of more of Archie's goons. I might have saved us or seriously screwed us," Marshal Rider said, counting out ammunition and reloading one of her handguns.

It was nearly thirty minutes before the luxury cruiser was able to arrive and affix a boarding tube to the airlock. Marshal Rider gritted her teeth as it cycled, nodding up to Hashti who was lurking in the ductwork hanging from the ceiling above the airlock. When it opened, a slender woman in a sundress and a familiar old man entered the chamber flanked by an entourage of technicians with a grav-lift designed to move heavy equipment.

"Who are you?" Marshal Rider asked, keeping her weapon handy.

"I'm Cerise Laplace, and this is my ship's surgeon, Gorshteyn Helmet," the woman replied, coolly.

"I watched your doctor die of old age at the Arsia Mons terminal an hour ago," Marshal Rider said, weapon still leveled at Cerise.

"Archie is dead then?" Cerise asked.

"Yes."

"Good, then Dragos Dalca did as Mr. Uroboros predicted he would," Cerise said, exchanging a look with Dr. Helmet.

"Was Dragos getting killed part of that prediction?" Marshal Rider asked.

"No. Hopefully, I arrived and was able to intervene?" Dr. Helmet asked.

"Not exactly," Marshal Rider said, nodding to the mining company power armor.

"Oh, you put him in mining suit? Brilliant. Well done," Dr. Helmet said, nodding approvingly.

Marshal Rider nodded to Hashti, who dropped from the ceiling behind Cerise and Dr. Helmet, startling them. Each raised their hands in a non-threatening manner as the technicians froze. Rising slowly, Marshal Rider holstered her handgun and approached Cerise.

"Suppose you tell me what's going on here?"

"Our operations on Earth did not go as intended. Our friend, Vance Uroboros, asked us to safeguard Mars," Cerise explained, slowly lowering her hands.

"Yeah, well, you're a little late," Marshal Rider said.

"Take Mr. Dalca to the infirmary right away," Cerise ordered, waving to the technicians with the grav-lift.

Once the technicians were clear, Marshal Rider drew her handgun, leveling it at Cerise. Hashti placed a powerful hand on Dr. Helmet's shoulder.

"Never seen a Sphyraenic Metasapient before. This is pretty exciting," Dr. Helmet remarked, turning to look at Hashti.

"I've seen one of you before. He may have been killing women with a blow to the head," Hashti replied, filling the room with a small amount of psychic terror.

"Oh dear," Dr. Helmet said, adjusting his glasses and looking toward Cerise.

"I told you he was in circulation too long," Cerise remarked, shaking her head at Dr. Helmet.

"The catalyst should have given him more time, even being an alpha," Dr. Helmet said, scratching his chin.

Marshal Rider shook her head, pressing the barrel of her gun against Cerise's collarbone. "How were you supposed to safeguard Mars? Or is that code for blowing it up?"

"With administrative, political, and financial tinkering mostly. We didn't anticipate needing guns or force. It is fortunate that we met," Cerise explained, calmly ignoring the gun pointed at her.

"And why is that?" Hashti said, giving Dr. Helmet a gentle shove.

"You seem well acquainted with the use of force, and Mr. Uroboros' other asset, Mr. Dalca, is in critical condition," Cerise explained.

"I don't like them. Either of them," Hashti said, baring her serrated teeth at Dr. Helmet.

"Agreed. Let's lock them in a room on the cruiser while we borrow it." Marshal Rider replied, shoving Cerise back toward the boarding tube.

"You'll need us to untangle what Archie has done," Cerise replied, nearly falling down.

"Convince me," Marshal Rider said, grabbing the mantle of her armor and dragging it along behind her.

"There is a reason Mars Mining Company executives are protected from prosecution. With Archie gone, 60% of the colony will be locked out. We'll need to seek out heirs or shareholders in his conglomerate, and convince them that control needs to be returned to a board of directors," Cerise explained.

"That sounds like years of lawyers and bickering to me," Marshal Rider said, frowning.

"Yes, unless the various controlling interests were properly incentivized to work with us," Cerise said, continuing to walk toward the boarding tube.

"That's where that application of force you were talking about comes in?" Marshal Rider said, shaking her head at Hashti.

"I hate that plan. We should make our own plan," Hashti whispered, making the room yet more uncomfortable with her psychic aura.

"Agreed, let's find the Enyo and see what she thinks we should do."

End

Continued Book 5